W9-AVC-124

The Liability of Love

The Liability of Love

A Novel

Susan Schoenberger

SHE WRITES PRESS

Copyright © 2021, Susan Schoenberger

All rights reserved. No part of this publication may be reproduced, distrib-
uted, or transmitted in any form or by any means, including photocopying,
recording, digital scanning, or other electronic or mechanical methods,
without the prior written permission of the publisher, except in the case of
brief quotations embodied in critical reviews and certain other noncom-
mercial uses permitted by copyright law. For permission requests, please
address She Writes Press.

Published 2021
Printed in the United States of America
Print ISBN: 978-1-64742-130-4
E-ISBN: 978-1-64742-131-1
Library of Congress Control Number: 2021900226

For information, address:
She Writes Press
1569 Solano Ave #546
Berkeley, CA 94707

She Writes Press is a division of SparkPoint Studio, LLC.

All company and/or product names may be trade names, logos, trademarks, and/or registered trademarks and are the property of their
respective owners.

This is a work of fiction. Names, characters, places, and incidents either
are the product of the author's imagination or are used fictitiously. Any
resemblance to actual persons, living or dead, is entirely coincidental.

For my beautiful children,
AJ, Jenna, and Claire

And in memory of
Karen O'Brien
(1960–2015)

Author's Note

I dedicated my first novel, *A Watershed Year*, to my parents, who always supported whatever I did, even when they didn't quite understand why I needed to spend years working on manuscripts that no one would read and more years pursuing agents and editors and publishers like my life depended on it.

My second novel, *The Virtues of Oxygen*, was dedicated to my husband, Kevin, who never once asked why I spent my precious pre-work hours and weekend mornings crouched over my laptop in the living room. Or why I had to drive an hour to speak at a library event that three people attended.

I had always planned to dedicate my third novel, if there was one, to my three children: AJ, Jenna, and Claire. I imagined them seeing the dedication page with their names on it, hovering in the center like writing on a sheet cake. And it's there, and I am amazed by all three of them, each one a beautiful, artistic soul. AJ, the writer. Sensitive and so agile with words, though the troubled world weighs on them more than I wish it would. Jenna, the actress. Gifted, generous with her talent, devoted to entertaining others no matter the cost to herself. Claire, the illustrator. The trauma and joys of life flow through her hands, and she captures them in a way that leaves me in awe. I worry for them, because the life of an artist is not an easy one, and yet, I think they will be okay.

But the dedication page is not theirs alone. I started this novel in 2014 with the encouragement of two of my best newspaper friends, Theresa Sullivan Barger and Karen O'Brien. Both had been behind me from the beginning of my writing career, lifting me up when I was pounded by rejection, reading the roughest of drafts and telling me they were good, worthwhile, promising.

We were all in our early fifties when this book had its start, but Karen never made it to her late fifties. Her cancer diagnosis was shocking, but less shocking than her decline and death six months later. She was a strong, vibrant woman with a perfect smile who laughed easily and loved her family fiercely. We lost her way too soon. If she were here now, she would tell me that this story took so long to emerge because it needed time to percolate. She would tell me it was worth the wait.

—1—

Margaret

Like many girls who came of age when the women's liberation movement was upending America, Margaret was a tangle of contradictions. She both enjoyed and resented being told she was pretty, unsure of which reaction Gloria Steinem would approve. When the feminists marching in the streets said girls could do anything boys could do, Margaret agreed but knew instinctively they would despise her if she tried. She was an excellent student and aspired to be a good Catholic, but at night in her twin bed, romantic fantasies filled her head. She dreamed of the day she would graduate from the all-girls Bishop McGarvey High School and meet a boy who would tear down the walls she had flimsily constructed.

Some of this could be blamed on *The Thornbirds*, which Margaret read multiple times, devouring the tale of a young Australian woman who can't have the handsome Catholic priest she loves except for one passionate week during which they conceive an illegitimate child. In Margaret's senior year of high school, her mother Caroline saw Margaret holding a dog-eared paperback copy and made a point of telling her that relationships were a little more complex than novels sometimes made them out to be. Margaret nodded because her mother was dying of breast cancer, but secretly, she held onto the

1

dreamy notion that she would meet a boy in college and finally learn what it meant to be so in tune with the universe and so deeply in love that nothing else mattered.

The spring of Margaret's senior year was filled with award ceremonies—she was the top math student in her class—and the signing of yearbooks and graduation festivities, and yet, she could not enjoy any of it. Her mother had died that January, leaving an absence so profound that it became a presence, shadowing her as she shuffled from one class to another, pressing between her shoulder blades as she ate in the noisy cafeteria, sitting heavily in her gut as her father, Richard, steeped in his own grief, told Margaret she would have to attend college in Hartford. Trinity had offered Margaret the biggest scholarship, and her father needed her on weekends in his failing dry-cleaning store. Trinity was an excellent school, but it wasn't Boston College, where she had also been accepted and which had a leafy suburban campus lifted straight from her romantic dreams.

When it was time to leave in the late summer of 1979, Margaret and her father loaded the old Chrysler sedan with almost all of Margaret's possessions: bedding, clothes, shoes, toiletries, a boombox for her cassette tapes, decorative pillows, Smith Corona typewriter, reference books (dictionary, thesaurus, a new copy of *Strunk and White*), mini-fridge previously used by both her older sisters, desk lamp, bulletin board. Filling in the spaces in and around her things were grief, love, and longing, in that order, with a few small pockets of resentment tucked into the passenger seat footwell.

As her father, Richard, backed down the driveway, he said something about needing to repaint the porch, which seemed to Margaret completely inappropriate for the situation. A thunderstorm had ripped through the neighborhood of careworn Victorians the night before, cracking limbs and drenching the small front lawns, sending rivulets of mud over the cracked granite curbstones and into the street. In its aftermath, the sun filtered through the dripping leaves and branches and bounced off the shiny aluminum flashing on their neighbor's new roof as if to say, *All is never lost.* It was all so moving and powerful and transitional, and yet, her father seemed not to recognize the moment for what it was.

Margaret waved until her sisters, who were in their late twenties but still lived at home, were out of sight. Then she flipped down the passenger-side visor to block the sun's glare as her father's car detoured around a thick tree branch in the street and carried her away from her childhood. Nothing was as it should be. Her mother should have been sitting where she was. She should have been in the back seat, wedged between her new comforter and a milk crate full of books, bristling with anxiety and excitement. Her father should have been telling embarrassing stories about his own college years, alternately winking at her mother and watching the road. Instead, she and her father talked about the weather: how hard it had rained the night before, how much it had rained that summer, how likely it was that it would rain again. Fifteen minutes later, they pulled up near her dorm. Her father helped her move in and said good-bye with a tight hug but no tears since she would be back home the following weekend and every weekend after that. Margaret's mother's illness had brought them to the brink of bankruptcy, which meant that Margaret and her sisters all had to help until Richard regained his footing.

Once the bed was made and her clothes put away, she wandered the charming walkways and manicured quads that linked the grand red stone buildings and their Gothic archways, thinking of how Trinity was in Hartford, but not of it. Just a few blocks away, the drug dealers did a brisk business behind the corner stores, one of the few options for employment. It was all too obvious that wealth and privilege grew on one side of the wall, poverty and desperation on the other, and she could hear her mother reminding her, *There but for the grace of God go I.* The college had given Margaret a full ride because the income from the dry-cleaning store barely kept a roof over their heads. She appreciated the help, and yet she worried that everyone she passed on the charming walkways and manicured quads would somehow know she was there on someone else's dime. A poor, motherless child.

No longer required to wear the pleated, plaid skirt and white cotton blouse of her Catholic school uniform, Margaret was free to forge a new identity, and she did. The money she had saved from summers and weekends sweating inside the dry cleaners had allowed her to buy some new clothes, mostly jeans and T-shirts and sweaters with Scandinavian patterns like those she had seen in the college catalogues, as well as bikini-cut underwear to replace the girlish cotton briefs that came up to her belly button. At the hairdresser, instead of the usual trim, she had her hair cut in long shoulder-length layers and asked for—and immediately regretted—the blunt bangs her mother had always told her would be a mistake. She donated three pairs of old saddle shoes to Goodwill and bought platform clogs that required practice before she could walk in them without risking an ankle sprain. She wanted to look like a young woman and not a girl. Girls didn't fall in love in the way that women did, and despite her mother's warnings about relationships being complicated, she was certain that an epic *Thornbirds* love awaited her on the other side of one of Trinity's Gothic archways. She just had to walk through the right one.

Her roommate was a tall, solemn girl from outside Chicago who played lacrosse. They got along but weren't close friends, which was fine with Margaret. It gave her time to consider the boys, for whom she had a burning curiosity, having gone to all-girls schools for the previous six years. Of the boys she had met at the occasional coed dance or math team competition, not one seemed even remotely suitable for her romantic yearnings. Instead, they seemed intent on speaking loudly and punching each other, or wrestling like puppies. College boys, she hoped, would belong to an entirely different species, one that knew how to walk upright with an arm around a girl's shoulder in a way that looked like they were seamlessly joined.

A month or so after orientation, at one of the first parties she attended, Margaret found herself talking to another freshman, a tall boy in a fresh-from-the-bookstore Trinity sweatshirt who had blond hair, freckles, green eyes, and extremely long feet encased in white basketball sneakers. David was from Michigan. David wanted to study political science. David saw himself running for office one day. David's mom and everyone in high school called him Davey, but now that he was in college, he had decided to go by David. As the party wore on and beers were consumed, David led her to a quiet corner where he brushed the blunt bangs she was already growing out back from her face and leaned in for a kiss. She was sure, as his pale, chapped lips loomed large, that he would sense her inexperience and regret his choice, but she closed her eyes anyway and waited until his wet, beery mouth was on hers and his tongue was pushing through her lips, past her teeth, into the vicinity of her tonsils. It was terrible but also not terrible. After a while, she pushed on David's chest a bit, and he released his suction.

"Um, thank you," she said with a formality she knew was wrong as soon as she heard it. "I have to go now."

David nodded, looking confused.

"Okay, well, see you around."

It was midnight when she left the party and went back to her dorm. At least she had been kissed. Was kissable. Was looking forward to trying it again and improving her performance. As she passed the lounge on her floor, she heard music coming from the beat-up spinet tucked into an alcove beyond the ping-pong table and looked in to see who was playing.

A small group stood around the piano while someone pounded away on "Heart and Soul," adding embellishments and jazzy interludes in and around the familiar melody. She recognized the person playing the piano as a sophomore named Fitz who lived down the hall and had helped Margaret the week before when she couldn't open a window in her dorm room that had been painted shut. He was a large person, both tall and wide, which she found somehow comforting. Whenever she saw him, he seemed to have a cadre of friends around him, though he wasn't boisterous or overly chummy. There was a calmness, a density about him that drew people to him like a planet with many orbiting moons.

"Margaret," he called when she started to turn away. "C'mon over. Can you play the piano?"

She wanted to go back to her room and imagine what her mother might say about her first real kiss, but Fitz had a gravitational pull that could not be ignored. She approached the piano. "Sorry, I never learned an instrument."

"At least, you never tried," Fitz said, launching back into "Heart and Soul." "My parents paid for ten years of lessons, and this is all I can play."

His friends all laughed, and Margaret envied them. They seemed unashamed to be standing around a piano when they were supposed to be pounding beers or downing shots of Jägermeister on a Thursday night, when, Margaret had discovered, college weekends began. Fitz had been unduly modest about the piano. He next played a variety of Christmas tunes, which he said his parents had forced him to memorize, and they all sang loudly on "Jingle Bells" and "Deck the Halls" and "Joy to the World," though it was only September.

Then Fitz stretched and yawned.

"I'm done for the night," he said. "I have class at eight at tomorrow. And I've learned from experience that Schmidt doesn't take it well when you nap during his lectures."

Almost immediately, the group around the piano dispersed, and Margaret was sad to see them go. She and Fitz walked down the dimly lighted hall together, and he paused with her as she found her key in her backpack and opened her door, which her roommate had decorated with pictures of cartoon cats holding lacrosse sticks.

"Thanks," Margaret said.

"For what?"

"For including me, a lowly freshman."

He chucked her lightly on the shoulder.

"Hey, kid, we were all lowly freshmen once. Until just a few months ago, I was one myself."

"Well, I appreciate it."

She gave him a wistful smile.

"Homesick?"

"Not really. My family's in Hartford."

"Seriously? Me, too. I thought I was the only one. I'm here because my father and grandfather went here. It's kind of a family tradition."

"Well, my mom died earlier this year, so I didn't want to be too far away. My dad needs me at his store on the weekends."

"I'm so sorry. That must be hard."

She didn't know Fitz well, but his sympathy struck her as genuine. She suddenly realized that David, of the awkward kiss, hadn't asked her a single question about herself. She also realized that the presence of her mother's absence would be gone someday, and when it was, she would have to grieve all over again.

"It is hard," she said. "Thank you for saying that."

"Rest well, okay. And let me know if there's anything you need. I'm right down the hall."

She closed the door to her room, thinking now about Fitz, whose height and heft somehow made him the least threatening boy she had ever met. What a kind person. What a generous and solid person. His size, while it was the first thing she noticed about him, seemed to melt away when he spoke directly to her. She liked him, and in the way of relationships made early in college, she knew he would be important to her. She just didn't know how.

—2—

Fitz

Fitz returned to his dorm room and flopped down on his bed, replaying the moment a few weeks before when he'd seen Margaret for the first time, remembering how his chest had turned inside out, exposing his organs for all to see. She had been hurrying across Trinity's main quad during orientation. Thick notebook cradled in one arm. Torso a violin. Face so perfect it hurt his eyes, and yet he couldn't look away.

When he discovered that she lived in his dorm and on his very floor, he was unnerved. Too close for comfort. How would he survive with his heart outside his chest, vulnerable to the elements? As he helped her open her painted-shut dorm room window, he wondered how she failed to notice his heart's arrhythmic clatter.

Such a girl, Fitz knew, would be unlikely to welcome his affections because he weighed well over two hundred pounds. Two sixty-five, to be exact, about seventy-five pounds overweight for his height, according to his doctor. His mother, who had never weighed an ounce over her ideal body weight except when she was pregnant with Fitz, thought the doctor was being kind.

Genetics on his father's side might have been partly to blame, but after a freshman psychology course, Fitz believed he could trace his weight problem directly to the moment in second grade when his mother suggested he might want to lay off the Oreos his regular babysitter handed to him whenever he cried. Before that, it had never occurred to him that crisp chocolatey cookie sandwiches with a perfect layer of cream filling could be limited. That any food could be limited. In fact, the mere suggestion that he should restrict his consumption of delicious treats had opened a chasm of hunger in his young boy's body that seemed to have no end. It blossomed into obsession with food in all its variety, from the spicy samosas he could buy in Hartford's North End to the delicate whipped-cream-and-fruit-filled cakes that were a South End specialty. Before going to sleep, he thought about what he would eat for breakfast; at breakfast, he thought about lunch; at lunch, dinner. In between there were glorious snacks: Ruffles potato chips with sour-cream-and-onion dip, Milky Way bars, hard and soft cheeses, Freihofer's mouth-watering and slightly salty chocolate chip cookies. His mother advised him to chew on raw vegetables when he felt the urge to eat between meals, but he found carrots and celery tasteless to the point of being offensive. Only calorie-dense foods could appease the cravings that pursued him throughout the day like a pack of rabid wolves.

Without his mother's micromanagement, he had gained another fifteen pounds since starting college. In the main cafeteria, where he ate most of his meals, a soft serve ice cream machine offered two different flavors. And though the food was unlimited with his meal card, the cafeteria was not open all day, which meant that he had to eat enough to sustain himself until the next time he could pile as many dishes as he wanted on his blue plastic tray.

When his parents had dropped him off at the start of the semester, they had insisted on visiting the cafeteria to assess the potential for Fitz to follow a new diet his nutritionist had created for him. As soon as Arlene and Hamish walked through the broad double doors, a student with the physique of a sumo wrestler passed by with an enormous bowl of chocolate ice cream dotted with gobs of peanut butter.

"The only thing safe in here is the salad bar," Arlene told him. She pointed toward the dessert section of the cafeteria line, where squares of chocolate cake with thick vanilla icing sat waiting for takers. "See that? Poison."

"Some people like cake."

"It's criminal. I'm going to have a talk with the dean."

Hamish had never been thin, but he was the chief executive of an insurance company and rarely seen in public without a suit that disguised the excess weight he carried around his middle. A football player in high school and at Trinity, he could fool himself into thinking that at least some of his bulk was muscle. He put his hand in the air and rubbed his thumb against his fingers.

"I can feel the grease," he said. "Remember, if it's fried, ask for grilled. For what we pay in tuition, the dean should be out here spoon-feeding you."

They were right, of course. Fitz did need to eat differently, and maybe Margaret would be a good incentive, though more likely she would be snapped up long before he could drop the weight of a full-grown Labrador Retriever. He imagined her joining the group of girls who treasured his friendship. He could do with a little less treasuring, but such was the life of a boy who didn't turn out the way his parents had hoped.

When Fitz was ten, Arlene sent him to fat camp. He was four and a half feet tall and weighed 145 pounds, which put him well above the hundredth percentile in the charts on which the pediatrician tracked the one metric where he was expected to underperform. His mother, he knew, was both concerned and embarrassed. The other boys at the private school he attended had arms that grew no wider than the sleeves of their Izod polo shirts and the long, athletic legs necessary to board the camp sailboats on which they spent their summers. These, along with sandy blond hair and blue eyes, were achieved through generations of natural selection. The dark-haired chubby outliers like him tended not to reproduce.

His classmates had various names for Fitz, or Billy as he was then called in school, but the unimaginative "Fatty" stuck because it was alliterative with Fitzhugh. School was a daily trial. They found myriad ways to insult him without getting caught, filling his desk with empty candy wrappers and making subtle farting noises when he walked by. At lunch, he would sit by himself in the high-ceilinged dining room with exposed wooden beams and methodically eat every morsel on his tray. The big-boned cafeteria ladies tried to soothe him with looks of sympathy and the occasional extra dessert, but the boys wouldn't let him eat in peace, taking turns getting up for more napkins or ketchup so they could pass him while coughing "Fatty" into their slender hands.

The teachers weren't much better. In fourth grade, Mrs. Peterson cast him as Augustus Gloop, the gluttonous boy in *Charlie and the Chocolate Factory*, which had compelled his mother to plan a family trip to Portugal that necessitated Fitz dropping out of the play. His fifth-grade teacher Mrs. Handy, no ballerina herself, had been the one to suggest the fat camp.

"He has such a hard time making friends," she told Fitz's mother when she picked him up one day while he stood there listening, his enormous cheeks burning. "Slimming down might make him a happier boy."

To his great surprise, fat camp had been the most enjoyable summer of his young life. Instead of stumbling around the tennis court at the country club or pretending to be sick to get out of swimming lessons, he was surrounded by other fat children, many of whom were fatter than he was, which made him less self-conscious. That was also the summer he discovered his special ability to bring people together.

"Kitchen raid at midnight," he whispered to eleven-year-old Arnie, a cabinmate who tipped the scales at 180. "Tonight, we feast."

Fitz, Arnie, and a twelve-year-old everyone called Pudge had bonded in the first week over their desperate need to consume more than the twelve hundred calories allotted each day. Between long hikes and the twice-daily trips to the lake for swimming and boating, they were starving even when they were eating. Hunger unleashed in Fitz a resourcefulness that had previously remained dormant. One night, he had followed the kitchen staff back to their bunkhouse and saw through a screen door the key to the locked walk-in refrigerator. It was left on a hook for the morning shift. That night, Fitz, Arnie, and Pudge snuck into the bunkhouse for the key while the night kitchen staff smoked pot around a bonfire near the beach and the morning kitchen staff snored in their beds. The kitchen raid produced a random smorgasbord: cold chicken legs, leftover rice, vegetable medley, sugar-free Jell-O, dietetic bread. Each bite exquisite because it was forbidden.

The camp was in the verdant northwest hills of Connecticut, far from the prying eyes of tony Fairfield County, from which it derived most of its clients. It looked more or less like any other summer camp with its dormitory-style cabins surrounding a grassy hill on which was planted a towering pole that flew an American flag. But the cabins had no bunkbeds for safety reasons, and the dining hall was located out of sight down a sloping walkway below the athletic fields, a symbolic arrangement not lost on the campers. Meals were not served family style or cafeteria style but were individualized according to each camper's doctor-approved meal plan. Fitz, whose doctor had banned both breads and sugar, would trade under the long tables with Arnie, who couldn't have any fat: A hard roll for half a Salisbury steak or a fruit cup for a slice of avocado.

"Hook me up," Pudge said when he found out that Arnie had smuggled in a bag of Starbursts.

"Buck a piece."

"You suck, man," Pudge said, handing over a five and picking out his favorite flavors of individually wrapped, artificially flavored bliss.

The camp's black market thrived. Fitz's mother had given him spending money for laundry and other incidentals, and he used it to buy Doritos at an exorbitant markup, which meant that he washed his clothes only twice that summer. Late at night, he, Arnie, and Pudge would make a tent with their sheets and pool their contraband, scarfing it down when the counselors had their evening meeting.

"Did you see Cindy down at the lake today?" Arnie was on his stomach plowing through a single-serving bag of pork rinds he had acquired from a security guard who had access to the outside world.

"Bikini girl?" Pudge asked.

"Oh, yeah. She flaunts that big old belly. The counselors made her change."

Fitz unwrapped an orange Starburst and sucked on it to make it last. He had missed Cindy in her bikini and was sorry he did. Most of the girls wore extra-large men's T-shirts over their matronly one-piece bathing suits. Being fat was even harder for them, and yet, they cheated as well. Camp legend had it that one girl smuggled a dozen cans of Betty Crocker frosting through a false bottom in her suitcase.

Fitz later found out that the camp took this kind of cheating into account when formulating meal plans. It also had strict rules about body mass index, which had to be more than twenty-five. Otherwise, apparently, the camp would have been flooded with teenage girls who thought they needed to lose ten pounds.

At the end of six weeks, Fitz had lost eighteen pounds and had grown an inch taller, but still looked overweight. When his mother arrived to pick him up, he detected disappointment in her eyes, even as she smiled and congratulated him. She must have expected the thousands paid in camp fees to deliver her a son who didn't need to shop in the husky department. A son who could see his toes while standing.

As he stood on the scale his mother had delivered to his Trinity dorm room right after visiting the cafeteria, he understood what a dilemma his weight had created for her. It disrupted her assumption that her family would be picturesque and perfect, that wealth and attractiveness went hand in hand, but most of all that she had set a good example. How could a woman with such exquisite control of her calorie intake end up with a fat son? Her friends must have looked at her with pity, wondering what she had done wrong and congratulating themselves for not making the same mistake, whatever that may have been.

He stepped off the scale and tried to imagine putting his beefy arms around the slender Margaret. It was an image, even in his mind's eye, that didn't make sense, and so he pushed it away, wishing he could do the same with the cafeteria's maddeningly addictive chocolate cake.

—3—

Margaret

Freshman year dwindled to the final few months, and Margaret had yet to spend a weekend on campus. She took the city bus home every Friday afternoon to join her sisters behind the chipped Formica counter, forcing a smile as customers handed over their pit-stained Oxford shirts and rumpled pea coats with old tissues and receipts wadded in the pockets. As the cleaned clothes rustled by on the conveyer belt, Margaret tried to emulate her mother's love for the business. "Handle every item," Caroline used to say, "as if its owner is watching." But Margaret had never loved the store, which was hot and loud and steamy and full of chemical smells that seeped into her pores. The intimacy of handling people's soiled clothing made her uncomfortable. The only part she liked was the big old-fashioned cash register, which made a satisfying noise like a bicycle bell every time it opened or closed.

When her sisters, Lauren and Annabelle, were young in the 1950s, Richard's dry-cleaning business had been so successful that he had expanded into four suburban towns, a chain with nine locations and dozens of employees. Then came the explosion of synthetic, machine-washable fabrics, and a third child, Margaret, almost a decade after the first two. Margaret's childhood had been one of contraction: moving from a grand house in the suburbs to the smaller one where they now lived in Hartford; Catholic school instead of prep school; a chain of stores back to one that struggled to stay open. Being older, her sisters had felt the contraction even more keenly, and Margaret always felt they somehow blamed her for it.

Margaret picked up a rumpled white linen dress with a red wine stain and marked it with a tag that would signal it needed special attention. People tended to procrastinate with their stained items, balling them up and stashing them in a bag until they had enough to warrant a trip to the dry cleaner. It was a bit like confession, where Catholics collected their various sins and brought them to the priest, expecting him to perform miracles of renewal, no matter how stained their souls, making them whole and new again. The process wasn't "dry" either. Margaret sometimes wondered at the lack of curiosity in the general public. No one ever asked her exactly how it worked. As long as their wool sweaters and linen pants came back pressed and smelling fresh, they had no need to know that said items were tossed into a machine that looked pretty much like the one they had at home and soaked in solvents before being dried. The secret was really in the pressing, a machine that used vacuum technology to hold down the fabric and make perfect creases, and a steam iron that could take the wrinkles out of a Shar Pei. If those machines ever got cheap enough for the average person to buy, she thought, the entire dry-cleaning industry would collapse.

After her final shift on Sunday, her father drove her back to Trinity, insisting the whole way that Margaret take the next weekend off.

"You're missing out on college life."

She *was* missing out on college life and hadn't kissed another boy since David of the white tennis shoes, but she didn't want her father to feel that way, so she lied.

"Have you been in a fraternity basement that reeks of beer? It's not all that appealing."

"You'll be home soon for the summer, and I'll feel guilty if you don't at least stay at school for one weekend. C'mon. Your mother would have wanted you to enjoy college."

Richard looked as if he hadn't had a good night's sleep, or a day's peace, since her mother died. His eyes grew red, which meant that Margaret had no choice but to comply.

"Okay, one weekend."

"And do something fun. Act like you're in college. That's an order."

"Yes, sir."

So, that next Friday, she stayed at school and took an extra shift at her job in the theater box office, a cramped closet outside the main auditorium on campus where she sat selling tickets and balancing the books for the theater department. At least she would make a little extra money.

It was the closing night of a production of *Macbeth* in which a junior named Anders had played the title role to great acclaim. On Saturday, after helping to break down the set, Margaret was invited to the cast party held in a senior's off-campus apartment, and she went, pleased that she would be able to tell her father how social she had been. She watched Anders from afar as his admirers brought him drinks and listened to his amusing stories about flubbing a line or being forced to pantomime when he forgot to reset his prop sword. She admired his modesty. His talent was obvious, plus he was the most beautiful boy Margaret had ever seen. Liquid brown eyes. Cheekbones likes switchblades. Hair shorter than the style of the day but perfectly suited to his face. She never would have approached him, but they suddenly came face to face in the kitchen as she was rummaging around a counter piled with bags of potato chips looking for a bottle opener. Her heartrate increased alarmingly.

"Margaret, right?" he said, flashing the perfect white line of his teeth. He seemed to have more of them than the average human. "I've seen you in the box office. I'm Anders."

"I know, I mean, hi, yes, I'm Margaret." She found it difficult to access the part of her brain that formed sentences. "You were amazing in the show. I didn't see the whole thing at once, but most of it, at different performances. I stood in the back."

Anders put the beer bottle he had been holding on the counter and leaned on one elbow as if he planned to stay a while. His eyes were so dark she couldn't distinguish the irises from the pupils. He looked down, then back up, sweeping her into a rip tide with the curl of his long, dark eyelashes.

"Shakespeare's always a challenge. I'm afraid I don't do him justice."

Just then, three drunk girls came into the kitchen and pulled Anders by one arm into the living room so he could tell his prop story again. Margaret was about to leave—her night complete knowing that Anders even knew her name—when he was suddenly there helping her with her windbreaker.

"Let's get out of here," he said. "They're all wasted."

It was warm for a spring night. They wandered the campus talking about life and art and whether or not Ronald Reagan, who was impossibly old and ridiculous, would be elected president. It seemed so simple in the moment, a boy talking to a girl, but underneath the calm tone of Margaret's voice was a current of expectation and a clear understanding that this stunning boy found her attractive. He told her as much as they sat on a low stone wall with the sun rising.

"You know, I've noticed you before."

"You have?"

"Of course, I notice all the beautiful girls."

She felt her face flush as Anders leaned toward her, tucking a stray hair behind her ear and kissing her. It wasn't a terrible kiss, but a perfect one.

Two days later, Anders stopped by her room with a single pink rose. He was on the audition circuit for TV and commercial work, he told her, but he would be back from New York City in a week. They set up a date, an actual dinner date, for the first week in May. He kissed her again, very softly, as she stood holding the door with its lacrosse cats now peeling and torn after an entire academic year of holding their webbed sticks.

"Oh, that guy," Fitz said when she mentioned Anders as they were posting fliers for an end-of-year dorm barbecue. "I've seen him around. Seems a little full of himself."

Margaret found this presumptuous. She hadn't asked Fitz, who had become one of her closest friends, his opinion. She tried to brush it off.

"You'd think that, wouldn't you? I'd be full of myself if I looked like him. But he's really not. Tape, please."

Fitz handed her the roll. "What makes you say that?"

"He's very thoughtful. Maybe even old-fashioned. I don't know how long he'll be around, though. He's already auditioning for professional acting jobs."

They moved down the hall and taped up the last of the fliers. Fitz pulled the sweatshirt he'd been wearing over his head, giving Margaret an accidental view of his bare belly spilling over the top of his jeans. She found it surprising that Fitz was so heavy since he never seemed to eat anything when she was around.

"From what I hear, he's always hitting on freshmen."

"Come on."

"Just be careful, okay? I don't trust that guy."

Margaret frowned and tucked Fitz's warning into a back corner of her brain, where it fraternized with other warnings she had dismissed, such as the perils of an unpapered toilet seat and the danger of swimming within thirty minutes of a meal. Instead, she chose to remember, as she studied for finals in a quiet carrell deep inside the library stacks, that of all the girls on campus, Anders had chosen her. Was it weird, she wondered, that she already loved him? They barely knew each other, and yet no other word could describe the unfiltered joy that came upon her when she thought about him. Yes, she was in love. It didn't make any sense, but that was how she felt. Stupidly in love, blindly in love, open to whatever might happen, ready to experience the kind of heart-stopping connection she had read about and seen in movies. It scared her a little, and yet, she felt she had been preparing her whole life for one such as Anders Salisbury.

The next week, Anders arrived for their appointed date in a rusty white Toyota Corolla he had borrowed from a friend. She wore the dress she had purchased for the awards night in high school at which she had received a citation from the American Legion for good citizenship in addition to all the top math awards. The dress was cornflower blue, a fitted A-line with a wide black belt that emphasized her small waist. She had borrowed a pair of black heels from her roommate, whose feet were a half size larger, which meant she had to concentrate on squeezing her toes when she walked to prevent their flying off.

After a dinner of Chinese food for which Anders insisted on paying, they went to an art house movie theater in downtown Hartford for a showing of *The Rocky Horror Picture Show*, which Margaret had never seen before and found both intriguing and disturbing. "If I'm lucky, I'll be up on one of those big screens one day," Anders said as they left the theater, and Margaret thought he was being modest. Of course, he would be up on one of those big screens one day. On the way back to campus, Anders pulled the Corolla into an expansive city park and drove to a secluded area surrounded on three sides by trees. As Anders turned off the engine and set the parking brake, Margaret waited in the dark, her heart pulsing in her ears, her body filling with anticipation like a balloon stretched to the breaking point. Something, she knew, was about to happen.

Without saying anything, Anders leaned over and kissed her. A beautiful boy had his hungry mouth on hers, in a way she had always imagined. Then, in a way she had not imagined, his kisses became more forceful and heated, as if he wanted to weld his face onto hers. With their foreheads still touching, Anders climbed over to Margaret's side of the car and pulled the lever that released her seat into the reclining position. She tried to ignore the seatbelt buckle digging into her hip and the awkward position of her legs as his weight pinned her down. In quick succession, Anders ran one hand roughly across her chest, then reached down toward his belt.

In the tight, dark space, he struggled with his pants, his shoulder pinning Margaret against her seat. When Anders reached under her dress, it triggered a brief, horrible flashback to a math team competition at which a boy she didn't know had slipped his hand up her skirt and snapped her underwear. A high-pitched voice in her head said *Stop*, but it was drowned out by the distraction of Anders' hands—how could there be only two?—moving fabric, exposing skin, finding access. Her heart pushed against her ribs as she realized she could not move out from under him.

"Don't!" she said, struggling against him. "Stop! Please stop!" But he didn't stop. His hands were pushing her thighs apart and shifting her underwear to the side and then something hard was pushing against something inside her that was unyielding until it wasn't. A flash of pain, a number of forceful thrusts, a loud groan, and then it was over. Anders fell back into the driver's seat.

"Oh, God. Thank you. Thank you. Thank you. That was amazing. Thank you."

A robotic voice in her head was now clear as a public broadcast system. "Warning," it said, pointlessly. "Abort, abort." Immediately, she moved her clothing back to its normal position, her breath rapid and shallow, a burning sensation between her legs. She looked over at Anders, who was zipping his pants and straightening his jacket, then starting the car with a brisk turn of the key. She was glad he couldn't see her face, chafed and burning, in the dark.

When they arrived back at school, Anders parked the car near her dorm and leaned over to kiss her, and she let him, numb now and confused. He was tender again, sweet. He told her she looked beautiful in the moonlight.

"I'd walk you to your door, but I told Mike I'd have his car back by midnight," he said.

She opened the door and got out—mind racing, heart heaving, body on autopilot—giving him an awkward wave.

"Thanks for dinner."

"Anytime." He shifted the car into gear and offered her a snappy salute, as if he were shipping out for war, then drove away.

Back in her room, she took off her dress and laid it over a chair, then wrapped herself in her bathrobe.

"How was your big date?" her roommate asked without looking up from the book she was reading on her bed.

Margaret heard herself answering "Fine," because it didn't seem fair to burden a solemn and unsuspecting lacrosse player with what had just happened to her, whatever it was. She walked down the hall to the bathroom where she found some blood on her underwear, stuffed it into the trash can, and took a long shower in the hottest water she could tolerate. Back in her room, she dug around in her dresser until she found a pair of her old high-waisted, white cotton briefs and put them on along with a long flannel nightgown, climbing into bed and hugging her knees to her chest. Her brain was on fire, and she did not sleep all night, replaying what had happened in her head, looking for a scenario in which she did not feel used and humiliated and ashamed.

As daylight appeared in the dorm room's one window, it occurred to Margaret that Anders might come over to apologize: *I got carried away, I should have stopped, I'm so sorry.* She began to shake violently, and needing more layers, got up, put on her robe again, and climbed back under the covers. She could never be in the same room with him again. The thought of even seeing him on campus made her sick, so sick that eventually she had to run down the hall to the bathroom to vomit. Dizzily, she brushed her teeth, then felt her way back toward her room in the half dark as Fitz was leaving his room in a suit and tie. He took one look and gently guided her by the elbow to the common room, blessedly empty. She sat, shaking again, on a stained purple sofa with Fitz balancing on its arm. He let her cry and handed her wads of tissue, patting her back like a big, gentle bear.

"You don't need to tell me what's wrong, but you can. If you want."

Her confusion had evolved into a primal sort of fear. She couldn't explain, even to herself, how she had lost control of her own body within a few short minutes in a dark car. She pulled her bathrobe tightly around her throat.

"I know you went out with Anders last night," Fitz said, his voice dropping. He looked over his shoulder to make sure no one was in the hall. "And you wouldn't be this upset unless he did something terrible. Am I right that he did something terrible?"

Margaret nodded and dropped her head toward her knees, crying harder.

"You need to report him."

Margaret lifted her head, staring at Fitz through a curtain of tear-soaked hair.

"Report him? Where?"

"The police, Margaret. If he did what I think he did, it's a crime. A felony."

She pictured herself in a small interrogation room having to tell strange grown men in uniform, their faces rough with five o-clock shadows, what had happened to her body. It was not possible. She stopped herself from shaking by sheer force of will.

"I don't think you understand. I went with him willingly. I knew something would happen."

She pulled a misshapen, purple throw pillow over her lap. If anyone else found out, this befouling of a body over which she had always had perfect control would define her. She would be damaged goods, as her catechism teacher had once described girls who lost their virginity before marriage. She regretted running into Fitz. He didn't seem to grasp how important it was for her to keep this a secret, have a good cry and forget, forcing it down through layers of consciousness until it disappeared into the murky basement of banished memories.

"At least go to the clinic. Talk to a counselor, or campus security. You have to tell someone, so he won't do it again."

She put the pillow back and calmed her voice. "It wasn't like he planned it. He was just overexcited or something."

"Why are you making excuses for him?"

"Promise me you won't say anything. To anyone."

"But—"

"I don't want anyone to know. I just want to forget about it. Promise you won't say anything. Promise."

Fitz let his big head drop down to his chest. He looked defeated.

"Okay, but if you ask me, that guy knew exactly what he was doing. I would not be surprised if he's done it before."

Margaret shook her head. She couldn't allow herself to believe that Anders was a serial predator because it would mean he'd seen her as an easy mark, nothing more. She stood up. She would take another shower and get dressed. She would study all day in her room. All she needed was some time, some distance, and for Fitz to stop talking.

"I'll be okay. Really," she said, wiping the back of her hand across her nose. "Where are you off to in a suit?"

"My parents' club. The required monthly breakfast where my mother yells at me for eating bacon."

Margaret mustered a smile to send Fitz on his way. She hated to admit it, even to herself, but he had been right about Anders. It was too late, though. The damage was done. She returned to the bathroom and brushed her teeth again. If she could have maneuvered the tooth-brush around in her brain to scrub away any trace of Anders, she would have. She never wanted to think of him again.

Three weeks later, home for the summer, Margaret lay in her twin bed realizing that she had missed her period. She ran through her mental calendar and determined that she was at least a week late. On top of that, her breasts were so tender that she flinched when she rolled to her side. They were sometimes sensitive before she got her period, but this was different. This tenderness was accompanied by uncharacteristic heaviness and swelling. It seemed impossible, but with a dread that grew until it took her breath away, she wondered if she might be pregnant. People said it rarely happened the first time, but it did happen. She didn't have to ask herself how God could be that cruel. Her mother's death was evidence enough.

Margaret felt sure that what had taken place in the borrowed Toyota Corolla was meaningless to Anders, a boy who raked up girls like autumn leaves, yet it could send her life irretrievably down the wrong track. Careless gratification for him, confirmed by the fact that she hadn't heard from him or seen him after their date, could be devastating for her. She threw off the covers and went into the bathroom, hoping to find that she had gotten her period. Nothing. She sat on the edge of the bathtub feeling faint. She couldn't imagine carrying a baby, her young body distorted and distended, and yet good Catholic girls didn't have abortions. It was, she had been told over and over, a mortal sin.

A blurry week went by, during which Margaret breathed in dry-cleaning fumes at work with abandon and kneaded her abdomen until it was bruised, hoping to create an inhospitable climate for the speck inside that had already transformed her body. Her stomach was still tight and flat, but she felt as if she had been invaded, her veins stretching to accommodate more blood, leaving her light-headed.

After her sisters fell asleep, she would get up each night and look up abortion clinics in the phone book, writing the numbers in ink on her hand, but in the daytime, she couldn't make the calls.

The next Sunday, when her father and sisters went to church, she feigned illness and prepared to call Fitz. She hated to trouble him, but he would know what to do. He seemed like the only person who could help her. Then, just as she picked up the phone, a strong cramp folded her in two. She stumbled to the bathroom and made it to the toilet just in time for a rush of blood to fill the bowl. Over and over, her abdomen seized, and whatever cells had been growing in her unready uterus gave themselves up. Crying with relief, she cleaned herself with handfuls of toilet paper and closed the lid of the toilet, then sat on it until she could breathe normally again. When she heard the door open—her father and sisters coming back from church—she flushed the toilet without looking.

"You okay in there?" her sister Lauren called.

"Just threw up," she said. "Feeling better already."

"Ugh, stay away from me."

"Will do."

After cleaning the bathroom with shaking hands, she crawled back into bed, depleted. She prayed then, thanking God for sparing her from the guilt, shame, and embarrassment of either having a baby or not having one. Now she would not have to decide. Maybe God had taken pity on her, so alone in her childhood bed, so desperate and confused. She put an open hand on her belly and tried to slow her breathing. But as she lay there, something else occurred to her: What if her desire to end this pregnancy had turned her womb into a hostile place? Or what if Anders had done something to damage her permanently? How would she know until she actually wanted a baby?

If her dear, sweet mother had been alive, maybe she could have asked to be taken to the doctor. Maybe she would have found the words. Instead, she lay on her side and felt her organs, including her heart, curling inward, shrinking a bit to protect themselves. It was clear now. Being open to the universe was no longer a viable option. The walls would have to go up again, and this time, they would be constructed from concrete. In the meantime, she had dodged not a bullet but a grenade. And she was grateful. It meant that as long as she didn't look back, she could move ahead.

—4—

Fitz

Fitz sat on a bench overlooking the main quad. After four years, he knew Trinity's rhythm, how it rippled with energy and high expectations in the fall, fell into an alcoholic hibernation through the long, snow-cluttered New England winter, then burst into bloom for the all-too-short springtime. It was late April now, and the crab apple trees were in full blossom, the small white petals floating down, sweetening the ground like sifted confectionary sugar. Spring had always been his favorite season until this year when he would be graduating.

He checked the next two weeks in his planner, which was heavy with graduation activities, parties, and good-bye coffees and drinks. It would be hard to enjoy any of them. He wondered how long he could sit on this bench before anyone noticed he wasn't where he should be.

The week before, his father had picked him up and driven him over to NatCo, which Fitz's great-grandfather had founded, where Hamish was the CEO, and where Fitz had been accepted into the executive training program. When they walked into the imposing headquarters building with its Georgian columns and its marble floor, his father's secretary greeted them with an employee badge for Fitz.

"I've got your office all set up on the third floor," Hamish said. The expression on his father's face was one Fitz had never seen before. He might have called it joy.

Fitz pretended to be pleased but wanted to enjoy his last weeks at college and wondered why this abrupt transition to the real world couldn't have waited at least until he had his diploma. His father led the way up a wide staircase to the third floor, then down a hallway half the length of a football field before turning into a small outer office where a secretary who looked to be in her mid-twenties was ensconced behind a desk with a phone set that looked like something an air traffic controller might use. His father glanced at the name-plate on the secretary's desk.

"*Brenda* here is going to set up your appointments and training sessions so you can hit the ground running on Day One," his father said, gesturing toward the young woman, who looked sweet and slightly frightened. She had a round face and big brown eyes, and her hair looked surprisingly stiff and styled close to her head, though maybe that was the corporate look. Fitz was used to the girls at college with their curled bangs and feathery wings and hair teased to the texture of an old shag rug.

"Nice to meet you, Mr. Fitzhugh," Brenda said. She stood up and came around the desk to shake his hand. "I look forward to working with you."

"Nice to meet you as well," he said. "But please, call me Fitz."

His father gave a small shake of his head—the insurance industry would be the last to abandon its formality—and Brenda nodded. She showed them to Fitz's own, inner office, which was also small but elegantly appointed with a desk that took up almost half the room and two small chairs in front of it. A set of hardcover reference books was already on the shelf of the built-ins that lined the far wall. The window behind the desk had metal blinds on it, and Fitz hooked a finger on one slat to peek outside. Below him and as far as he could see was the employee parking lot. His father's office, on the other side of the building several floors above, had two large windows with a view of the gold-domed state capitol.

"The higher up you go, the better the view," his father said, looking toward back toward Brenda, who abruptly mustered a smile. "Am I right?"

"Absolutely, sir," she said, smiling now a little too emphatically. Fitz could see that part of her job was to summon up whatever expression the higher-ups wanted to see. Every executive's attempt at a clever riposte, no matter how lame, had to be acknowledged and rewarded. How exhausting. Whatever they paid her, it wasn't enough. He gave her a sympathetic look, though she seemed not to see it.

His father then took Fitz to the executive dining room, where they joined Hamish's top deputies for an artery-narrowing lunch of roast beef, gravy, and mashed potatoes that would have appalled Fitz's mother. Fitz had met most of them at dinner parties during his elementary and middle school years when he was trotted out to play a piece on the piano before going to bed. Over the course of two hours, they indoctrinated him into the NatCo culture and gently ribbed the boss.

"Your father's been talking about this day since you were five years old," Cal Trowbridge, the chief finance officer, said. "He's been holding on to that office for the last year, I kid you not."

"Guilty," Hamish said, eliciting laughs all around.

Fitz could see that this was a proud moment for his father, though no one had ever asked him if he wanted to work in the insurance industry. He once came home from school and told his mother he wanted to be a fireman, which had made her laugh in a way that told him how completely absurd that would be. In their milieu, he eventually learned, the only acceptable jobs required showering before work, not after.

"He personally picked your secretary from the typing pool," Peter

Green, his father's top legal counsel, added. "I hear she can type eighty words a minute."

"She's easy on the eyes, too," Cal said. "And let me tell you, I've seen some cows in that typing pool."

They all laughed and nodded in agreement. The young woman refilling their water glasses paused just long enough for Fitz to notice, then went about her work.

"Heifers!" his father said to more raucous laughter. "I've got to tell human resources to stop recruiting at the livestock convention."

They were all in stitches. Fitz looked down at his plate, which he had cleaned, sopping up the gravy with the soft, bland rolls that had been left in a basket on the table. No one seemed to notice he wasn't laughing. He looked around at the other tables of men in their black, navy, and dark gray suits, consuming their meals without a thought for the tired hands that had prepared them. This was where he would be expected to hold forth, to bray and bluster like the rest of the donkeys.

About a month before, Fitz had gone to a career center fair for seniors and taken a free Myers-Briggs test. The test told him he was insightful, creative, and caring, best suited for a job where his creativity would serve others. Some of the suggested careers were counselor, fitness trainer (ha!), dancer (double ha!), and musician.

Most of his fellow 1982 graduates had no idea what they would be doing when they were catapulted after college into the worst recession in decades. But he envied them. He envied that space to carom from job to job and fail and struggle until they found what suited them. Instead, he was looking at the rest of his life, the life his father had offered like a family heirloom, and he saw no way out.

In his last week at school, Fitz threw a graduation party in his suite. If he had to leave college, he would at least make himself a lasting memory to carry him through the first month or two at NatCo. It was also a way to spend a little more time with Margaret before he had to leave. Though Anders had left school early to pursue his acting career, and though Margaret seemed to have put her freshman year trauma behind her, she was still extremely cautious around men and went out only with groups of friends. Of late, she had seemed more at ease, and it cheered him to see her become more social.

Margaret arrived at the party in a summery yellow top with straps that tied in bows at her shoulders and a wide skirt with old-fashioned telephones printed on the fabric.

"Do you like it?" she said, holding out the skirt. "I got it at a thrift shop. It's from the *fifties*."

She said "fifties" like it was a better time, a simpler time, but Fitz knew that was a false image perpetuated by TV shows like *Happy Days* and *Laverne & Shirley*. Margaret would have hated the actual fifties, when she probably wouldn't even have gone to college unless she wanted to be a teacher or a nurse.

"It's the bee's knees, or whatever they said back then," Fitz said, hugging her. "I'm glad you're here."

He moved toward the kitchen to make Margaret's favorite—a rum and Coke—but she hadn't followed him. A girl from his history of cinema class handed Fitz a shot of Fireball, and he tossed it down. The apartment was crowded. Even as the heat of restless bodies surged around him, he could feel Margaret's presence through the walls as if she were emitting radio waves. He searched through the packed hallway and the living room, certain she hadn't left but unable to find her. Friends brought him drinks and asked him about his plans after graduation and thanked him for the party. When he finally moved back into the kitchen, there she was in her yellow top and her telephone skirt, her back to him. A junior named Steve who played in some idiotic rock band was talking to her, gesticulating as if he were explaining something she might find difficult to understand.

The air rushed out of Fitz's lungs so rapidly that he thought they were collapsing. Stupid-fucking-handsome Steve. Stupid-fucking college parties where people who weren't even invited showed up, bold as brass, and went right into your kitchen and drank your beer like they owned the place. Then a revelation born of fatalism and inebriation: There would always be a stupid-fucking-handsome Steve between him and Margaret. She would never see him the way he saw her.

All around him, people laughed and talked and drank, and he considered many of them friends, but he realized with a cold certainty that few of them would even notice if he left his own party, not even Margaret. Fitz drank from his beer bottle and noticed that the television was tuned into a soccer game, though no one was watching it. He wished he had the body of one of the players, even the ones with ham-hock thighs that were not as perfectly sculpted as Steve's. Any body but the one he had.

His mother's voice echoed in his ears. "Beer? Is that really a good choice, Billy? You might want to think about it."

It would be hard for him to lose weight but not impossible. He just had to buckle down, exercise, eat less, drink more water. When fewer calories went in than out, he would see his body change. He would feel lighter, more energetic. It would take time, but eventually, he could look like one of those soccer players if he really tried. Then women might look at him differently. They might tilt their heads at the angle of flirtation. They might imagine kissing him instead of telling him their problems.

After two more beers and several more shots, Fitz could feel the party dwindling through his haze. His friend Paul, an enormous defensive lineman who made Fitz feel less self-conscious about his size, slapped him on the back on his way out the door. "Good party, my man." Fitz suddenly felt the need to lie down, but people were hugging him and shaking his hand, and the room seemed to expand and contract like his already throbbing head. He felt a tap on his shoulder and turned around to see Margaret there, looking slightly concerned.

"Are you okay?" she said. "I don't think I've ever seen you this drunk."

"I'm nah drunk."

"Let's get you to bed. C'mon."

Fitz felt Margaret's small hand close around his large one as she led him to his room, shooing out a couple making out on his bed. He sat down heavily and let Margaret take off his shoes, then tipped over like an uprooted tree. The room spun around him, and he felt sick to his stomach. Margaret unfolded a blanket and put it over him.

"Sleep it off, big guy," she said, leaning over to kiss him on the cheek.

He caught her hand as she turned to go, and though his tongue did not cooperate with his brain, his thoughts were lucid and sober.

"Mah-gret," he said. "I need to tell you summ-thin."

"It can wait."

"No, now. I nee to tell you." The room had stopped spinning, and in his field of vision, Fitz could see only Margaret's sweet and beautiful face. It filled him up in a way that food never could.

"Okay," she said, her tone indulgent. "What is it?"

Even blitzed, he knew he might regret saying words he could not take back, but he couldn't stop them. He simply had to say something, or his head would explode, plastering the apartment with his obsessive thoughts and anxiety.

"I love you, Mah-gret. With all my heart. With all my soul."

She pulled her head back slightly. She was smiling, but it was a strange smile, a sad smile.

"I love you, too, Fitz. Now get some sleep."

He fell asleep thinking, *At least she knows.* But when he woke up in the morning feeling like regurgitated garbage, his breath still reeking of beer, Margaret's smile came back to him. In the harsh light of day, he understood that it wasn't sadness he had seen in her face but pity. He looked down at his stomach and grabbed a handful of flesh, shaking it. That was why Margaret couldn't love him the way he loved her. There was simply too much of him to be of any value.

He rolled painfully out of bed and went to the kitchen for aspirin. Luckily, he was leaving college and, if he tried hard enough, he could avoid her for the rest of his life. Gradually, painfully, he would forget her. It was the only solution. His head felt like an anvil and his stomach like a cesspool. On the positive side, at least he wouldn't feel like eating for a whole day.

The only thing Fitz liked about his job was working with Brenda. She was shy when he first started, afraid to interrupt him, and apologetic when she had to remind him about some meeting or phone call. Slowly, though, she had become warmer and more friendly. Brenda, he felt, was like one of the trifles his mother liked to serve to her book club. The top layer was whipped cream, light and airy and perfectly pleasant, but further down was the payoff—rich custard and fruit and the sherry-soaked sponge cake that used to give him a slight buzz when he swiped the leftovers and took them up to his room. Brenda had some fruit and custard in her, of that he was fairly sure. The sass and spunk of a sherry-soaked sponge, well, that remained to be seen.

As Fitz passed by Brenda's desk, she handed him several pink phone message slips and a black coffee. He thanked her, then shut his door, intending to immerse himself in the quarterly report his father had asked him to prepare. With some effort, he opened the folder and began rereading what he had written about risk management in tornado-prone areas. The bar charts blurred and danced. He took a sip of his coffee, put a hand on his forehead, and rubbed it, warding off a migraine. The blinds were closed, but the jailed sun found weaknesses in the bars, slipping inside.

Risk was something he thought a lot about. It's not a risk, for example, when you fall in love, as he had fallen in love with Margaret, because that can't be helped. The heart wants what it wants, or so he had learned in a college English class that had briefly touched upon the poems and letters of Emily Dickinson. The risk enters when you admit that love to the object of your affection, and no policy exists to spread the risk around, which is the whole point of insurance. But what if there were? What kind of premiums could be charged to indemnify the owners of hearts so fragile they could be stopped cold by a single indifferent look? When he thought about it, the potential for rejection insurance was unlimited. After all, Lloyd's of London had insured Betty Grable's legs and Dolly Parton's breasts. Why couldn't his company insure a heart? Only half in jest he was writing "Heartbreak—New Division?" on his scratch pad when Brenda tapped lightly on the door.

"Yes?"

"May I come in?"

"Of course."

The door opened a crack, and Brenda, always careful to take up the least amount of space possible, slipped past it and closed it again. She was carrying a second cup of hot coffee and the planner on which she mapped Fitz's schedule with colored felt-tip pens. She sat in one of the chairs in front of his desk and crossed her legs.

"Your father called a few minutes ago," she said. Her pursed lips went to one side and then back to center again. "He's looking for the tornado report."

"This?" Fitz said, nodding toward the papers on his desk.

"That's the one."

Someone had once told Fitz that secretaries always fell in love with their bosses, but he didn't believe it. Still, a tiny part of him, a fingernail's worth, wanted to think it was true. At least somebody would love him.

"Do you like working here, Brenda?"

She started as if he had asked for a massage. It was more of a personal question than a professional one, and yet, he felt entitled to know the answer.

"Of course, I do," she said, straightening the hem of her skirt. She touched her hair, which never varied or moved, but floated almost above her head like a hair-sprayed halo. The style made Fitz think of his sweet, old, mostly deaf great aunt Harriet, who had to be at least fifty years older than Brenda.

"Why?"

"I'm not sure what you mean."

Fitz propped one arm on the desk and rested his chin on the palm of his hand. His noggin was an empty stage. The pain was standing in the wings, fidgeting behind his left eye. Soon it would insist that he open the curtains and listen to its brutish, hours-long monologue, but for now, only the overture was playing. He tried to focus on Brenda.

"What exactly do you like about it?"

"Well, I think you're very nice, of course . . . and the location is convenient. It's not too far from where I live." She paused. "The cafeteria has a good salad bar."

"But the work itself. What do you like about that?"

Fitz wasn't sure how Brenda filled her days, but mainly, she seemed to function as a human alarm clock, reminding him of meetings and calls and deadlines. She handled his correspondence, but there wasn't much of that. She answered the phone. She took numerous messages from his father, who refused to call him directly or visit his office.

Brenda looked confused. She touched her hair halo again, and Fitz could almost feel its stiff texture on the nerve endings of his fingers. He guessed that she wore it that way even on weekends.

"I guess I like being useful."

"And you are," Fitz said, though it made him sad to think that her work life could be described with such an anemic term. Useful was better than useless, but there was a fine line. If you're too useful, you're vulnerable to being used up. He ran a few lines through the report as Brenda sat there, hands folded on her lap. Then he scribbled some notes in the margin and handed it to her.

"This should shut him up for an hour or two," he said, pinching the bridge of his nose as Brenda slipped through the door as unobtrusively as she had come in. He chose that moment to recommence his wallowing over Margaret, as if it were an important assignment he had been neglecting. She had called him earlier that day to get together, but he had put her off by blaming his job. "I do nothing but work, eat, and sleep," he had told her. "And sometimes I can't even sleep."

He had tried to cut her out of his life, hoping she would gradually fade from his thoughts, but this had failed. First, because she was persistent in calling him, though she never once brought up his confession of love. And second, because she came to him in his dreams. In one that was eerily literal and recurring, he and Margaret walked around a seedy amusement park eating caramel corn. When they entered the funhouse and looked into the mirrors, she was absurdly skinny, and he was obscenely fat. He had not seen her in person since he had graduated five months earlier, and he wanted to keep it that way. His new plan was to put her off until he lost a substantial amount of weight. Otherwise, they made no sense together except on terrible sitcoms, and the fault of that was all on his side. When the pain of his migraine began, he felt as if he'd been cored like an apple, the essential parts of him removed and left to dry in the unsympathetic sun.

—5—

Brenda

Brenda removed her wig and placed it on the Styrofoam form that sat on her vanity. She wished she could afford a better one. This one itched, and its hair—though it was actual human hair, unlike the synthetic ones she'd had before—had started to dry out. She was saving up for one with a layered cut and curved bangs like all the girls were wearing.

She ran a hand over the smooth surface of her scalp. Her affliction had a name she had been forced to learn when she was too young to understand its lifelong implications: alopecia. She sat down in front of the mirror and pulled off her fake eyelashes, two twisted spiders, then swiped each eye with makeup remover to get rid of the leftover glue. What looked back was a cloth-bodied baby doll put through the wash one too many times.

Then she smiled, remembering that Mr. Fitzhugh had asked her a personal question earlier that day. Her answer—some nonsense about the salad bar and feeling useful—didn't matter. Only that he had thought about her and how she felt inside.

She lay down on her bed under the pink canopy her father had made for her when she was in the fifth grade. The canopy was dusty and sagging now, but she couldn't bring herself to ask her father to take it down. She opened a textbook from her intermediate French class. Only three courses away from getting her bachelor's degree, though Mr. Fitzhugh didn't know that. She would surprise him one day, walking in with her diploma. Maybe he would look at her differently then. Maybe he would stop mooning over some girl named Margaret, whose picture he kept in his top right-hand drawer underneath the list of phone extensions that Brenda updated for him every month or so. It was strange to her that Mr. Fitzhugh didn't have a girlfriend. She worried that he thought of himself as unattractive, which wasn't true. Yes, he carried around a few more pounds than he should, but so what? He had a beautiful smile. Kind eyes. She only needed to look at his face to forget the round stomach that he mostly hid under dark suit jackets anyway.

She shut her book. She imagined Mr. Fitzhugh leaning over her, staring into her dark eyes, kissing her tenderly. Soon enough, it would be winter, and she could wear the stylish hats that covered her wig. Outdoors anyway. Fewer children would follow her with their questioning eyes, trying to figure out what didn't fit. She and Mr. Fitzhugh would walk out to the parking lot together one day while it was snowing. Her long fake lashes would catch the snowflakes, and he would brush them gently away.

The smell of her mother's Wednesday night meatloaf drifted in. At six thirty, her mother, father, and older brother, who worked in an auto-repair shop, would take the same places they always took at the kitchen table, and her father would mumble a perfunctory grace. They would eat quietly, each of them wondering when the tableau would finally change. Her brother was dating a girl her parents considered a tramp, but still, he had the best chance of shaking things up.

For Brenda, it was different.

Technology, at least, had allowed for vast improvement in wigs. Natural hair woven into a softer scalp net. More strands per square inch. But without any hair to anchor it with bobby pins, her bangs still occasionally migrated over one ear, and the wig still had to come off at night.

It won't matter to someone who loves you, her mother told her, but this caused an essential dilemma. Should she convince someone to love her and then reveal the shocking truth? Or should she reveal the truth before the love developed, hoping it wouldn't preempt it? She had never been able to figure this out, and so her weekends were quiet, spent reading and studying or making sandwiches for the homeless after church on Sunday.

"Brenda, Brenda, Brenda," her mother would say on some of those Sundays as Brenda sat at the same table where she had seen the first clump of hair fall into her mashed potatoes at the delicate age of twelve. "Don't let life pass you by." As if life were a convertible traveling in the left lane, speeding along next to Brenda's compact Chevy, about to leave her in the dust unless she performed some cinematic highway stunt and vaulted herself into the passenger seat. But that was ridiculous. No woman who wore a wig would willingly get into a convertible anyway.

At dinner that night, Brenda waited for her father to serve himself and pass the meatloaf. Her plate had a thin crack in it, and she stared at it, wondering if her mother would ever throw it away. Nightly, she tested where the cracked plate would land, pulling a stack of four plates from the cabinet and starting with her father's place at the head. It almost always came to her.

If Mr. Fitzhugh ever came to dinner, she would go out and buy new plates, something modern with a bold color, red or blue, or an edgy, asymmetrical pattern. She imagined him looking around at the same worn furniture and lace curtains they'd had since the sixties, the ancient hissing radiator, and the broken windowpane her father had covered with a piece of cardboard. He would be kind, though. He'd tell her mother what a lovely house it was.

Sadly, Mr. Fitzhugh only left her thoughts when she was absorbed in a novel or watching a particularly gripping movie. He carried Brenda around in his suit jacket pocket without even knowing it. Helpless. Hopeless. That's how she felt every time she entered his office and saw his sweet round face.

—6—

Margaret

When she was four and a half, Margaret began taking ballet. It was her mother's idea, but she went along with it, sitting through the tugging of her hair into a tight bun, the wrestling of small, uncoordinated legs and feet into thick pink tights, the leotard that pulled on her shoulders in an uncomfortable way. It was all worth it for the tutu, the bouncy spray of tulle that circled her waist and made her feel like a princess. She wasn't allowed to wear it during class, but her mother would let her put the tutu on at home as a reward for the boring positions and pliés.

One day after class, she changed from her ballet slippers into her Keds and ran out the back door in her leotard and tutu. The boys next door were playing in their backyard, digging trenches in a large sandbox their father had built for them.

"Hi," Margaret said.

The boys, Peter and Michael, were four and six, respectively. Both had blond hair buzzed down to the scalp and bare chests brown as acorns. They were outdoor children, always building forts and jumping out of trees and firing at each other with pretend guns they had fashioned out of broken toys and sticks and rubber bands. Margaret admired their intensity, although she rarely saw the point of their peculiar boy games, which seemed to involve an excessive amount of preparation and very little actual playing.

"Hi, Margaret," Peter said. He was the nicer one and the one in her class at preschool. They sometimes sat next to each other at snack time.

"Go away," Michael said, digging harder.

"What are you playing?"

"War," Peter said. As if Margaret would know what that was.

"How do you play?"

Michael stopped digging and looked at her, eyes pausing on the tutu.

"It's not for girls. Go home."

Margaret didn't want to go home. Inside, her mother would be cooking dinner, and her older sisters would be in their room, listening to forty-fives or daring each other to call boys on the phone. She wanted to play war, which, while inscrutable, seemed like it might be more fun than forcing her feet into unnatural angles and listening to the same piano piece over and over again. She pushed the tutu down and stepped out of it, tossing it on the grass.

"I can play now," she said, looking at Peter, who looked toward his brother.

"No, you can't," Michael said. "I told you, it's not for girls."

"Why not?"

"Because after we dig these trenches, we're going to have a battle. And that means we're going to shoot and kill each other. And girls can't do that."

"Why can't they?"

Shooting and killing held no interest for Margaret, but the sand beckoned. Ever since the sandbox had gone in next door, she had wanted to dig and play in it, to push around the great mounds of soft crystals. On one occasion when the boys were inside, she had filled a small bucket and brought it over to her own backyard, dumping it into a hollow at the base of a large maple tree to create a miniature beach for her Barbies.

Peter looked at her and shrugged. He had no authority when his brother was around.

She tried again.

"Why can't girls play?"

Michael picked up a branch from the weapons stash outside the sandbox. He aimed it at Margaret as though holding a machine gun.

"Pow, pow, pow," he said. "You're dead."

"Am not."

"Are too."

"Am not."

"You're dead."

The argument made no sense. She was standing in front of him, clearly not dead, yet he would not acknowledge it. Margaret retreated to her own rusted swing set, which had been new when Lauren and Annabelle were young, and watched the boys as they dug their trenches and gathered more weapons, including a stash of pinecones. It was the pink tights, she thought, and the leotard that prevented her from joining them. She pried the back of one of her Keds free and kicked it off, flinging it high, then the other. She got off the swing and peeled off the uncomfortable leotard and the suffocating tights. Free now in only her underpants, bare chested like the boys, she approached the sandbox again.

"Now I can play," she said.

Michael stuck his shovel in the sand. Peter looked at her, slowly shaking his head.

"You're in trouble," Michael said, and he clambered out of the sandbox and ran to the back door, calling his mother. Before Michael's mother could be summoned, Margaret's own mother came into the yard and saw Margaret's clothes in various places on the ground.

"What's going on out here?" She picked up Margaret's leotard and tights and approached the sandbox, where Margaret stood trying not to put her thumb in her mouth in case Michael came back outside. He would call her a baby.

"Girls aren't supposed to play war," Peter said without looking up. He kept digging, even though he had passed through the sand and was now hitting dirt.

"Is that so?" Margaret's mother said, stifling a smile that somehow made Margaret even more ashamed. She had done something unspeakably wrong, but she didn't know what, only that it had to do with the difference between girls and boys. Michael must have been right: Girls couldn't do the same things as boys. But no one had told her. No one had explained the rules.

"C'mon, Margaret," her mother said, leading her back inside. "We're going to play something way better than war."

That day formed one of her earliest and most vivid childhood memories: her mother taking her small trusting hand and leading her away from the sandbox, then drying her tears of confusion and rocking her as she sucked her thumb and fell asleep before dinner.

This well-worn memory came back as Margaret glanced out the kitchen window while scrubbing an abandoned saucepan coated in a dried cheese sauce with the consistency of grout. Her parents' small house had once been a marvel of efficiency, but it functioned more now as a Museum of Failure with appropriately low attendance figures. The overhead lights in the kitchen flickered and buzzed. Cabinet drawers gaped at the seams. Grime had worked its way into the holes of the salt and pepper shakers, stopping them up. The presence of her mother's absence could now be found in the layers of grease and dust she would have regularly removed. Every room, but most of all the kitchen, smelled of aspirin and Ben-Gay and habitual despair.

"Stop fussing with all that," her father said from his recliner on the enclosed porch just beyond the kitchen. "Come sit by me."

Margaret dried her hands on a cleanish corner of a crusty dishtowel and walked out to the porch, sitting down on a cold metal folding chair next to her father's brown corduroy recliner, which he had titled back to elevate his feet. In better days, he'd had eyes like a summer sky. Margaret's elementary school friends had been shy around him because he had been the most handsome of all the young fathers with his pressed shirts and his thick, dark hair. Now his hair was receding, mostly gray, and the color of his irises had faded into winter sky just before the first snow. Like a Polaroid exposed too long to sunlight or the photocopy of a photocopy, his colors had lost saturation. Maybe all fathers faded, but hers was ahead of the normal curve.

They sat in silence, staring through the mesh screen at the bird feeder outside. The feeder had only a trace of seed inside it, but a male blue jay landed on it, grooming his colorful wing in a shaft of late September sunlight. She liked to imagine her father sitting here, identifying the different species indigenous to central Connecticut, content in solitude, though she suspected he was often lonely even though all three of his daughters now lived with him. It was as though Caroline's death had permeated the house and kept them all in a state of lugubriousness and decline. Margaret tried to resist its pull, but her sisters, who had grown up with a cleaning woman, seemed to have accepted it as the new normal.

"Remember when your mother bought that?" Richard said. "We started calling it 'the squirrel feeder,' but we never took it down. She used to love to come out here and watch the squirrels when she was sick."

"I remember."

"She wanted so much for you, for all three of you," he said, sipping from a glass of water Margaret had placed earlier in the recliner's built-in cup holder. "She'd be so proud of your job and all."

Margaret nodded. When she had graduated that spring,

accounting seemed like the perfect job for an introvert who needed to help manage a family business. The numbers didn't care about Margaret's past or why she sometimes felt so ashamed of what had happened with Anders that she couldn't imagine anyone touching her again. The numbers weren't jealous or needy. They existed in their own peerless, orderly world and lived by unchanging principles. It was never their fault when things didn't add up. The blame was always external, and finding it was like solving a mystery. She had been so pleased to get a job offer at one of the bigger accounting firms in Hartford, especially since her grades had suffered a bit after freshman year, but she was already finding the office ecosystem difficult to navigate. Accounting had turned out to be more about the faces and names attached to the numbers, the men with briefcases who opened their tabbed folders and made cryptic notes with their engraved Cross pens, then told her she was even prettier when she smiled.

Her father shifted in his recliner. A cloud passed in front of the sun and the porch dimmed and cooled, bipolar September tipping away from summer into autumn mode. Margaret rubbed her upper arms to ward off a chill.

Richard smiled and turned away, pointing again to the bird feeder again and saying exactly what he had said just a moment ago. "Remember when your mother bought that? She used to love to come out here and watch the squirrels when she was sick."

Margaret turned her head to cry quietly, and by the time she was empty of tears, her father was asleep, snoring softly. She found her mother's favorite crocheted afghan in the living room and tucked it around her father, kissing him on the forehead. Who lost their memory at sixty-one? The doctors said early onset Alzheimer's was uncommon but not rare, and yet it seemed like an obscene joke to see it visited on three sisters who still hadn't recovered from losing their mother.

Margaret had thought about finding a small apartment, but it made more sense for her to live at home, propping up the dry-cleaning business as best she could and helping her sisters take care of Richard as his memory failed. She tried to pretend it didn't matter that the shower could only be turned on using a pair of needle-nose plyers, or that the markings had rubbed off on the washing machine dials, creating a sort of Russian roulette for each load of laundry. She scrubbed each room in turn, but the dinge persisted, impertinent and stubborn.

A few weeks later, summer finally conceded to autumn. Margaret was attacking the kitchen sink with steel wool when Lauren walked in to place a dirty sandwich plate on the counter. The age difference had made it difficult for Margaret to be close to either of her sisters, but now that she had moved back to the family home as an adult, she realized it wasn't only that. She and Lauren, for example, were almost opposites. Lauren was tall and extroverted, Margaret petite and introverted. Lauren loved movies, Margaret books. Lauren liked to cook and make messes; Margaret cleaned them up. Their only real connection was a deep love for their parents and a fervent wish that both had been less fragile.

Lauren began, "So this guy I'm dating, Henry, is having a party on Saturday. It's a bunch of his friends who teach at the Harwood School. Most of them are guys, so I told them I'd bring along my sisters. You're not busy, right?"

Margaret looked up from the sink. Lauren had never invited her to a party before. Immediately, she pictured a bunch of awkward male teachers with wide striped ties and slight paunches hanging over their khakis. In fact, a party with a bunch of men she didn't know sounded like her worst nightmare.

"Yeah, no thanks."

"It's not like a blind date or anything. Henry just wants to have a nice party, and I thought you'd enjoy it."

Margaret pulled out the spray nozzle and rinsed the sink. Her mother had managed to keep the enamel bright white, but she could manage no better than an indolent puce.

"You know I'm not big on parties."

"I'm stuck, okay?" Lauren said. "Henry promised his friends there would be women there. Show up, have a drink or two, and then leave. That's all you have to do."

Just then Annabelle scuffed into the kitchen in a robe and fuzzy purple slippers. She had recently dyed her hair red on an advertorial's promise that it would bring out flecks of gold in her eyes, and her heavy maroon lipliner made Margaret think of French mimes. Annabelle was much more attractive, Margaret thought, when natural and unvarnished. She was taller than Lauren and a little stout, though not unpleasantly so. As the baby of the family, who suddenly became the middle child when Margaret arrived, Annabelle at least occasionally played the peacemaker.

"Are you going to this party?" Margaret asked.

Annabelle cracked the refrigerator, stared at its contents, and then closed it. She opened a cabinet and took out a jar of peanut butter, found a spoon in the utensils drawer, opened the jar, and stabbed the spoon inside.

"Of course," she said, pulling the spoon out and licking it. "It'll be fun. You should come."

Margaret had nothing planned for the weekend. Maybe it wouldn't hurt to meet some new people. Fitz would talk to her by phone but never seemed to be available face-to-face, and most of her other college friends had fled to Boston or New York. She was still too new at work to socialize with anyone there.

"What time does it start?"

"Eight. So you'll come?" Lauren said.

"If you insist."

"I do."

—

On the day of the party, Margaret examined the options in the suit-cases and boxes where she kept her clothes since every closet in the house was already full. The dresses she wore to the office were too formal, and the sweatshirts, T-shirts, and jeans she wore outside the office were too casual. She had no desire to go shopping, where she would be tempted by beautiful things she had no business buying. Her salary was decent, but she pumped a good half of it into the dry-cleaning business to keep it solvent so Richard could maintain his health insurance.

"What's the dress code?" she asked Lauren, who was in her bed-room painting her nails a candy apple red.

"I'm wearing that," she said, pointing to a bright red crop top and a pair of high-waisted black jeans draped over a chair.

"Can I raid your closet?"

"Help yourself," Lauren said.

Margaret slid the hangers down the rod. She passed an entire safari—leopard, cheetah, zebra, tiger—before spying a light blue dress with a narrow waist, a full skirt, and puffy sleeves.

"How about this one?"

"That's one of my hideous bridesmaid dresses. I've been meaning to get rid of it."

To Margaret, the dress had an odd, rumpled, storybook quality. She wanted, for some reason, to rescue it from the dark recesses of Lauren's closet, and she liked the subtle message its eccentricity would send: Keep away. She had learned through her experience with Anders that appearing approachable could have unforeseen consequences.

"I kind of like it. Do you mind?"

Lauren shrugged as Margaret took the dress into the bathroom to steam out the wrinkles while she took a shower. An hour later, Lauren bellowed from the living room.

"Margaret, let's go."

As Margaret entered, her father, who was seated on the couch with a cup of tea, took in a quick breath.

"My God, Margaret," he said, eyes reddening. "You look just like your mother."

Lauren tugged on her top and dug around in her purse for her car keys as Margaret smiled at her father and kissed him on the cheek. She followed Lauren and Annabelle out the door, hoping they wouldn't want to stay at the party until the bitter, stumbling end, but at the same time knowing they would. Once her sisters had turned thirty, the air of desperation around them grew and became a thing people avoided, which meant they tried even harder. Margaret wanted them to find a way out of the weird codependency that had developed when Caroline got sick, but Richard's illness had only made it worse.

Ten minutes later, Lauren drove up to a homely split level with a long line of cars in front of it. Annabelle reapplied her lip liner in the visor mirror as Margaret sat like an afterthought in the back seat. Over the house, the moon functioned as a spotlight, casting a yellow glow on the tops of the trees and on the house itself.

"If either of you meet someone for me, give me the signal," Annabelle said, running a thumb along the corners of her mouth.

"Which is?" Margaret asked.

Annabelle peeked around the headrest.

"A squeeze on the upper arm. With a subtle nod toward the intended victim."

With all the animal prints in their closets, Margaret would have thought that her sisters liked to be seen as prey, but that was a ruse. Hunting was the metaphor they most often used when talking about relationships. Singling out the limping gazelle. Spearing the slow-moving boar. They also discussed men in terms of their "potential," which always reminded Margaret of her high school physics class and the other meaning of potential, as in the energy possessed by a something like a raised weight or a compressed spring. Her sisters were all potential, waiting for someone to release a latch and catapult them into a better income bracket. Part of her felt sorry for them, and part of her admired them for the openness they still had to love.

The three of them walked up to the front door in the same formation they had used in the car: Lauren on the left, Annabelle on the right, and Margaret two steps behind. Lauren tugged on her midriff, sucked in her stomach, and turned the doorknob. Once inside, they found themselves in a tight vestibule with half a staircase going up, another half going down. Lauren and Annabelle headed up, toward the lights, toward the conversational din, toward Madonna insisting in her nasal bray that she had made up her mind to keep the baby. Margaret was drawn to the quiet of the downstairs but reluctantly followed her sisters.

"Henry!" Lauren said as they entered a crowded living room choked with people wedged on and around an enormous, sectional, Ultrasuede sofa the color of a Tootsie Roll. "We're here!"

Henry, who sported the unfortunate combination of prematurely receding hairline and unibrow, pushed his way through the crowd and put an arm around Lauren's waist, pulling her tight.

"Therz ma lady," he said, all rubber lips and roaming hands, one slipping into the back pocket of Lauren's black jeans. It was only eight thirty. Margaret gave Henry another hour before he passed out at his own party. Lauren threw her head back and laughed; Annabelle disappeared into the crowd. Left alone, Margaret found small gaps in the crowd to advance toward the dining room in search of food.

The spread was meager. Two bowls of tortilla chips with accompanying bowls of watery salsa that were almost empty. The mandatory divided plastic container of crudité that hadn't been touched except for gouges in the central well of Ranch dressing. Some congealed chicken wings. A paper plate piled with erratically cut brownies. She sighed and filled a napkin with crudité and chips. Her crunching seemed to echo in her ears, and in the way of people with no one to talk to in a crowded room, she felt as if she were on stage and under a klieg light.

When she finished her snacks, she sought out the bar for a rum and Coke. She brought the drink back to her quiet corner and attempted to watch the others in the room as though they were on TV. She closed her eyes for a moment, imagining a lovely sunroom at the house Fitz's father had pressed him to buy, tilting back in a recliner with a view of the landscaped, heated pool he had told her about, though Fitz's decorator would no more incorporate a recliner than hang a piñata from the living room ceiling.

She was about to attempt conversation with a group of women in padded-shoulder jackets clutching white wine spritzers when a man approached her.

"Need a refill?" he said, though her glass was more than half full.

He was a man of average appearance, almost startlingly so. Average height, average weight, though maybe a few extra pounds around the middle. He had medium brown hair and brown eyes, a nose neither large nor small, lips neither thin nor thick. His clothes were casual, but his pants were not of the cargo variety, which she saw as a plus. He was neat and clean, smelling of Ivory soap. His only distinguishing feature was that, unlike anyone else at the party, he had approached her.

"I'm fine," she said, raising her drink to point out the obvious.

He started to turn away—which was what she had intended for him to do—but then something made her stop him. She didn't want to spend her evening in the corner alone or fend off the sloppy jousting for attention that would emerge fairly soon, given the pace of the drinking she saw around her.

"So, how do you know Henry?"

The man looked surprised that she had spoken to him. He took a quick sip of the beer he was drinking and cleared his throat.

"We're both teachers at Harwood."

Margaret's sisters had gone to a school like Harwood with imposing architecture and bow-tied deans when her father's dry-cleaning operation was a mini-empire. So Average Man was a schoolteacher.

"What do you teach?"

"Seventh grade history." He rocked back a little on his heels and took another sip of his beer. "Pretty much your basic survey of the world from the beginning of recorded time."

Margaret noted the sense of humor, though she was more focused on the man's shirtsleeves, which had the crisp look achieved by a commercial presser. He had his shirts laundered. As the daughter of a dry cleaner, this impressed her.

"What do you do?"

"I'm an accountant."

"How do you know Henry?"

"He's dating my sister. I was kind of dragged here to balance out the genders."

She found herself conversing easily with Average Man, though his eyes kept darting to the sleeves on her sister's storybook dress.

"I'm Douglas," he said, extending his hand.

"Margaret. Nice to meet you."

What followed was a long conversation whose details Margaret had mostly forgotten by the next day. She did recall feeling, though, as if she had finally learned what most people did, or aimed to do, at parties. It was a revelation, really, that a man she had just met could talk to her like a person, maintaining eye contact once he had stopped staring at her sleeves, listening to the sentences and phrases she uttered, offering appropriate responses. The only other person who had been able to talk to her this way was Fitz, and in recalling that, she felt the pang of loss. He seemed to have slipped into a whole new life that didn't include her except for the occasional phone call. His confession of love before he graduated had surprised her because she had never considered him in that way. But afterward, she had turned the possibility over in her mind and found herself intrigued, maybe even interested. Then again, drunken confessions of love didn't necessarily count. Maybe he didn't even remember saying it. She wanted to talk to him in person about it, to sort out her own confused feelings, but he kept avoiding her. Lately, she had accepted that he didn't make time to see her because it wasn't important to him. Fitz had moved on.

Gradually, the crowd in the living room thinned, and Margaret walked outside with Douglas. It was after midnight, and Lauren and Annabelle had slipped away from the dwindling scrum to unseen parts of the house. Douglas asked if he could drive her home, but she said she would wait to make sure her sisters got home safely.

Douglas opened his passenger side door, rummaged in the glove compartment and found a torn scrap of paper and a pen. He asked for her number with an earnestness she found endearing. She hesitated, though. She could imagine kissing him—his mouth would taste of sharp cheddar and beer—yet she guessed that his palms would be unpleasantly damp. He had been forced to peel the fragment of an envelope or, perhaps in his eagerness judging by the weight of the paper, a car manual, from his warm hand before handing it to her.

Douglas waited, motionless, as she clicked the pen several times with her thumb. She had been surprised to meet a man who, it seemed, would not rush her, a man who would not startle her into doing something she had no intention of doing. His patience convinced her to take a risk. She wrote her number down on the damp slip of paper, leaning on the cool car hood beneath the spotlight moon.

—7—

Douglas

Since arriving at Harwood, Douglas had spent most of his time in a panic writing elaborate lesson plans, scripts almost, to limit the cotton mouth that sometimes attacked him in the classroom. Prep school was nothing like the public school at which he had done his student teaching and his long-term subbing, where the high schoolers seemed more interested in fondling each other or covering their undersized desk-chairs with crude graffiti. The prep school students had planners and bought the suggested supplemental texts. They had no doubt been exposed to classical music and opera since birth. He sometimes feared they knew more than he did.

He had gone to Henry's party only because one small cluster of synapses in his throbbing brain told him he needed to relax.

"It'll be a blast, man," Henry had assured him. "Lots of beautiful babes."

This had turned out not to be true, with the exception of Margaret, who was standing by herself, one forearm crossing her abdomen, holding an elbow as if her other arm were tired. She had a highball glass of what appeared to be a soft drink and wore a knee-length dress with wide puffy sleeves. The dress made her appear thin and fragile, lonely and at a loss, a little like Princess Diana. He wanted, for reasons that could only be explained by the three beers he had consumed on an empty stomach, to rescue her.

"Need a refill?" he'd asked, though her glass was half full.

"No, I'm fine," she said in a not-at-all-fragile voice, holding up her highball glass, which stood in relief against her puffy shoulder.

He had started to turn away—more than one woman in his short life had told him to get lost in much the same way—but she spoke up.

"So, how do you know Henry?"

"We're both teachers, over at Harwood."

"And what do you teach?"

"History. To seventh graders. In public school, they call it social studies." Other words came out of his mouth, but he couldn't remember them. "What do you do?"

"I'm an accountant. I graduated in May, so I'm new to it. . . ."

A pleasant hum arose in his ears as other words followed. He suppressed an urge to touch one of the puffy sleeves. Did the fabric stay inflated on its own or was there some kind of filling, as it were, that kept the sleeve's shape? In his search for clues, his eyes traveled to the face above the puffy sleeves. She was, he thought, very beautiful. Too beautiful. He considered fleeing but couldn't think of an excuse to leave the conversation. Instead, the alcohol inside him casually suggested that he double down.

"I'm Douglas," he said, extending his hand.

"Margaret. Nice to meet you."

At this unexpected exchange, Margaret smiled in a way that Douglas could only describe as grateful, and it occurred to him that the loneliness he had detected earlier was genuine.

As the party wound down, Margaret walked with Douglas to his car. He opened the passenger door and the glove compartment, tearing off a corner of the car manual, and after a moment of hesitation during which he surreptitiously wiped his sweaty palms on his pants, she scribbled her phone number on it, leaning on the car hood in the cool night air. He found himself strangely moved by the delicate tendons in her neck, which caught the moonlight as she looked up and handed him the small scrap of paper. She reminded him of a ballet dancer. Strong and agile, but also frangible and weightless. A mysterious contradiction.

For days after Margaret had given him her phone number, Douglas carried the torn scrap of car manual, transferring it from the back pocket of his casual pants to the jacket pocket of his blue blazer, and then to the front pocket of his teaching khakis. He rubbed it like a talisman until the paper became soft and pliable, almost like fabric. The numbers written in pen became smudged with the oils from his fingers but remained legible. He would marvel at the wonders that might be bestowed upon him should he avail himself of their power to connect him with a beautiful stranger. Seven digits, dialed in a certain order. The combination to the lock. The incantation. And he had them in his possession. Finally, three days after they had met, an amount of time he had been told would seem neither creepily eager nor uninterested, he dialed, his hands shaking slightly, glancing at the paper as if he had not already memorized her number.

In the way of casual decisions made in the precious and precarious window of young adulthood, Douglas's move to Hartford had set everything in motion. He sometimes looked back and wondered why he hadn't put more thought into it.

After both of his parents' deaths only six months apart—his mother of lung cancer two months before his twenty-fifth birthday and his father of emphysema four months after it—he had been forced to sell their small family home in Pittsburgh to pay off the medical bills. For two weeks, he had examined the evidence of their tightly circumscribed, smoke-filled lives, tossing most of it in a rented dumpster. In one box, he found an old, folded road map of the United States with a line drawn in pen along Route 66, perhaps a trip they had wanted to take but never did. He spread the map on the worn kitchen table and examined the country in all its pastel glory. Nothing tied him to Pittsburgh with its emptying steel mills and its deserted downtown. And he was a teacher, which meant he could move almost anywhere. His finger, as if on a Ouija board, moved west toward the pale rose of Illinois.

Chicago? He had been there once on a high school trip for the Model United Nations and had found its broad boulevards and aggressive street vendors intimidating. Large cities in general made him question his ability to cope with a crisis. His finger took him north and further west.

Montana was a light blue rectangle that held the promise of vast, cloudless skies but little else. What did one do in Montana besides ride horses and sigh at long vistas of nothingness? He needed a certain density of people and services: convenient gas stations and grocery stores and a place to take his button-down shirts to be cleaned.

California, green as a slice of avocado, was enticing. He had never been. The Beach Boys had painted for him a mental picture of sunshine and surfing and tall blonde women in bikinis. The ocean, though, would always be on the wrong side. He imagined himself waking up at night and feeling as if he were lost.

The South didn't seem like an option. Heat made him lethargic, and he hated sweet iced tea, which is what he had been served at lunch and dinner daily on a college service trip to build houses for the poor in Louisiana.

He looked to the East. He wasn't fond of crabs or seafood in general, so the Mid-Atlantic had nothing compelling to recommend it. The Northeast then, where there was rumored to be an appreciation of history. During his student teaching in Pittsburgh, a parent had gone to the principal after Douglas gave his son a failing grade for failing to complete any of his assignments, and the principal had unilaterally raised it to a D so the boy could play football. The Big Game. As if that mattered more than understanding the past.

From what he had read and seen in movies, New York's blue-gray and New Jersey's purple were both encased in a toxic smog. He examined the relatively small geographic area of New England. Except possibly for Portland, the pale yellow of Maine was out. Too cold and too rural. Vermont in light green and New Hampshire, pink as a pig's ear, suffered from small populations that took themselves and their maverick reputations too seriously. Rhode Island, a tiny spot of tangerine, seemed like the odd relative no one speaks to at family picnics.

That left Massachusetts and Connecticut. Boston did not appeal to him with its strange relationship to the letter "r." He might not even understand what people were saying. The rest of Massachusetts (in peach) was a big blank to him, towns and small cities with generic names like Springfield. Connecticut, though, was a comforting soft brown. Hartford, he knew, was a small, manageable urban area. For many years, it was the home of Mark Twain, who had been the subject of his senior project in high school and remained a fascinating figure for him. He could stroll the streets Mark Twain had strolled, visit his home, feel the shade of the same towering trees that had once cooled the great writer. He could start with Hartford, anyway. If it didn't work out, he could always move. That was as far as he thought about the decision, from which he could trace in a straight line the fourteen applications he had sent to secondary schools in the Greater Hartford area, the job he had landed at Harwood, and the party that led him straight to Margaret.

On their first date after meeting at Henry's party, Douglas took Margaret to a quirky little pizza place with dollar slices and cheap beer, hoping to impress her with offbeat charm since he couldn't afford an expensive restaurant. He made a show of pulling out a stool for her. Unsure of what to say, both of them watched the TV mounted above the counter as they waited for their slices to warm.

"Oh," she said, pointing at the screen. "I know that guy."

Douglas looked up and saw a rather large man speaking to a local news announcer about a road race sponsored by the insurance company he apparently represented.

"Sweetest guy on the planet," Margaret said. "We met in college."

Douglas took a sip of his beer. The question had to be asked.

"Just a friend?"

"Yes."

"He wasn't interested in anything more?"

Margaret looked back toward the television. Her eyes, for a moment, lost their focus.

"We came from two very different worlds. His family belongs to a country club. Old money and all that. Mine is always one step away from bankruptcy."

"Well, he's kind of on the heavy side. Maybe he thought you were too beautiful for him. Either that, or he doesn't like women."

"Come on."

"I thought you were too beautiful for me. I attribute my bravery to two gentlemen: Mr. Anheuser and Mr. Busch."

Margaret took a small sip of beer. She seemed to be contemplating whether or not to change the subject.

"He said something once, but he was drunk. That doesn't count."

"It doesn't?"

"Of course not."

Margaret paused, then sighed, pulling her shoulders back. He had no idea what she was thinking.

"Let's not talk about college. Tell me how you ended up in Hartford."

Looking back, that had been one of the highlights of their early relationship. He had felt so close to her that night. The spark was undeniably there on his end. Seemed like hers as well, though he found her hard to read. When he took her home after that first date, they had stood on the front steps of her father's house for a long awkward moment until she leaned over and kissed him goodbye on the cheek. Normally, he would have seen that as a rejection, but her smile as she turned to go inside was an invitation to keep trying. He decided then and there to accept the challenge.

—8—

Fitz

Hartford retained traces of its glory days: the grand Wadsworth Atheneum, Mark Twain's brick fantasy of a home, the gold-domed State Capitol, the venerable Bushnell Theater. But G. Fox's enormous department store wasn't what is used to be—they barely changed the window displays anymore—and whole neighborhoods were pockmarked with abandoned buildings, giving rise to a general habit among residents of peeking through curtains and blinds to make sure their cars were still sitting where they had been parked. Its residents tried to like Hartford, but it was too close geographically to self-satisfied Boston and overachieving New York. It was the moping loner of a cousin about whom the adults spoke in whispers. Lack of motivation. Not living up to potential. Perhaps a drug problem.

That afternoon, Fitz and his father, Hamish, sat at a long, glossy table in a lawyer's downtown Hartford conference room to discuss litigation over a claim. Fitz studied the view while his father and the lawyer talked. From twenty stories up through floor-to-ceiling windows, the tree-lined Connecticut River appeared to bump a friendly elbow into the city's perimeter. Up close, the river was a brackish liability, sucking in inexperienced boaters and homeless alcoholics by the dozen every summer.

Really, though, almost everything was a liability. Doors, stairs, windows, cribs. The equipment of everyday life maimed and killed people every day. It was right there in the risk management reports that few outside the industry ever saw, but Fitz had to carry that information around in his head. It sometimes left him wanting to warn young mothers and fathers when he saw them out with their death-trap strollers. The lawyer tapped the table to get his attention.

"It's important that we speak with one voice here. The claim is being denied on the basis of intent to die. That's the language we all need to use."

The lawyer picked up his pen and underlined the words, turning his paper so that Fitz could see it. *Intent to die.*

"What exactly does that mean?" Fitz asked.

Hamish coughed. The lawyer leaned forward, both elbows on the slick wood of the conference table. He was a thin man, most likely a smoker based on the color of his teeth. Fitz hated these meetings, where he was mostly an observer, but his father wanted him to know every aspect of the business.

"This policyholder had end-stage cancer, so we are taking the position that his car accident was intentional," the lawyer said.

"You're saying it was suicide."

"That's correct."

"And that means we wouldn't have to pay the accidental death claim?"

Hamish gave Fitz a look that suggested he shut up. He chose to ignore it.

"You're telling me that this guy couldn't possibly have crashed his car accidentally."

"Think, son," Hamish said before the lawyer could answer. "He was at the end of the road with his treatments. His doctors say he was despondent. I'm not surprised his wife is suing, but we have a strong case."

Fitz looked out the window again. A large bird, a hawk maybe, flew by, dipping one wing to turn on the wind. How magnificent it would be to sail on the breeze instead of smelling the ash-tray breath of a lawyer who had no difficulty procuring the "language" that would keep the company's books clean, even as it failed a family that had paid its premiums like everyone else. The lawyer sat quietly, fingers tented.

"What did the police report say?"

"Inconclusive," his father said. "He went off the road and hit a telephone pole."

"Did he leave a note?"

"Not that I'm aware of, though I'm sure the wife would have destroyed it."

"So, you blame her."

"I don't blame anyone, but we're within our rights to contest the claim. If the litigation goes against us, we'll pay what we owe."

"In the meantime, this widow and her family get nothing, and they have to pay a lawyer to even hope of seeing a penny."

"It's a ten-million-dollar policy."

"Which they paid for."

"And which we have every right to contest."

Fitz crossed his arms. Despite spending millions on advertising that touted the company's personal and compassionate service, his father tended to view policyholders who tried to collect as panhandlers. Sure, there were a few unnecessary whiplash collars and the occasional arsonist looking to bail out a failing business, but nothing to justify his father's default mode that all claims had a potential loophole. But that's what it took to succeed. Keep the money flowing in, not out. Make the shareholders happy. Crack down on grief when it requested compensation.

At one end of the conference room was a large blue and green glass bowl on a pedestal. Fitz left his father and the lawyer to finish the paperwork and wandered down to look at it. The edges were curved and crimped like some fantastical sea creature, which made it beautiful but useless. Fitz stifled an impulse to pick it up and throw it, although the carpeting was so thick maybe it wouldn't even break.

He turned back to the window and sighed. Lint trap of an afternoon. Exhaust billowing up from the rush-hour streets below. Dark clouds mugging the horizon. Below, in the leafless gray of late November, bridges crossed the river, and beneath those bridges lived homeless men and women whose worldly possessions fit inside a rusted grocery cart. Did they ever look up and wonder about the suited men and women working in the high rises above them, sipping dark roast and fretting about their pension funds?

"Son—"

Fitz turned around. Both the lawyer and his father were standing, apparently waiting for him. In the world of business, his father was a shark who, much to his chagrin, had raised a manatee who preferred munching on placid groves of seaweed to following a trail of blood.

"We're done here," his father said. "Let's go."

Fitz followed him out and into the elevator, his mood dropping with each floor. Margaret had called him twice in the last month and suggested getting together, but he had given her more excuses about work. Even with all his dietary restrictions—no bread, no sweets, no fried foods—he had lost only twenty-one pounds since his graduation more than a year earlier, and he didn't want to see her again until she might look at him differently. Until he might look at himself differently, too.

Seventeen sycophants sat solemnly.

Fitz began a poem in his head as he watched his father conduct a meeting of NatCo's board of trustees. His father had invited him to sit at the table and observe.

"It's a rare opportunity for someone at your level to watch the inner workings," Hamish had said before the meeting. "Pay attention."

Most of the people in his management training group would have stabbed their own grandmothers to sit where he was sitting, and yet, he would have traded places with them gladly. Being the favored one made him feel like fraud, but his father saw it differently, regularly pointing out how grateful Fitz should be.

"If my grandfather hadn't founded this company, and my father hadn't turned it into a national powerhouse, you and I would be sitting here with nothing."

His father assumed the whole family would be stuck in a Depression-era time warp if Great-Grandfather Fitzhugh hadn't taken a crack at the old insurance business. But that was absurd. The Fitzhughs would have found their way. Instead of insurance titans, they might have been poets and teachers and car salesmen and librarians, and why would those modestly compensated professions have made them any less respectable or worthy? His father had the same attitude about money that Fitz had about food. Any suggestion that it might be restricted left him pale and shaking.

Some board member was pointing to a chart on an easel and asking questions about a subsidiary of the company. Fitz's boredom reached a threshold he had never before experienced, even during the etiquette classes his mother had force him to attend as a child (*The cream soup spoon has a larger bowl than the oval soup spoon*). His vision blurred, his thighs felt numb, and his left eyelid began twitching. He shifted in his chair and rubbed his eyes. He must have made some sort of involuntary noise because the board's attention suddenly turned to him.

"Did you have a question?" his father asked.

I have many questions, he thought. *Why I am here? What is my purpose in life? Does a cream soup spoon really do the job any better than an oval soup spoon? Better enough to require an entirely different class of spoons? Seventeen sycophants sipped soup with a spoon.*

"No, sir," he said. "Please continue."

The presentation began again, sounding to Fitz's ears like a distant swarm of bees, rising and falling on the wind. If life were short, as many said it was, how could a board meeting bend time so that one afternoon could feel like an eternity? Fitz pulled a pen from the inside pocket of his suit jacket. He reached under the long, elegant table around which the seventeen sycophants solemnly sat. In his own tiny act of rebellion, he wrote upside down as best he could: HELP.

After the meeting, he returned to his office to find Brenda and another secretary, Lydia, flipping through a *People* magazine. Brenda slapped it shut as soon as she saw Fitz, and since Brenda rarely socialized when she should be working, he blamed Lydia, who seemed to devote herself to distracting other people as though she were paid for it.

"You went to Trinity, right, Mr. Fitzhugh?" Lydia said. She had none of Brenda's poise or restraint. "Did you know this gorgeous man? He was there around the same time you were."

Lydia opened the magazine to a full-page article about Anders Salisbury starring in his first feature film. In the photo of Anders, a beautiful young actress with long blond hair had her head buried in his shoulder as if they had been sculpted as one piece, the artist carving only a fine line to indicate their separateness. A shudder passed through Fitz's body. Anders seemed to be staring directly at him, mocking him with his toothy grin.

"Not someone I admire," he said, after sorting through and rejecting the language that first came to mind. He wondered what Brenda and Lydia would think if he ripped the photo from the magazine and threw it in the garbage.

"Well, he's a looker, I'll tell you that," Lydia said. "I just thought you might have the inside scoop."

"I don't."

Lydia frowned and picked up the magazine. "Sorry I asked," she said, then turned to Brenda, "but we're still going to see this movie."

Fitz left them and closed the door to his inner office. He sat down and dialed Margaret's work number. His hands were shaking so badly that he kept misdialing, but he persisted. She answered on the second ring.

"Hi, you," she said.

She sounded uncommonly upbeat.

"How did you know it was me?"

"We have this new system that shows us the number of who's calling, which means I don't have to pick up when Trinity calls me to ask for money. So what's up?"

Fitz twisted the phone cord around his index finger. He hated that he would spoil her mood.

"Have you seen the latest issue of *People* magazine?"

"You know I don't read those except when I'm at the dentist's office."

"I just didn't want you to see it without being prepared."

"Prepared for what?"

His finger was beginning to turn blue, so he unwrapped the phone cord.

"It's Anders. He's in a movie—a real movie—called *Deadbolt*. There's a feature about him. I thought you should know."

He listened intently, but Margaret said nothing. He began to wonder if something was wrong with the phone.

"Are you okay?"

"I'm here," she said, her voice flat. "I'm fine."

"You're fine? Why are you fine?"

"I've put that behind me."

"I'm sorry, what? How have you put it behind you?"

"I don't think about it. And neither should you."

This struck Fitz as impossible, or at least his brain didn't work that way. The more he tried not to think about something, the more it crept into his consciousness, sneaking in around the edges he had folded and crimped like so much aluminum foil.

"You know it's not too late to report it," he said.

"I appreciate your concern, I really do. But the less said about that person, the better."

"If you say so."

In theory, he understood. Margaret couldn't change the past, so she chose to pretend it never happened. But he could tell her from his own experience that trying to forget something, or someone, could have the opposite effect.

"I can hear my boss galumphing down the hall."

"Okay, talk to you soon."

When Fitz closed his eyes and rubbed them, the image of Anders and the young actress rose in his mind. *Deadbolt* looked idiotic, but Fitz could tell from the adoring look on the young actress's face that millions of other women besides Lydia would want to see it anyway. The son of a bitch would not be erased no matter how much Margaret wished for it. It came to him that there are primitive men who swing through life with machetes, only vaguely aware that clearing a path for themselves might have a negative impact on the flesh-and-blood creatures who live in the environment they're destroying. Blithely, they move along, never looking back to see what devastation they might have wrought, judging only how quickly they can reach the next watering hole, rewarded at every stage for their efforts. Treated like heroes.

—9—

Margaret

When Douglas dropped down on one knee near the Bushnell Park carousel in the spring of 1984, about six months after they met, Margaret thought he had dropped some change or needed to tie his shoe. His shoes never seemed to stay tied, which mildly annoyed her. Then she noticed the small, black velvet box he had pulled from his pocket. He was holding it with two hands, one supporting the other, as if the box were much heavier than it looked.

A few thoughts flashed through her mind in that moment: 1) Douglas was proposing; 2) he had chosen a public place where she could not think about it for more than a few seconds without disappointing everyone around them; 3) there was no reason at all that she shouldn't say yes.

"Margaret, you are the best thing that ever happened to me," Douglas said in a way that sounded rehearsed. "And I know this is fast, but I've been thinking about this day since we met. Will you marry me?"

For a moment, Margaret imagined telling her mother she was engaged, and it took her a heavy heartbeat or two to push aside the crushing realization that Caroline would never know. Then she tapped Douglas on the shoulder, wanting him to get up, to speed the whole process along. "Of course, I will," she said, because of course she would. It made perfect sense, and what a relief to be done.

Done with dating, though she had gone out with very few men. It had been four years since what happened with Anders, and until Douglas came along, she was still terrified to be alone with a man except for her father and Fitz. Now she would never have to worry about dating again.

Done with living at home, sleeping on the bent-frame pullout couch in the living room, walking her father back to bed in the middle of the night when he would leave his bedroom, fully dressed, thinking it was time to open the store.

Done with sleeping alone. Done with wondering how she would ever have a normal relationship. Done with all her worrying and fretting about the past. Douglas had patched over her broken places without even knowing she had them. In his presence, she could almost feel herself getting ready to welcome the universe again.

"Of course, I will," she said, and they kissed to the applause of the women waiting for the carousel with runny-nosed children who turned away in embarrassment.

The ring was slightly disappointing, though she would never admit that to anyone. It had small sapphire baguettes around the diamond when she would have preferred something simpler, but she wanted to keep the moment as perfect as possible.

"Do you like it?" he whispered as they walked through the park holding hands. "Be honest. We can take it back if you don't."

"I love it," she said, dropping Douglas's hand and holding her own hand to admire the diamond as it caught the sun. "It's beautiful."

Suddenly, she was starving and led Douglas to the popcorn vendor, who stood next to a woman selling giant balloons on sticks. The popcorn was so salty it almost burned her tongue. The grass was especially green that day, the air sweet. She felt alive in a way she hadn't since her mother died because Douglas loved her enough to imagine how they would move forward together, intertwining their lives in a most improbable but completely expected way.

Fitz would be surprised. She imagined him opening the wedding invitation, pleased that he could stop worrying about her and whether she would fully recover from the trauma of Anders. She pictured dancing with him at her wedding, which would be simple and modest and elegant. Her sisters would be her bridesmaids. Her father, she hoped, would have enough of his memory left to enjoy the ceremony. By the time she threw the empty popcorn box in the garbage, she had the whole thing planned.

A few days later, Margaret poured herself a cup of coffee in the break room at work and sat down at one of the orange laminate tables. A cloying brown sugar smell emanated from a coffee cake on the counter where employees left their group binge offerings.

She had been sent off to wait while a technician installed a computer terminal at her workstation. As she took her first sip of coffee, a fiftyish secretary she had met a few times, but whose name she had forgotten (Helen? Ellen?), entered the break room with a mug shaped like a cowboy boot.

"Margaret, right? How's it going?"

"Fine, thanks."

By "fine" she meant worried about her father and his disintegrating memory, jittery because she'd already had too much coffee, and self-conscious of her ring and the questions it invited, but none of these to the extent that she would trouble a virtual stranger. The secretary smiled and poured her coffee, then groaned when she saw the cake.

"This place is a sugar addict's nightmare," she said, taking a thick slice and toppling it onto a paper plate. "We are so bad."

Margaret smiled and nodded as the woman sat down, uninvited, at her table. Helen/Ellen had a plastic fork halfway to her mouth when she noticed the ring.

"Now wait a minute. What," she said, pulling her head back dramatically and looking over her glasses, "is that?"

Margaret began to fold one hand over the ring but realized it was too late. She held out the fingers of her left hand in the standard pose, as if she were a dog waiting for someone to shake its paw.

"Oh, my God. It's beautiful. You must be so excited!"

As Helen/Ellen was exclaiming over the ring, Margaret's boss, Frederick Gray, a balding and pear-shaped man with a nasal voice, came into the break room. He took his time pouring a cup of coffee then sauntered over, pulling out a chair in the manner of someone who owned it. His general demeanor was that of a landlord who didn't bother with leases and could kick out his desperate tenants at any time. "What's this now?" He held out his hand, and once again, Margaret was forced to extend her paw.

"Congratulations," he said, tilting her hand so the diamond would catch the light. "Who's the lucky man?"

Margaret had disliked her boss at the first sight of him, with his combover and his belt worn too high on his rotund middle. He reminded her of a science teacher she'd once had in middle school, so smug that he knew what the students didn't. We can learn, she always wanted to tell him. Have your forgotten that it's your job to teach us?

"His name is Douglas Gayleman. He works at Harwood."

"Really now? My kids went to Harwood. Great school."

Margaret nodded along as Mr. Gray waxed on about Harwood and a headmaster who had left years ago, wondering if she could find an excuse to leave. She still had more than half a cup of coffee in front of her, so she took a long sip and immediately regretted it as the caffeine pulsed alarmingly in her veins.

"It's a shame, though," her boss said, pulling a white cotton handkerchief out of his pocket and swabbing his nose with it. "I didn't think we'd lose you so quickly."

The blood rose in Margaret's face. She looked down at her coffee, which had a few grounds floating in it, not wanting to look at Mr. Gray, whose skin had an unhealthy pallor and texture that made her think of bread dough. "I hadn't planned on leaving."

"I'm teasing!" he said, glancing toward Helen/Ellen, who returned his look with a smile that made Margaret wonder about their relationship. She seemed a little too familiar with him, eating her cake without checking her lips for crumbs, as though she were sitting in her own kitchen.

"It's 1984, Fred. You can't assume she's going to leave just because she's getting married."

"You're absolutely right, Helen. It's 1984. I keep forgetting."

Margaret put her left hand under the orange table. She liked her work. The numbers spoke to her in soothing ways, and when she could bring them into balance, she felt a sense of peace and order. If she could have avoided anyone over forty, all of whom seemed compelled to remind her how young and inexperienced she was, her job would have been perfect.

"I plan to be here for a very long time," Margaret said. "Really, I do."

"I'm sure you do," Mr. Gray said, putting his handkerchief back in his pocket. "I'm sure you do."

Helen stood up and patted Margaret on the back, which made her feel like a kindergartener who had just told an outrageous fib.

"I really didn't need that cake," Helen said, tossing her paper plate in the trash. "Oh, well. Back to the salt mines."

Margaret went back to her desk, wishing she could hide the engagement ring. A future with Douglas seemed like the right decision, but all the steps along the way were fraught with expectations. Douglas's especially. She was still terrified of letting someone else command her body, demand of it something she wasn't sure she knew how to give without losing herself in the process. Douglas, bless him, accepted it, though he was all for a short engagement. She felt the diamond with her thumb and turned it so it faced her palm.

—10—

Fitz

Fitz's secretary, Brenda, had left one of her mother's homemade chocolate-frosted cupcakes on a napkin on his desk. These cupcakes were irresistible to him, and normally, he would have peeled the moist paper from the cupcake's squat little body and consumed it in three bites, licking the frosting from his fingers. Instead, he pushed it to one side. Dread had taken over the lease where his bottomless appetite once resided.

That morning, he had opened a thick cream-colored envelope without glancing at the return address, thinking it was for another of the endless string of galas and fundraisers on the charity circuit, for which men and women of a certain income bracket donned tuxedos and full-length gowns and spent the evening outwardly admiring, inwardly critiquing each other's taste. As an aside, some starving children or exhausted greyhounds got a check in the mail. He tried to avoid these as often as possible.

This envelope was something different, though. It requested the honor of his presence at a marriage. The woman he loved, the woman he had pined for since his sophomore year of college, was about to walk down the aisle with someone she'd met barely a year before. The cloying chocolate smell was making him sick. He picked up the cupcake, walked to the deserted outer office, and threw it in the garbage, hoping the night cleaning staff would remove it before Brenda returned in the morning.

He slid down to the floor with his back against Brenda's desk. Maybe Margaret loved the guy. Maybe she felt for him what Fitz felt for her. The vagaries of the heart were many. Nobody, for example, could explain why his parents had been married for thirty-some-odd years without maiming or killing each other. There had to be some love, a placemat at least, under the heaping bowl of bickering.

In the low-pile beige carpet, he traced a heart with his fingernail, wrote Margaret's initials and then his with a plus sign in between. If he could have cut out his heart and laid it there as a sacrifice, he would have.

Now it made sense that Margaret hadn't been in touch with him lately. Her calls had become less frequent as he kept putting her off with one excuse or another, thinking he'd surprise her when he was finally down a full twenty-five pounds, and he was almost there. The last time they spoke by phone might have been three or four months before.

"It's ridiculous," she had said. "We live in the same city, but we never see each other."

"Talk to my father. He won't let up. I'm in this stinking office morning, noon, and night."

"Even on weekends?"

"Most of them, sure. It's basically hazing."

"Maybe you need a different job."

"You're right, I do. I'll work on it. In the meantime, what are you up to?"

She had paused.

"Well, I'm seeing someone."

This didn't surprise him, nor did it especially worry him. Men would always pursue Margaret, but she was understandably wary.

Thus far, she had never had a serious relationship and didn't seem eager to pursue one. It was why he thought he still had a chance once he was a slimmer man whose professions of love might be taken seriously.

"Tell me about him."

"He's a teacher at a small prep school. Harwood."

"A teacher? Where'd you meet him?"

"At this party my sisters dragged me to. He's nice, though, you'd like him."

"If you say so."

"No, really, you would. He's very humble. Not one of the pretty boys."

Fitz didn't believe it for a minute, but he had said nothing, done nothing, and now Margaret and this teacher person were about to be married. He would have to congratulate her and send them an expensive present. He wouldn't go to the wedding, though. It would be too much to see her walking down the aisle, all in white, toward the man who had eviscerated his hope, disemboweled his dream.

Two weeks after the invitation arrived, Fitz called Margaret.

"Hey, you," he said, trying to sound cheerful. "What's this about you getting married?"

"I know, it's crazy," she said. "But my dad isn't doing so well, so we decided to have a short engagement. You're coming, right?"

It had been warm for September in Hartford that morning, yellow leaves drifting down toward the heated pool through beams of light, and Fitz had already swum sixty laps. This was his new morning routine now that he could only choke down a slice of dry toast for breakfast. He shivered and pulled his robe tighter around him. The air in the breakfast nook of his house, the one his father had badgered him to buy as an investment, seemed thin and inadequate.

"Is that what you want?"

"Of course, it's what I want."

He moved the receiver away from his mouth and covered it with his hand. Sighed. Pulled it back.

"The thing is, I have plans to be away that weekend."

"What plans?"

He looked down at a magazine his decorator had left behind. *Believe in Belize: Tropical Trends in a Sunlit Paradise.*

"I'm going to Belize."

"On business?"

He should have changed out of his wet bathing suit before making the call. He felt pale and impotent sitting there. He hadn't yet turned on the heater, so the water had been cold.

"I have some meetings, but it's more of a vacation. I'm taking someone."

Long seconds ticked by and Fitz began to hear the ambient sound of the phone line, a low, furtive buzz that grew louder and more intrusive the longer he listened. The air was almost entirely gone from the room now. He struggled to pull in a breath.

"Someone? Who?"

"Just someone."

"A friend?"

"Kind of."

"Do I know her?"

Another long pause. Wounded pride gave him license to make it good.

"I met her at a charity event. We hit it off right away."

"So, you're taking her to Belize? Doesn't that seem a little sudden?"

That was rich. So rich he had to stop himself from pointing out the irony of that question coming from Margaret. Here she was about to hitch her star to some teacher she barely knew who would always have a mortgage. Literally mortgaging her future.

"Not really. We've been seeing each other for a few months."

"You can't change the date?"

"I've already got the tickets, and like I said, I'm working the vacation around some meetings. And she already asked for the time off. I'd be in the doghouse if I asked her to change it now."

"What's the name of this mystery woman?"

He glanced into the next room. The decorator had recently brought over a recliner, which he had ordered after Margaret had mentioned several times how comfortable they were and how her father rarely sat in anything else. It had been on back order, and he had forgotten about it. It was sitting near the fireplace in the pointlessly designated family room, still wrapped in plastic.

"Cline," he said, clearing his throat. "Rachel Klein."

As he said this, he stood up and, stretching the coiled telephone cord, walked over to the recliner. He sat down, despite the damp bathing suit under his robe, despite the plastic on the chair, and tilted back. It somehow felt more truthful to lay in the clingy arms of Rachel Klein.

"That makes me very sad," Margaret said, sounding far away. "Are you sure you can't change your plans?"

"It's not like you gave me much notice."

"I know. I'm sorry about that. Things seemed to happen so fast."

Fitz guessed that Margaret knew she would marry Douglas right away, probably within minutes of their first meeting, just as he had fallen in love with Margaret from the moment he saw her on the Trinity quad. This was the problem with having a relationship that existed mostly in your head. Margaret knew so little of what Fitz was thinking, and he sometimes forgot that. She didn't know how carefully he had considered the speed of his courtship, how his plan had been to deepen their relationship through their long, meandering phone calls, and then to show her how beautiful and fulfilling their lives could be once he lost the weight he had always intended to lose. He wouldn't have expected her, or anyone, to look past the outer Fitz that had eaten and obscured the thin and radiant inner Fitz. Now he had a choice. He could let her go, or he could risk putting his heart outside his chest again, this time without copious amounts of alcohol to assist him.

"I just—" A pause.

"You just what?"

"I just hope you know that I love you. And I want the best for you."

"Without a doubt, you are the sweetest person I have ever known. I love you, too."

He took a deep breath and closed his eyes. This was the fulcrum on which his life would change, one way or another. Simple words in a particular order. A high stakes risk that no company would ever insure.

"No, Margaret, I love-love you. Not just as a friend."

She was quiet then, so quiet he could hear the compressor on his pool kick on. He could hear the cycle shift on his dishwasher and a truck backing up down the street. He could hear Margaret's shallow breathing and his own weight shifting in the plastic-wrapped chair. Finally, she spoke.

"Oh, Fitz."

"I told you already, that night before I graduated. When you were putting me to bed."

"You were drunk out of your mind, remember? I didn't think you really meant it, or at least I wasn't sure, and you've been avoiding me ever since."

So she hadn't rejected him only for his size, maybe not at all. This was a revelation, and it gave him hope.

"Margaret, you can still change your mind."

She was quiet again, so quiet he could hear her swallowing. So quiet he could hear what sounded like an insect burrowing in the wall.

"It's too late now, Fitz. I thought you'd moved on. Besides, we've paid the deposit, I have the dress. I couldn't do that to Douglas. He's been so good to me."

The quiet that followed had a different sort of quality to it, one that Fitz could only liken to being underwater on the verge of suffocating. It was the eerie quiet that happened after the last beat of a heart.

"Do you love him?" Another endless pause. "Margaret, do you love him?"

"Of course, I do. I wouldn't marry someone I didn't love."

He cleared his throat again. "Then I wish you every happiness, my friend."

He put the receiver on the floor, tilted the recliner back as far as it would go, and closed his eyes. He could still hear Margaret speaking on the other end of the line, calling his name, but he fell into a kind of twilight sleep in which he imagined that Margaret suddenly realized it was Fitz she loved. She would call off the wedding and show up at his house, demanding to confront this "Rachel Klein," and he would lead her to the recliner, and they would fall into it, laughing, reconfigured from parallel lines into right angles, intersecting at last.

As Margaret's wedding day dawned six weeks later, Fitz stood on his bathroom scale and somberly noted that his weight had dropped fifteen pounds from the time he had received the invitation. His appetite had not returned. He could only vaguely remember how good it felt to fill his mouth with cake or his secret vice, Big Macs with extra special sauce acquired at late night drive-throughs. Side order of shame. Now he ate only when hunger forced him, chewing absently on whatever happened to be around: bruised apples, leftover pizza, cold noodles. It all tasted the same.

He looked out the bathroom window into the backyard. Saturday. Fall. Fresh pumpkin pie of a day. Promising for a wedding if the sun stayed out, bathing the landscape in the golden radiance particular to New England for a few weeks every year. Margaret would be up already, maybe sipping coffee with her sisters. He couldn't picture her in a wedding gown and veil, his brain protecting him from that kind of heart-twisting beauty. He put his bathing suit on and walked down the back stairs into the family room on his way to the pool. The doorbell rang. He crossed through the kitchen and dining room into the foyer and put his eye to the front door peephole.

It was his father, dressed in a suit and tie. Fitz opened the door, gut churning. In no version of the universe could his father be standing on his doorstep on a pumpkin pie Saturday with good news.

"Let's talk," Hamish said, leading the way toward the kitchen. Once there, he looked around. "Can you get some coffee going?"

Fitz filled up the carafe and poured the water into the coffeemaker, then measured a few scoops into the paper filter, hit the brew button. He rarely drank coffee at home, and never until after his laps.

"To what do I owe the pleasure of your company?"

"Sit."

Fitz sat on a stool at the counter, wishing he had at least a T-shirt on to cover his still-substantial belly.

"We need to talk about how you resolved the Anderson case."

"On a Saturday?"

"I don't get a day off." Implied in this: *You, who will run the company one day if I have anything to say about it, will never get a day off either.*

Fitz shivered. The coffee maker hissed. He jumped off the stool and poured his father a cup. Hamish sipped, grimacing.

"You call that coffee?"

Fitz shrugged. Hamish put the rejected cup on the counter.

"You settled a case that didn't need to be settled. Curtis Anderson had a preexisting condition, and he lied about it."

His father had his hands on his ample hips, and in this posture presented to Fitz a vision of himself in thirty or so years: jowls forming, blue veins bulging near graying temples, pants bagging across an ass that had somehow been absorbed into his body and repurposed into a formidable paunch, although Fitz already had a head start on that.

"He said he didn't know about it. His medical records didn't mention any heart condition."

"The ones they gave you."

"Not every case needs to end in a lawsuit."

Fitz crossed his arms. There were benefits to the position his father had: lavish vacations, access to power brokers and politicians, expensive houses, fast cars, bespoke suits. Beautiful women, too, some even more beautiful than Margaret. But it took its toll, and not only on the body. Above a certain level in the company, moral compasses were confiscated. In their place, standard issue, were divining rods for wealth. The rich got richer, not because they were better or smarter or more dedicated to their jobs, but because the correct tools were handed to them with very explicit instructions.

Hamish took his terrible coffee off the granite counter, sipped and grimaced again.

"Get your head on straight, son. This is a business, not a charity."

And there it was. His father was right. Fitz wanted to run the business like a charity, and that was unfair to the shareholders. He lacked the essential gene required to put the company's interest before those who bought its policies, and though his intentions might be admirable on a case-by-case basis, it wasn't sustainable. He was completely unsuited for the role he had been groomed from birth to play. Then again, if he walked away, he would drop into an income bracket not seen in his family since his ancestors had fled a failing farm in Northhamptonshire in the eighteenth century.

"You're right. It won't happen again."

"What I'm saying is, you need to look at this from a corporate perspective."

"I get it. I was wrong."

The cup of coffee went to his father's lips again, but he put it down before taking a sip. The space between his eyebrows narrowed until they were almost touching.

"There is no mercy among shareholders. It's not always pleasant, but you do what you have to do. Eventually, you'll understand how that benefits the whole company."

His father suddenly seemed to notice that Fitz was wearing only his swim trunks. His brows resumed their normal positions.

"Going for a swim?"

"Planning to."

"Good for you. Get your exercise while you can."

A prediction or a threat. Fitz didn't know which.

—11—

Margaret

The shoes were perfect. White satin with a three-inch heel that made her feel tall but didn't cripple her feet. The dress wasn't terrible—lace overlay, cinched waist, cream puffed at the shoulders like Princess Diana's wedding gown—but she would have preferred something less dramatic. Her sisters had fallen in love with this one, and she had decided to give them the pleasure of choosing it.

Her fingers trembled slightly as she smoothed on foundation and traced her almond-shaped eyes with the deep indigo liner the woman at the cosmetics counter had insisted she buy. Something blue. Her sisters had wanted to help with her makeup, but she had sent them to pick up the bouquets instead, planning to have it all finished by the time they returned so she wouldn't end up wearing maroon lipliner.

Her heart hitched suddenly, and she dropped the eyeliner, putting a hand to her chest. This was it. No going back, not after they had paid for the DJ and the three-tiered raspberry-filled cake and the absurdly small champagne bottles to give as favors. She took a long, slow breath, picked up the eyeliner, finished the job. Dusted on a little setting powder, no blush because she already looked flushed. Applied some lipstick, pressed her lips together. Done.

She untied her robe, tossed it on a chair, exposing the silky lingerie

Annabelle and Lauren had given her at the bridal shower. She slipped on the requisite garter and felt like a three-dollar saloon whore. Douglas had been so patient. That night, she would try to show him how grateful she was.

Her heart hitched again. What was it? Doubt? Everyone had doubt on their wedding day, it was more or less mandatory. She unzipped the plastic casing around her dress, ran a hand down the lace. She took the dress off the hanger, letting it drape across her arm, where it was no more than a collection of fabric, most of it synthetic, judging from the fairly modest price. Here it was benign, without power. Once she put it on, she would be The Bride, and the day would revolve around her, which made her feel slightly nauseated. People would be staring at her all day. But not Fitz, who apparently still loved her and wasn't coming to see her marry another man. It troubled her to hurt Fitz. He was her North Star, the person around whom she felt most like herself and most comfortable and most loved, and yet, he had avoided seeing her for two years now, letting her assume he had a new and better life that didn't include her. There was something else as well. Only Fitz knew what had happened to her in college. If she chose Fitz, she could never forget about Anders. In the part of her mind where fear held sway, the two of them were inextricably linked.

The gown had a row of tiny faux buttons down the back and a secret zipper on the side. She stepped into it carefully, as if climbing aboard a boat, and pulled it up, slipping hands through the voluminous sleeves. The hem drooped on the ground, deflated, until she edged the zipper up. She dragged the long train across the room to where the white satin shoes were waiting on the floor, turned out slightly, reminding her of Mary Poppins. She put them on. Transformation. It all came together. The long dark hair—half up, half down—the sleeves wider than hips, the cinched waist. In the mirror, she saw herself but didn't, half of her hiding in the corner where she could pretend it was all a game.

He was a good man, Douglas. He had already helped her find an assisted living place for her father, where someone would fix his meals and check on him until he was sick enough for the adjacent nursing home. These were the boxes that had to be checked in the orderly, shuffling line toward his premature death. Her sisters were grateful to Douglas, they were all grateful. It had become too much for them to handle at home, too hard for them to watch.

Her heart hitched for a third time. What was love anyway? It couldn't have been what she felt for Anders, though at the time, she thought it was. Once, when she was seventeen, she had gone to visit her mother during one of her hospital stays, and from the doorway she had seen her father kneeling on the hard linoleum floor next to the adjustable bed. His hands were clasped in supplication, his forehead touching the mattress. Her mother, bald head swathed like an infant's in a soft pink cap, had her hand on the back of her father's neck. His neck had looked so white, so exposed at the edge of his hairline where the barber shaved it close, and her mother's hand so calm and sure, so protective. That was undoubtedly love.

A few months before they were engaged, she had caught Douglas studying her profile while they stood in line for ice cream at a farmer's market. His gaze was like a paintbrush against her skin, a bold attempt to trace each angle and plane, to memorize it. She had clasped his hand, then squeezed it, and he had flushed. That might have been love. Or maybe she just enjoyed being admired.

Her sisters would be back soon. She placed the veil on top of her head and covered her face, ready to face the priest, though she feared that he might see the stain on her soul, the baby she had wished away. Seeing through the veil was like being inside the confessional. *Bless me Father, for I have sinned.*

She and Douglas were compatible in so many ways. She liked his laugh, his small even teeth, his short sandy brown hair. She liked the way he listened, even when she spoke about accounting principles, nodding at appropriate intervals. He was a good man, and he loved her. They would sometimes be happy. If she waited for the mythical *Thornbirds* connection, she might end up like her sisters, who drifted from loser to loser as the years slipped by.

She heard a short knock at the door and then it opened. Annabelle stuck her head inside.

"You're already dressed!" she said. "I thought we were going to help you."

"I got antsy. You know how it is."

"Frankly, I don't, but—"

"Is Lauren out there?"

"She's getting her dress on. The flowers are all set."

"Come back when you're ready and we'll walk out together."

The door closed, and she was alone again, frothy white and breathless, afraid to sit down. This was it. The organist was playing the prelude, and she could feel the bass notes vibrating through the floor. In another hour, it would all be done, and she would be Mrs. Douglas Gayleman, Margaret Gayleman. Her modest engagement ring would be joined by a band of yellow gold that would ward off unwanted attention like Wonder Woman's bracelets. A relief. She and Douglas would move into a small house in the suburbs. It was all as it was supposed to be. Her heart swelled. She wouldn't look for problems where there were none. Douglas loved her. He was a good man. She loved him back, and if she didn't love him with the burning passion of a thousand suns, that wasn't such a bad thing. The heat was there, but she could approach him without fear of getting burned. It was enough.

Another knock at the door. The hitch again. Her father stood motionless in the hallway in a suit purchased for him off the rack, pants hems touching the ground, sleeves down to his knuckles. He had been too impatient to let the tailor measure him for alterations. Lauren was holding his arm, as if he were the one to be walked down the aisle. Annabelle was down the hall, waiting for them in the vestibule.

"Hold on to Margaret, Dad," Lauren said. This had been rehearsed the night before, but her father needed reminding. Time for him was like a loose-leaf binder, the pages turning constantly, each one as blank and new and disconnected from the others as the last. Margaret took her father's other arm and they walked together down a long cinderblock hallway with a dropped ceiling. This part of the reception hall attached to the church looked like a school building, which it might have been at one time. Margaret felt her feet in her shoes, but the rest of her was floating at a comfortable remove.

She glanced at her father, who was looking at the floor ahead, concentrating on his short steps, as if he might suddenly find himself at the edge of a pool or a cliff, because every few minutes offered a virtual rebirth, eyes squinting into the dawn of a different day. The four of them waited near the doors of the chapel, out of the line of sight of those in attendance, listening for the music to change.

Lauren dropped her father's arm and reached over to adjust Margaret's veil.

"That's better," she said, tears forming. "It was all crooked."

Margaret's father turned to her, and she thought she saw a flash of recognition, but then it was gone.

"Are you getting my juice?" he said.

This was not how she had pictured her wedding, and yet she smiled. Her father wouldn't remember it, but she would enjoy the memory of having him there.

"Let's go get your juice together."

The organist thumped the first chords of the "Wedding March." Annabelle walked in first—step, together, step, even though they had been instructed to walk normally. Lauren followed, nodding her head to the assemblage like a beauty queen. Then Margaret approached the open doorway with her father, who smiled at the pop of flash bulbs. A gift.

Margaret gripped her father's arm, looking toward Douglas. Amid a thousand thoughts, she wondered if she had been wrong to reject Fitz, even as Douglas stood waiting at the altar for her. Then, about halfway down the aisle, her father suddenly stopped.

"Where is my juice?" he said, his voice rising over the music.

Margaret tried to nudge him forward, but he refused. People from nearby rows urged Richard along with their eyes, but his feet stayed planted. "You said you would bring my juice."

From amid the flower arrangements at the end of the long aisle, Douglas gave a short waist-level wave, as if to suggest they had forgotten about him. Lauren, Annabelle, and several guests surrounded Richard, volunteering to take him outside, but he wouldn't budge. Margaret couldn't move. The crowd surged around her, making it worse. Her father was stamping his feet now.

"Juice, juice, juice."

It was a mistake, all of this. They shouldn't have rushed the wedding. She looked back toward the vestibule, seeking an exit. This could be her excuse to leave, call it a postponement and then gently explain things to Douglas. People shouldn't be allowed to meet at a party, eat some overpriced restaurant meals together, and then sign legally binding documents that braided their lives and finances together, unbraided only by costly litigation. That this happened all the time made it no less bizarre. The faces around her looked confused, upset, which only verified her misgivings. Her bones felt hollow inside her sisters' choice of a dress. All of this was wrong.

Suddenly, though, there was Douglas with a cup of juice in his hand, gently guiding Richard to the vestibule. Margaret watched in wonder. Where had he gotten the juice? Of course, the reception was right next door. He had dashed over and raided the bar.

Two friends of her mother's agreed to sit with her father while he drank his juice. Everyone resumed their positions and the organist picked up where she left off. Margaret could feel every eye in the place, aside from those of the organist, trained on her, wishing the ceremony along. They had waited long enough. She smoothed her gown. At the end of the aisle, she could see Douglas beaming at her. Slowly, she began heading toward him, and with the first step, her body came back to her. She was perspiring after all the tumult. She could feel the scratch of the lace on the bare skin of her back, the strands of hair stuck to the sweat on her neck, the surprising weight of the bouquet in her hands.

Ahead of her, wearing a morning suit that looked a little silly on him, was a good man, a kind man. He stood there, shifting from one foot to another, looking as if he needed to use the bathroom. Together they would be good citizens, care for her father as he declined, vote even in mid-term elections, support public radio, redeem her traumatized womb. She had been wrong to have such doubt.

When she reached the front, they formed the usual triad. She on the left, he on the right, the priest facing the congregation. She smiled at Douglas, almost shyly, proud of his quick thinking and how he had saved them all from further embarrassment. She glanced out toward the crowd of friends and family and saw their relief: They hadn't worn control-top pantyhose and neckties and toe-torturing shoes for nothing. Margaret and Douglas exchanged vows, traded rings, said, "I do," sealed it with a short but emphatic kiss.

They walked down the aisle, hands clasped and swinging. Sweetness and light. It was over, and now they were paired, conjoined, a mixing of souls. Asunder-proof. Margaret felt the hitch in her heart again, but this time it was a release. She would stop wondering, worrying if she had made the right decision. It was done. She was done. The shoulder of Douglas's suit jacket pressed against her sleeve as they stood in the receiving line. A heavily pregnant woman with whom Douglas worked teetered up to them on pencil-thin heels, and kissed Margaret's cheek, leaving the imprint of her red lipstick on it.

Lauren leaned in, holding Margaret's chin and rubbing the lipstick off with her thumb.

"That's you in a year or two," she said, nodding toward the swaying belly.

"Maybe," Margaret said, because this was what she had set in motion, a whole series of cascading events that led inevitably to a new family that would replace her broken one. This was what she had signed up for.

Her cheeks began to hurt from smiling, but Douglas had enough enthusiasm for both of them. He would carry them through this. He would have a plan that would allay her doubts. He had found the juice, pacified her father. An older man she had never met pulled her toward him for a crushing hug. Douglas gave her a sympathetic glance and mouthed the words "my uncle." See, there he was, anticipating her needs, her questions. She had to trust that he saw their future more clearly than she did.

For what was the future anyway? She pictured it as a spiral staircase she ascended without being able to see more than the next few steps ahead. Now Douglas would ascend with her, and maybe he would show her the landings where they would rest and breathe and find comfort. Or maybe there were no landings. Maybe the staircase was the only thing. She could only hope that taking it with Douglas was what she was meant to do.

—12—

Douglas

Two months before the wedding, Douglas found himself on a floor of Macy's he never knew existed. He and Margaret walked slowly past the shelves of china patterns. Dinner plate, salad plate, bread plate, teacup, and saucer. Brittle quintet. His parents had never owned china, barely had enough utensils to feed the three of them on a daily basis, but Margaret seemed to think coordinated tableware was a prerequisite for married life.

"Which one do you like?" she had asked him, holding up two plates that looked identical.

"Whichever one you like."

"That's no help," she said, turning back to the black-suited salesman who responded with a practiced eye roll that told Douglas what he was thinking. Clueless grooms. They plagued his fiefdom.

Douglas had learned so many things since he had met Margaret; for example, that his ties were too wide and that he shouldn't wear white socks with brown or black shoes. He also learned that because their wedding was taking place during the day, he couldn't wear a black tuxedo like James Bond. Etiquette dictated a morning suit with tails, which made him look short and pudgy, like the man from the Monopoly game.

None of this mattered as he stood, breath rapid and hot, at the front of the church looking toward the vestibule where Margaret would appear at any moment swathed in layers of white like a present he would unwrap when they were finally alone. He still couldn't believe she had agreed to be his wife. When he had dropped down to one knee outside the Bushnell Park carousel, he wasn't sure she would even say yes, but the question burned inside him like a lighted match. He had bought the ring only three months after their first date and had been carrying it around with him, waiting for the right moment. Love, his first true and unmistakable love, had propelled him to act.

"Margaret." His voice had been shaking.

"What are you doing?"

His left kneecap had landed on a sharp pebble that dug into his skin, but he resisted shifting. It seemed necessary that he hold the pose.

"Will you marry me?"

Those in the line waiting for rides had noticed the telltale pose and began to gather around. The small box in his hands grew heavier with each passing moment. The women in line had their hands over their mouths, waiting breathlessly. For a few endless seconds, Margaret's face revealed nothing, and Douglas berated himself for choosing a public place, having thought it would make for a great story when they took their future children to the park for carousel rides. This is where Daddy proposed to Mommy, right here, on this very spot. But then she smiled shyly and tapped his shoulder as if knighting him.

"Stand up," she had said, finally. "Of course. Of course, I will."

The shoes he had rented with his morning suit pinched his feet. He shifted slightly, feeling the eyes in the room upon him like a laying on of hands as the organist played some vaguely Baroque filler music. Where was Margaret? He wanted to glance at his watch but knew that would make him look uncertain. He smiled apologetically at the few members of his family who had made the trip from Pittsburgh. His mother's brother and his wife, and two cousins from his father's side. A meager turnout, but still it was something.

Rustling could be heard in the vestibule, but then it stopped. Would Margaret's hesitation be the motif of their marriage? Once again, he still felt the sting of her momentary blankness following his proposal. Then, at the moment he had convinced himself that she had changed her mind and he would have to walk red-faced back down the aisle to inform the caterer that there would be no dinner, the organist switched up the music and Margaret's sisters began their slow procession. Margaret appeared in the doorway, more beautiful than he could have imagined.

The ceremony did not go smoothly. His faltering father-in-law almost ruined it with an infantile demand for juice, but he had thought quickly, secured said juice in the adjacent church hall where they would have the reception, kept everyone moving. His role in the family dynamic was already in place. He was the icebreaker, jamming through floes of hesitation or indecision. Greasing the rusty hinges. Finding the lost screw. It was a role he was happy to play.

The line at the bar was ten deep, but someone put a bottle of Budweiser into Douglas's hand and slapped his back so hard he lurched a half step forward.

"It's all over now, you son of a bitch."

Uncle Percy was his mother's only brother, a plumber who drove a pickup truck with silhouettes of arched-back women on the mud flaps that used to stir unnamable things in Douglas when he was younger. Percy and Douglas's mother had the same general shape, thick as tree stumps right down to the ankles, the same watery blue eyes. But Douglas imagined that his mother, even as a child, had always looked inward while Percy looked outward. His mother had been wary of other people, self-conscious about her less-than-perfect teeth, defensive as a badger in protecting her young. Percy faced the world like a Saint Bernard with a fresh bone, tearing into it with his big padded paws.

"I guess so," Douglas said, sipping the beer.

"Christ almighty, your mother would have loved this," Uncle Percy said, looking around. "It's a damn shame."

"Yes, it is."

"She died too soon, Dougie. Your dad, too." Uncle Percy clamped a hand on Douglas's shoulder, squeezing it hard. "You saved their marriage, you know."

Booze and nostalgia were about to bring on a confession Douglas didn't necessarily want to hear. He scanned the room, a riot of color, for Margaret in cool white.

"I don't think—"

"Your mother told me herself when you were a baby. She was about to leave your dad when she got pregnant. 'I guess we just needed a project,' that's what she said. You know what the project was? You, Dougie. *You* were the project."

Douglas more or less already knew that his presence had prevented his mother from dwelling on how her life had turned out. She could never do enough for him. She would come home from cleaning houses or hotel rooms and immediately set up the ironing board to press his shirts and pants for school. He never had the heart to tell her that the kids in middle school had nicknamed him "Crease."

"She had it hard," his uncle went on between slugs of beer. "No opportunity. And your dad didn't work steady, of course, so it was all on her. That's why she smoked those Newports like a God-damned chimney. Stress."

Douglas nodded, wishing that his mother could have seen him in this place, marrying this extraordinary woman, poised for a life not just three steps up the ladder from the one on which he had been born, but on an entirely different ladder. More like a fire escape.

"Dressed for success," his mother used to say as Douglas left for high school in the jeans and a button-down shirt she had ironed for him. "You don't look like anyone's stooge."

Unbeknownst to his mother, he was a stooge extraordinaire. His smiling confidence dissolved the minute he walked into the buffed linoleum hallways of Briarcliff High School, the same Pittsburgh institution his parents had attended. He navigated the distance between classes with eyes directed at knee level to avoid the bullies and their thrusting chins, but soon enough, Douglas's classmates discovered that his mother cleaned some of their homes.

"Better go home, Crease," Bruce Rutledge, his chief tormentor and son of a prominent lawyer, said one day. "Your mother needs you to take out my garbage."

Had she been there, Douglas's mother might have encouraged him to pound Bruce Rutledge into the buffed linoleum, but Douglas was not inclined to draw attention to himself, even in his own defense. So he turned away, his cheeks scarlet and heart racing, hoping they would leave him alone the next day. And the next day. And the next. But that was the best thing about high school. Eventually, it ended.

"Hey, Dougie, they want you on the dance floor," his uncle said, pushing him toward the band. Margaret was already there, her hand extended toward him, her face flushed and shining with a thin layer of sweat from dancing. The two of them would make a family now, big, boisterous bunch of kids, the crazy spinsters as doting aunts. No functioning grandparents, of course, but eventually he and Margaret would be the grandparents, matriarch and patriarch of an extended clan that ate Sunday dinner on folding tables stretching across two rooms. He reached for Margaret and pulled her close, one arm around her small waist, the other grasping her hand and placing it over his heart.

—13—

Margaret

Margaret's former self hovered above her as she lay in bed still half-asleep, fighting a wave of nausea. The apparition mocked her, eating a hamburger dripping with caramelized onions. Her gorge rose at the phantom smell.

"Crackers," she whispered, and Douglas jumped out of bed, ran to the kitchen and returned with a sleeve of Saltines and a glass of water sloshing across his hand.

She tried to sit up but couldn't. She put a cracker in her mouth, chewed it weakly, and dozed again before swallowing the bland paste that had formed on her tongue. In this twilight state, she floated over a moonlit lake, marrow quivering in her bones. She had no strength anymore. Something inside her the size of a grain of rice had hollowed her out, stolen her soul.

"Here," Douglas was saying, offering another Saltine. "You can't let your stomach get empty."

He tilted her boneless body forward and tucked his own pillow behind her. She took the Saltine, ate, sipped some water. The smell of phantom onions still saturated the air.

"I'm better," she said, wishing he would go away. She pressed cool fingertips on eyelids that had gone purple with burst veins. The day before she had thrown up six times.

"You sure?" He looked worried.

"I'm sure," she said, attempting a smile. "You need to get ready for work."

When Douglas left to shower, she sat up a little more and counted the days she had left to the twelve-week mark, when all the books said the nausea would subside. Twenty-seven. Each one an eternity.

Though they were young to start a family, Margaret had wanted to test her body and make sure it would function as it was supposed to, so slightly more than a year into their marriage, she was twenty-four years old and eight weeks pregnant. It had happened almost as soon as they started trying, so she hadn't been ready for the assault: the vomiting, the swollen and tender breasts, the aversion to smells. Down the road, she could expect the spreading feet, the enormous belly, the counterweight ass. She had seen it happen to friends and acquaintances, how they stopped wearing lipstick, donned dresses shaped like traffic cones, wore strange-looking wide-width loafers. But none of that mattered. After her initial shock, she had come to realize that a baby would be proof she had recovered fully. Good as new.

Another spate of nausea welled up inside her, and she leaned over and vomited into the plastic pail Douglas had set up at the side of the bed. When the sour contents of her stomach were out instead of in, she felt a little better. The squeak of the faucet told her that Douglas was finished with his shower, and for a generous moment, she was glad he didn't have to experience the ordeal that morning sickness had turned out to be. One of them had to be functional.

She sat up and blew her nose, then pulled down the covers. She would clean herself up, go into work, and distract herself enough to let her uterus to do the job it had been created to do. At that very moment, cells were dividing and learning their designated purpose:

you there, gallbladder; second row on the left, hair follicle; way in back, optic nerve. Between bouts of nausea, she would contemplate with awe this new human being inside her, a person who would eventually live apart from her body, with his or her own political party affiliation and ice cream preferences. She had a hard time imagining what that person would be like.

Douglas walked in, a towel wrapped around his growing waistline. In the weeks since they had learned of her pregnancy, he had gained five pounds from stress eating malted milk balls, while she had lost the same amount from constant retching.

"You puked?" he said.

"I did," she said. "But it's okay. I feel better."

"Let me get that."

"No, I'll take care of it. You get to school."

"Are you sure?"

"I'm sure," she said, toting the foul-smelling container with her to the bathroom. She could do this, push down the doubt and the fear, power through this months-long flu, because she was the miraculous vessel that would nurture a new life. She turned on the water, cranking it to full volume. As she stepped under the stream, nausea hit her again and she bent over, spewing yellow bile into the bathtub and watching it swirl around her feet.

Douglas and Margaret had purchased a tiny, tidy ranch in the south end of West Hartford, a growing suburb. It had been Margaret's idea to buy instead of rent, and to keep it small and affordable. She harbored a dream of retiring early and didn't want to be house poor.

"We'll pay it off in twenty years," she told Douglas. He had frowned at the shoebox bedrooms and the single bathroom, but the real estate market was heating up, so he agreed, fearing they wouldn't be able to muster the down payment for something larger. The neighborhood was a mix of young couples and older blue-collar families that had purchased homes in the 1950s and '60s, when they were new. The neighborhood's men appeared to gravitate toward hobbies that involved engines. The revving would start at about four in the afternoon every weekday and by nine or ten in the morning on Saturdays. Standing in her kitchen on a Saturday was like being immersed in a blender. Margaret had taken to wearing earplugs while doing the dishes.

Done with her shower, Margaret dressed and went to the kitchen. She needed to eat, but she feared opening the refrigerator, which was now a Pandora's box of evil odors that could send her running to the bathroom. Granola bars. She could usually choke one of those down with a little water. She ran the tap to get it cold, and while she was staring blankly at her unattractive counters, thought of Fitz in his grand house with a pool. He had told her about the granite countertops, and she imagined him now, casually making a sandwich.

They had not spoken since the momentous call before her wedding, but that morning, she had seen his picture in the newspaper at a charity dinner and noticed that he looked significantly thinner than she remembered. In the photo, he had his arm around a stunning blonde who was an anchor on the local evening news. She should have been happy that Fitz had found someone else, but happiness was not the emotion that came to mind. In part, she blamed the pregnancy hormones, which had twisted her brain so thoroughly she was always on the verge of tears.

Impulsively, she put the granola bar on the counter and picked up the phone. Fitz picked up on the second ring.

"Hello?"

"Hey, you. It's me."

There was a pause, during which Margaret realized she no longer talked to him frequently enough to have the privilege of calling herself "me."

"Wait, Margaret?"

"Yes, Margaret."

Another pause, during which she imagined him looking apologetically at the blonde anchorwoman studying the pages of a pool accessories catalogue.

"Nice to hear your voice. How are you?"

How to answer this. She was excellent, by any empirical standard. It had been mild for January in Connecticut. She had married a nice man, had a decent job, owned a house in the suburbs, was about to have a baby. She was healthy and young, some said beautiful. She was also miserable. She hadn't been given a promotion she thought she was due, her father was dying of an obscenity of a disease, her mother was gone when she needed her most, and she had thrown up twice in the past hour.

"I'm fine, well, pretty fine. How are you?"

There was a pause, during which Margaret imagined Fitz nodding to the anchorwoman to let her know he would be off the phone as soon as he could.

"I'm all right."

"I saw your picture in the paper today."

"It's not my favorite thing to do, but it's expected."

"You hide it well."

He let out a short laugh.

"Hey, can I call you back? I'm a little tied up right now."

He seemed impatient with her, and she wanted to cry, but again, maybe that was the pregnancy. It was a little like being drunk: too many emotions brought to the surface, stomach out of sorts, the impulse to call people with whom you once shared a bond.

"I'm sorry. I'll let you go."

Another long pause, during which Margaret imagined that Fitz was looking at his watch or sharing a smile with the blonde anchorwoman who had left the room and reentered with the newspaper or coffee. She heard him sigh.

"You just caught me at a bad time."

"Maybe we can have lunch or something."

She wanted to tell him about her pregnancy in person. Now that he was clearly over her and in a serious relationship, she wanted him back in her life. Over time, it had become obvious that Fitz was not the only reason she would be reminded of Anders. His first big movie, the stupidly named *Deadbolt*, had been a success, and she could no longer peruse the magazines while waiting in the grocery checkout line. His grinning visage was everywhere, looming from movie posters and newspaper ads. His basic looks hadn't changed, but he looked smoother and manufactured, as if someone had buffed and polished his body until it had the sheen of plastic. A bolt of panic ran through her every time she saw his picture.

"Sure thing," Fitz said, but he wasn't speaking directly into the phone, as if he had turned his head because someone had called to him from a distant room.

"Okay, bye." She placed the receiver gently on its cradle. She would have to be an adult now, the grain of rice in her abdomen demanded it, and adults knew that life had phases. The relationships in one phase didn't always carry over into the next, no matter how much you wanted to haul them along with you. Her stomach writhed, empty. She picked up the granola bar and opened the wrapper. The sweet smell of it almost sent her running back to the bathroom. Weeping openly now, she broke off a piece and stuffed it into her mouth with a trembling hand, choking it down with her tears.

—14—

Douglas

"Can you keep a secret?"

Marilyn Kim, who ran the headmaster's office, nodded and made a cross over her heart with a long, pointed fingernail the color of pomegranates. She was slightly plump and wore body-hugging jersey knit dresses, and Douglas always worried that his eyes might land in the wrong places. She had a way of smiling that invited confidences.

Marilyn looked over her shoulder to make sure the headmaster's door was closed.

"What is it?"

"I'm going to be a dad."

He thrilled to the words, to the beauty of new life and a new generation and all that it meant for who he would become. He and Margaret had agreed not to tell anyone until the requisite twelve-week mark had passed, but that was still almost four weeks away. He couldn't possibly wait that long.

Marilyn's shoulders dropped almost imperceptibly but enough for Douglas to notice, as if she had been expecting some gossip, maybe someone on the staff sleeping with someone else on the staff, which happened occasionally. She recovered with a smile that reflected back Douglas's own enthusiasm.

"Oh, that's wonderful. Congratulations! Your wife must be over the moon."

Douglas hesitated. He couldn't honestly say that Margaret was over the moon, more like on the moon, navigating the airless environment and the dusty craters. Her body seemed to be fighting for its sovereignty as this new entity claimed its resources.

"She's having some morning sickness. Not too happy right now. But the doctor says that's normal."

"She's still in her first trimester?"

"She is, so don't tell anyone, okay? She'd kill me if she knew I said anything."

Marilyn pressed her lips together and turned an invisible key. Douglas slipped out of the office as the headmaster's door began to open. How would he even teach class today between worrying about Margaret puking her guts out and how to pay for a crib, car seat, diapers, four seasons of new clothing every year, then toys and bikes and car insurance and college tuition?

The issue of money had already pulled up a stool at Douglas and Margaret's small kitchen table and sometimes wedged between them in bed, claiming its own space.

Their two full-time salaries should have been enough to live on, but her father's care took a sizeable chunk of their take-home pay. Margaret tracked every expenditure, down to the per-cup cost of their coffee. She bought Douglas a thermos after finding Dunkin' Donuts sugar packets in the pockets of his khakis before she did the laundry.

Love of money, the Bible said, was the root of all evil, but Douglas didn't love money, he hated it. He hated that it colored every decision he made. He hated that the fence around his parents' provincial lives had expanded only slightly for him and Margaret. He hated that money dictated the radius in which he could move.

"How about Mexico?" Douglas had suggested for a honeymoon, wanting simply to say that he had visited another country.

"We can't afford that."

"I've got a small retirement account. We could cash that in."

"That's insane! You can't spend your retirement money for a week's vacation. Do you know what that'll be worth in forty years with compounding interest?"

He did not know or care, given that he might not be alive in forty years, but Margaret was the expert in such things. They went to Cape Cod instead and stayed at a motel with damp carpeting, a dripping faucet that kept him awake at night, and a creepy manager who knocked on the door once a day to ask them if they were behaving themselves. If two poles marked the spectrum of people in the world—on one end, your raucous souls who lived, loved, laughed, and drank, wringing themselves out before they were fifty; on the other, your responsible bean-counters who eked out their pleasure in small doses well into their nineties, the memories long but not deep—he had married someone who leaned more toward the latter.

Douglas unlocked his classroom door and went inside, inhaling the odor of chalk dust and pencil shavings. The early morning light illuminated the desks as if they were set pieces in a play about to begin. He loved this moment when the air shimmered with the hope of a flawlessly executed lesson in which the sparks of knowledge would shower down on his students' heads.

Teaching hadn't been his first choice. He had majored in history at the University of Pittsburgh after bailing out of both the premed and engineering tracks. His mind refused to dwell on formulas. But now that he had a few years under his belt, he felt he had been destined for the classroom. Pedagogy fascinated him, and he studied how to take what he knew and deliver it in digestible chunks to the malleable brains of restless youngsters without boring them into comas. It was a never-ending challenge.

He was opening his attendance book when Howard Mitchell, one of his homeroom students, stuck his head inside the door. Howard, with his bendy-straw legs and arms, had the unmistakable look of a boy who had never willingly played a sport, a boy who was never without a book but couldn't read the room. A boy for whom recess was the worst part of the day.

"Mr. Gayleman?"

"Yes?"

"Can I ask you a question?"

"Sure."

Howard's prep school ensemble only served to emphasize his frailty, the jacket flapping around him like a loose sail. He approached Douglas's desk.

"Okay, so Jack McGreggor is walking around this morning like he owns the place, nothing unusual there, but he comes up to me and says, 'Howard, is that a booger in your nose?' and I put my hand up to my nose, and then he yells, 'Howard's picking his nose!' I'm sick of it, Mr. Gayleman. He won't leave me alone."

Howard's head was cantilevered on a thin stem of a neck that looked unable to support it. His indignation was justifiable, and yet, Douglas couldn't get too worked up about it. The sooner the Howards of the world stopped letting the Jacks of the world bother them the better.

"Let me tell you a story," he said. "When I was your age, I knew this guy, Bruce Rutledge. He used to—never mind, that doesn't matter. The point is that I wish I had ignored the guy. I let him bother me, and that gave him all the power."

"So I should let him say whatever he wants?"

"Not exactly. But what if you had a few comebacks."

"Like what?"

"I don't know, like if he tries that nose trick again, maybe tell him you're looking for his brain up there, or something like that."

Howard laughed, revealing his braces. He was so fragile, a stick figure come to life. These were the kids Douglas tried to protect, and yet he knew they would have to sort things out for themselves. Just as he had.

Look at me, he wanted to tell Howard. A dirt-poor schmuck brought up by uneducated chain-smokers, now married to a stunning woman, about to become a dad. This could be the happiest he had ever been. The future was a vast, amorphous cloud of endless possibility. He gave Howard's shoulder a light squeeze and sent him back outside until the bell rang.

Two weeks later, Douglas entered the headmaster's office, hands stuffed in his pockets.

Marilyn Kim gave him a smile that said they had a secret between them, only it wasn't a secret anymore, since Marilyn had apparently told most of the faculty, given the number of pats on the back and winks he had received.

"How's your wife feeling?" Marilyn said, looking up from the attendance sheets she had been sorting.

"It's over."

"What?"

"She had a—" He couldn't say it. The word was an abomination.

Marilyn pulled in a short breath, put a hand to her mouth.

"I'm so sorry," she said. "When?"

"Over the weekend. She had some cramps, some spotting. We went to the hospital, but it was too late."

Marilyn placed a hand on her heart and briefly closed her eyes. Then she stood up and came around to the other side of her desk to put her arms around Douglas, pulling his head onto the warm pillow of her shoulder.

"Are you sure you can teach today? I can find a sub if you want to go home."

Going home would mean facing Margaret, who had sent him off to work that morning as if she needed to be alone. When he left her, she was lying on her side in bed, knees tucked up under her chin, eyes wide open, staring at the wall.

"Are you sure you're okay?" he had asked her.

"I will be. Just give me some time."

"We can try again."

"I know."

But Douglas had to wonder. He wasn't sure if she envisioned the future as some vast, amorphous cloud of endless possibility, as he did, or as something completely different, maybe a deep underground lake with deadly rocks just below the surface. It could be anything.

He pulled away from Marilyn.

"I'll be fine," he said. "It's a good distraction."

For his first period class, he had planned a lesson on the submarine warfare of World War II, where small groups would be asked to reenact battles and decide whether to fire and reveal their position or stay submerged. But in the end, their high, sweet voices were too much for him. He called for silent reading and stayed at his desk peeling bits of dry skin from around his cuticles.

—15—

Fitz

After the loss of appetite that banished fifteen pounds came an inexplicable aversion to smells, particularly to onions, which he used to love. That accounted for another twenty. His personal trainer had been trying to get him to run for years, but his knees had outright rejected it. Too much compression. Now that the mountainous belly was mostly gone, he found great solace in jogging when it was too cold to swim, his subconscious in conversation with the exercise-induced endorphins. It was a bit like dreaming while in motion.

Margaret's phone call had set off alarms, but she couldn't call him while he was out running. She couldn't pry open the window he had deliberately painted shut if he didn't see or hear her. Or could she? Because here he was thinking about her again. This was how love rewired the brain. Like an autoimmune disease, it blazed new pathways when the old ones shut down. It ferreted out excuses and justifications to get what it wanted.

A slight incline stretched for a good quarter mile. His leg muscles were still in their infancy and whined for him to walk, but he plodded along in the cold anyway, studying the filigreed patterns of sun and shadow on the sidewalk. Why had she called? She had married

Douglas, and being a good person, he wanted to let her live the life she had chosen with no interference from him.

Though he usually ran only to the edge of Elizabeth Park, this time he turned into the park and followed the tree-lined pathways to a murky pond where young children in snowsuits cracked the ice around the edges with their fat little boots. He had been one of those children once, decades ago and in summer, delivered to the park by a substitute babysitter who had gone off into the woods after greeting a man she seemed delighted to see. She had left Fitz on a bench near the pond (*sit right here, stay put*), and at first, he had imitated the other children, throwing rocks and floating pinecones. Then he had cried, wandering on the paved pathways, until spotted by a white-haired woman who took him by the hand and led him to a police officer, who bought him an ice cream cone at the small café in the park and sat with him on a stone wall, cleaning up the drips that ran down his tear-stained arms with small napkins, until his parents arrived.

Children were so delicately calibrated. Why did so many adults think they were equipped for that kind of twenty-four/seven responsibility? It seemed to Fitz that only a small percentage had the temperament and patience to be excellent parents. And shouldn't excellence be the bar, given the long-term consequences?

Fitz slowed to a walk on legs of jelly near the stone wall where he had eaten the ice cream so long ago, the memory like an aging monument he passed time and time again. His parents had been angry with him. His mother, who didn't work but had an endless string of exercise classes, luncheons, and hair appointments necessitating the babysitter and her occasional substitutes, had shaken his shoulders. "Why did you let Beatrice go off like that?" as if he had had a choice. Guilt tended to ask rhetorical questions.

The path led him to a road that curved through the park, and he started jogging again. As he rounded a bend, he saw a 1970s era

Ford Mustang, red with a wide black stripe down the hood, driving in the opposite direction, going slowly but weaving a bit. It was the kind of vehicle certain men gifted to their reckless sons on the day they turned sixteen because "you're only young once." He turned his head to see if the weaving would continue, and it did. With no sidewalks along the road that traveled through the park, pedestrians in clumps of twos and threes jumped back onto the frosty grass as the car passed them.

Fitz tried to see inside as the car came toward him. There seemed to be multiple teenagers moving about and grabbing the steering wheel. The Mustang sped up alarmingly, then took a sudden lurch to the left and plowed into a young woman with a backpack crossing the road. She flew into the air, and for a brief and graceful moment, spread her arms wide and looked directly at Fitz before hitting the pavement with a dull thud.

Fitz sprinted to the woman's crumpled form as the Mustang squealed off. Hit. Run. The car's brake lights flashed its driver's momentary indecision but ultimately fear won out. Fear screeching right out onto Asylum Avenue where it would merge with the oblivious vehicles heading to grocery stores and shoe shops and school parking lots and dentist offices and vacuum repair centers.

"Call nine-one-one," he yelled into the air in several directions, and various onlookers ran toward the small café near the pond where they might find a phone. He knelt on the cold macadam next to the woman, who was gripping one of her legs around the knee and biting her lip. He couldn't tell how badly she'd been injured. Though he couldn't see any blood and felt certain she would survive, she needed to go to the hospital.

"Stay right here," he told her, as if she were about to flee. "An ambulance should be here soon."

Lamely, he patted her head. He had nothing to give her, no water, no ice, no blanket to prevent shock. He had nothing on his person except what he was wearing. His front door key was tied to one of his shoelaces.

"It's okay," he said. "Help will be here soon."

The woman, probably no more than twenty, had straight black hair and smooth skin and Asian features. She might have been part of the small Korean community that lived in Hartford. She rolled over to one side and tried to sit up, baring her teeth in pain. Fitz guessed that she might not speak English but the only foreign language in his arsenal was high school French.

"*Comment allez vous?*" he tried, but this had no effect, and the woman tried again to sit up. When she heard the ambulance siren, she cried out and tried to get to her feet.

"Let them look at you," he said. "You can't even stand up."

Two paramedics jumped out of the ambulance like paratroopers and ran to the young woman, who was sobbing now and shaking her head. She pulled her knee away when one of the paramedics, the more handsome of the two, tried to look at it.

"I don't think she speaks English," Fitz said. "But I saw what happened."

The less-handsome paramedic—nose too large for his face, eyes a muddy brown—took Fitz off to one side.

"We see this a lot. She probably doesn't have insurance."

Fitz understood. She might be here illegally. A trip to the hospital could be ruinous. In her mind, better to let the bones knit on their own, strange lumps pressing against bruised skin. And here he was, Mr. Insurance, unable to do anything about it.

"It was one of those Mustangs, red with a black stripe. It tore out of here."

"Did you get the license plate?"

Why didn't he get the license plate? He closed his eyes, vaguely hoping for his memory to deliver the moment back to him so he could look for the incriminating letters and numbers.

"No, I'm sorry. It happened too fast."

"Can you describe the driver?"

He knew what kind of person would drive such a car, but he hadn't actually seen the driver.

"I'm pretty sure it was a teenager, with some other kids in the car. But I didn't see them clearly. Only the car."

The handsome paramedic was trying to get the woman onto a stretcher, but she rolled away and tried hopping on one foot until she fell to the ground again. Fitz stepped toward her. He somehow felt responsible.

"We'll take it from here, sir. The police will want to talk to you since you're a witness." The handsome paramedic went to the woman's side and helped his partner load her onto the stretcher and then into the back of the ambulance, as two police cars came screaming into the park. The woman looked at Fitz with dark, pleading eyes. He followed the paramedics to the front of the ambulance.

"Do you have a piece of paper?" he asked the less handsome one, who was driving.

He was handed a notepad and pen, and he scribbled down his name and phone number.

"Give this to her, okay?" he said. "I can help."

"Sure," and then they were gone, sirens blaring, though the situation was not life and death, just life, that of a person who, he imagined, navigated a knife's edge trail while Fitz strolled along a flower-lined pathway half a mile wide. The troubles that had occupied every molecule of his brain when he had started his run now seemed pathetic. Looking through the other end of the binoculars did him good.

After talking to the police, he jogged home, and as he did, he formulated a plan. It called for raising money, a lot of it, but he had the connections to do that. And then it called for quitting his job. His father would lose it, but this plan was exactly what he had been seeking to escape the insurance industry, which had turned him from a man who brought people together to someone who hated meetings and stayed in his office alone as much as possible. It was also a way to stop his wallowing. It would take his mind off Margaret. And off Anders, whose terrible and popular *Deadbolt* movie had propelled him into the public eye in a way that poured acid into the wounds that he carried on Margaret's behalf.

He strode along, imagining a life where he woke up and didn't dread the day ahead. It would require making decisions that had far-reaching consequences, but he could do it. Onward, he thought, his legs propelling him home. There is no other option.

—16—

Brenda

B renda's French book was open to the page of irregular verbs that always gave her trouble, when Mr. Fitzhugh the Elder walked in. Though it was her lunch break—egg salad on whole wheat half gone—she shut the book and flipped open a steno pad.

"I'm sorry, he's not here. Is there anything I can help you with?"

Mr. Fitzhugh looked toward the open door of his son's office as if he weren't sure whether to believe Brenda.

"I guess I'll catch him later," he said, but instead of leaving, he sat down in the chair that faced Brenda's desk and stretched arms over his head, leaning first to one side and then the other. The remainder of her sandwich sat on its rectangle of wax paper, its sulfurous scent wafting through the air. She could almost see it drift over to the elder Mr. Fitzhugh's nose.

"Egg salad?" He pretended to shudder. "Not a fan. Now tuna's a different story. I could eat tuna seven days a week."

"Yes, tuna's always good." She glanced at her odiferous lunch. He had ruined it for her, just as he had ruined her study time.

"You've been here, what, a couple years now?" He shifted in the chair, settling himself. Brenda glanced up at the clock, but he seemed not to notice.

"I started in eighty-two. In customer service. I came upstairs when Mr. Fitzhugh started later that year."

"That was my doing," he said. "They told me you were the best typist in the pool."

She smiled in the way he wanted her to smile. If he wouldn't go away, she would at least leave him with a good impression.

"You picked the right executive"—as if it were her choice—"I can tell you that. This guy's going places. I hear he has connections." Big guffaw. She could see his back molars. One had a gold cap on it. "When's he getting back?"

Mr. Fitzhugh had left before lunch for a doctor's appointment about his migraines, but she felt certain he didn't want his father to know that. She pretended to check his calendar.

"Looks like he'll be back around three."

"Tell him I stopped by." He rubbed his chin, assessing her as if she were a mannequin in a store window, and stood up to leave. "Play your cards right and you could be upstairs in the corporate suite someday."

He didn't bother to ask, of course, but she hated cards. She leaned more toward board games like Risk and Masterpiece, which required some strategy instead of relying on the hand you were dealt. What she liked didn't matter, though. People like the man blocking her light in the doorway decided the game and held all the cards.

Right then, Mr. Fitzhugh the Younger came up behind his father. "Hi, Dad."

"Well, well." He pushed the sleeve of his suit jacket up with one finger and glanced at his garish watch. "Your girl here told me you'd be back at three."

She wasn't surprised he didn't remember her name, but he hadn't even bothered to turn his head a few inches to look at the nameplate on her desk. Her Mr. Fitzhugh gave her an apologetic glance.

"What can I do for you?"

"Must be nice to get outside the office, away from prying eyes," Mr. Fitzhugh the Elder said, stage winking at Brenda. Involuntarily, her smile got wider.

"Is there something you need?"

"Let's talk."

They went into the inner office and closed the door. Brenda let her face resume its normal resting position. She wrapped up the remainder of the egg salad sandwich and squeezed it into a ball. She would be hungry as the afternoon stretched on, thinking too much about the roast chicken (it was Tuesday) her mother would be making for dinner.

As a young girl, she had been told not to set her sights too high. College was for rich folks. We're simple people, her mother often said, meaning: We like good, simple food, seasoned with salt and pepper, and church on Sundays. We work hard, and our bathrooms are clean, and we stay out of trouble and politics, which are basically the same thing. One day, God will reward us.

But Brenda didn't like *only* good simple food. She had once gone on a class field trip to New York City and had ordered paella in a Spanish restaurant, not knowing what it was. Its layers and textures and complex flavors had been a revelation. The city itself had chased her at first, its subway exhalations hot on her ankles as she speed-walked down its crowded streets before she succumbed and allowed it to swallow her whole. She wanted that city, but also other cities. Paris, in particular. She wanted to sit at a café with the Eiffel Tower in the distance and order a meal in perfect French. She wanted the waiters to nod at her lovely accent, to admire her clothes and her shoes and the chic hat that covered her chic wig. Lilacs in bloom. Wicker bicycle baskets holding baguettes. Ennui and sadness and cigarette smoke and lost love perfuming the air. She would fit right in.

She would walk and walk and walk down every *rue* she had seen in her books, and she would tour every gallery in the Louvre: the

Mona Lisa, Winged Victory, Venus de Milo, the *Virgin of the Rocks.* By viewing these great works of art in person, she would own them. They would imprint on her brain, seep into her skin. Their greatness would feed her soul, make her a better person, erase her deficiencies. And no one would know her in Paris. No one would ask why she was alone.

She had read a quote in one of her French classes: "We all have enough strength to bear the misfortune of others." So true. She could look at Mr. Fitzhugh and wonder why he wasn't more satisfied with his privileged life, but people might say the same about her. Other than her alopecia, she was healthy. She had a job that gave her something to do every day, benefits, and a salary. But it wasn't enough. Not nearly enough.

The elder Mr. Fitzhugh left his son's office, buttoning his suit jacket and giving Brenda the smallest of nods. These men wore their jackets like armor, she thought, while the women walked around in their dresses and skirts, too much of their bodies exposed. Too many points of vulnerability. She missed her childhood, that oblivious age when she and her brother played with the neighborhood kids after dinner: bare feet caked with dirt, marbles on the stoop, muscles sweetly tired from swimming at the public pool, pigtails brushing the tops of her bare shoulders. The girls were just as tough as the boys back then, maybe tougher, but then one day she was twelve. Clumps of hair in her mashed potatoes. Breasts arriving, spirit shrinking. That's when everything changed.

—17—

Margaret

In the long, quiet months after her miscarriage, Margaret spent more and more time at the nursing home, talking to a man who didn't know who she was.

"Where are my shoes, Mother?" her father said, looking under the bed. "Did you hide them?"

The nursing staff had, in fact, hidden his shoes because he frequently tried to make a break for the outdoors. Margaret found this sad but understandable. Her father wanted to go home, wherever home might be in that muddled brain of his. She found it harder to accept that he called her *Mother*.

"It's very common," one of the doctors had told her. "His oldest memories may be his strongest. In his mind, he may be a young boy, so adult women will seem to him like his mother. And there could be a family resemblance."

"Your shoes are out being polished," Margaret said, leading her father to his recliner, the one piece of furniture they had allowed him to bring from home. This bizarre role reversal upset her, but she played her part like a trained actress. It seemed to soothe him.

Douglas rapped on the open door and stuck his head inside.

"The nurses put on a fresh pot. Want some?"

"Sure."

"Be right back.

Margaret searched around in her tote bag for a coloring book and crayons. This was their Sunday afternoon ritual now. Strangely, despite all his infirmities, her father could color beautifully. He even stayed inside the lines, though the colors he chose had no relationship to reality. Suns were black or silver, skin was periwinkle or heliotrope, and clouds were brown or yellow or tangerine.

He had been at the home for almost two years now, since the summer before she and Douglas got married. Margaret and her sisters split the costs that weren't covered by insurance, and her sisters, who had sold the dry-cleaning shop and opened a candy store, had been forced to take out a reverse mortgage on the family house. Her father was one of the youngest residents in the home, yet he blended in quite seamlessly in his soft shapeless sweatpants and food-stained sweatshirts, shuffling to and from the recreation hall as if he were polishing the floor with his socks. His hair and beard had grown long and white. He flailed his arms every time they tried to cut it.

Douglas came back with Margaret's coffee and set it on the hospital bed table fitted with wheels that Margaret had pulled over to her father's chair. He was coloring a cartoonish-looking donkey with a Mexican blanket on its back.

"Nice job," Douglas said, leaning down close to his father-in-law. "I like how you've done his ears."

Margaret smiled. Douglas had always been patient with her father, more patient than she had been. Perhaps, she sometimes thought, it was because he was used to working with children. A pinch of jealousy there. The nurses liked him better, too, reserving their most sympathetic nods and smiles for when he was in the room.

Her father picked up a brown crayon, made a mark on the paper, then threw it, hitting the wall. Margaret eyed him, wary. One crayon sometimes led to another, and then the whole plastic bucket dumped on the floor or, once, into the toilet. Her father picked up a blue crayon for the donkey's nose and kept coloring, now humming to himself. She let out a breath she didn't know she had been holding.

Children did this, too, didn't they? Their emotions bubbled up to the surface for years and years until they developed the second skin that kept them all inside. She turned to look out the window, where Douglas had installed a bird feeder to remind her father of home.

With no warning, the crayon bucket hit her in the back of the head. She whipped around.

"Dad! What the—"

Douglas put up a warning hand, ever the teacher. She bent down to pick up the bucket and gather the scattered crayons. Her father had picked up a new yellow crayon and was peeling its wrapper off in small precise bits.

"This seems like a good time to go," Douglas said. "Let me get Cheryl in here to settle him down."

Cheryl. Douglas knew all of their names and which shifts they worked. No wonder they liked him better. She kissed her father on his forehead and picked up her purse as Cheryl distracted him so she and Douglas could leave.

It was early June, and the warmth of summer that seemed so appealing when viewed at a distance from the other nine months of the year had descended in all its sweat-inducing, bug-laden glory. She wiped away the moisture that formed on her upper lip as soon as they left the air-conditioned building. On the way to the parking lot, Douglas took her hand, his fingers meshing into hers. The gesture unleashed a torrent of emotion: anguish for her father, jealousy of anyone whose father was not suffering from early Alzheimer's, self-pity. This was not how she had imagined spending Sunday afternoons at this point in her life. She kept looking for an end to the turbulence that had started with her mother's illness and chased her through college, but the calmer waters were always behind her.

Douglas opened the car door for her, as though she had just been released from the hospital. She had a sudden craving for junk food she never ate, Doritos and a Coke, or a hamburger with French fries. If she could digest them without getting sick it would verify that she was still young, still resilient. Maybe some chicken wings or nachos would overpower the nursing home smell that stayed on her clothes long after she left.

As he drove, Douglas seemed to be checking on her with furtive glances.

"What?" she said.

"You look upset."

"I am upset. My father threw a bucket at my head."

"He didn't mean to hurt you."

"I know that. It's just hard to see him that way."

"Of course it is."

She looked out the passenger window and caught a glimpse of herself in the side mirror. In it, she saw her own unhappiness. The plan had been to get married and, within a few years, have a baby who would take up every minute of her time and energy outside of work and make up for the unwanted baby she had lost after Anders— she could say it to herself now—raped her. God would forgive her, the balance of the universe would be restored, if she became a flaw-less wife and accountant and mother without a moment to think of anything else. Instead, the miscarriage she'd had with Douglas had left her to wonder if her body was capable of carrying a baby to term. There was a long torturous day during which she considered revealing the whole sordid Anders episode to Douglas but decided he would be devastated that she hadn't told him earlier.

Words then emerged that must have originated in Margaret's sub-conscious. She had no awareness of forming them.

"I think I'm ready to try again."

Douglas turned his whole body toward her, eyes wide. For a

moment she thought he might go off the road. After the miscarriage, she had flirted with the idea of leaving and letting Douglas start over with someone new who wasn't damaged, had no ugly secrets to conceal. Strange how she could hold that idea in her brain, and at the same time, move along as if it had never existed.

"Watch where you're going, mister," she said, pointing toward the windshield, laughing.

"Really?"

"Yeah, sure. Really."

"Man, oh, man."

She thought Douglas might want to wait, but apparently not. Maybe the need to procreate churned inside him as well. Maybe he was also drawn toward the round and luminous as she was, more keenly now because a troubled speck had been there, and then a grain of rice, exerting its power. Maybe they could both feel the harmony of the universe's rotating spheres, urging them toward wholeness.

Side view mirror again. Worried glance. Not words she could take back, so there it was. They would try again, and though Douglas didn't know it, she could say *third time's the charm*. She and a man who just happened to move to Hartford and show up at a party she attended had made a verbal agreement to manufacture a person, and that person could grow up to be a murderous psychopath or the doctor who cures Alzheimer's. More likely, though, just another needy soul seeking its place in the noisy and indifferent world. Like her.

—18—

Douglas

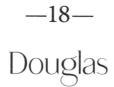

Procrasti-painting. That's what Margaret called it whenever Douglas came back from the hardware store with his plastic bags of supplies and a gallon of some new color. How about adding a chair rail in the dining room, she would ask? Or fixing the broken basement stair? Or retiling the bathroom floor? I'll get to those, he'd tell her, after I'm done painting. The truth was that those jobs were not soothing. They required mental energy. A calculator. Power tools. Painting was different. It transformed the space, and all it required was a little tape, a brush, a roller, and a Zen focus on the wall.

Margaret ducked her head into one of their two spare bedrooms, which Douglas was painting yellow. No pressure, he had said that morning. Yellow is neutral. Boy, girl, exchange student, litter of puppies. Everyone loves yellow. "I'll be back in a few hours," she said. "Lauren wants me to help sort out some insurance problem."

He pointed to the swatch of the yellow he had painted on one of the walls.

"What do you think?"

"I like it."

"It's called *butter*," he said. "It was between that and *goldenrod*."

"Great, now I'll crave an ear of corn every time I come in here."

The smile that sent Margaret on her way was only for show. An idea had come to him, and he had pushed it aside for a week, but now it needed his attention. He began taping around the trim, which he would paint a semigloss white. What if—he stretched a few feet of the blue painter's tape along the ceiling—this was not his life? What if he was supposed to marry someone else instead of Margaret? It was an ugly bruise of a question, and he pressed it, testing for pain.

He loved her, of course. And though the sex was not as frequent as it had been for the first few months, it was still satisfying, at least for him. He could never quite tell with her, but she didn't complain. He taped the corner. A cloud passed by the sun and the light dimmed, then returned so brightly that his eyes teared up a bit. He wiped them with the hem of his old, paint-splattered T-shirt.

He wanted a child, children, had always wanted them. Didn't almost everyone? His classroom was a front-row seat to the buck teeth, cowlicks, oversized ears, crude interactions, and careless cruelty of middle school, and if what he saw there didn't put him off, nothing would. But Margaret seemed less sure, despite what she had recently told him, and her ambivalence threatened all his assumptions. He had to ask himself, was she unsure about wanting a child, or unsure about wanting *his* child? He pressed the bruise again. Face it. She holds back. Emotionally, she never committed more than two thirds, or three-quarters, and maybe that's not enough to sustain a family. Maybe that wasn't enough to sustain the pregnancy that had ended.

He began taping the next wall. Then again, does anyone commit one hundred percent of themselves to a marriage? His own commitment might only be ninety or ninety-five percent. She had said she wanted to try again. Why not take that at face value? He worked the tape close to the baseboard, running his thumbnail along the seam to form a tight seal.

He went to find another roll of painter's tape in the garage and noticed, through the bay door that Margaret had left open, his next-door neighbor, Ollie, tinkering with his Harley. Ollie's property reeked of motor oil and testosterone, and Douglas avoided it when he could, but he had been spotted. Ollie waved him over.

"Painting?" Ollie said, nodding toward Douglas's T-shirt, an abstract catalogue of all the colors he had used since they moved in.

"One of the bedrooms," he said, pointing to a small swatch on his sleeve. "It's called *butter*."

"More like margarine, if you ask me. I had a grandmother called it oleo. Ever hear it called oleo?"

"Can't say that I have."

"Used to be you had to mix the oleo with a little tube of coloring to make it look more like butter. That's what she said, anyway."

Ollie ran the back of his thick wrist across his forehead, pushing up the bandana that had slipped down. A sheen of sweat was visible on his skin at all times, verifying the manliness of his pursuits, muscles always in the heat of motion. He had the build of a wrestler, but he was a short man, no taller than Margaret. This inadequacy, Douglas had decided, gave Ollie a keen eye for weaknesses that could be exploited in others.

"Saw your wife the other day," he said, rummaging through a gray plastic toolbox.

"Oh, yeah?"

"Dumping some flowers in the trash can. Do something to piss her off?"

Douglas hadn't given her flowers. He flipped through his mental calendar. No birthdays or anniversaries this month. She hadn't been promoted at work. Who else would be giving her flowers, and why would she throw them away?

"I'm sure I piss her off every day," Douglas said. Noncommittal enough for the story Ollie would tell his wife and his greasy friends. The whole neighborhood seemed to regard Margaret as an exotic animal whose every activity deserved close scrutiny and constant narration. It made Douglas protective of her.

One of Ollie's towheaded children came around the corner of the house with no shirt and a diaper sagging between her fat little bowed legs. He scooped her up and tossed her a foot and a half into the air. She squealed with glee and terror before Ollie put her down, leaving the dark imprints of his filthy hands on the bluish skin under her arms.

"Get," he said, swatting her toward the kitchen door. "Tell Mama to change your drawers." He turned back to Douglas, "Why do you think she was throwing them flowers away? They looked fresh, too."

"Bugs, maybe?"

"Could be," Ollie said. His eyes said the opposite: Check on your wife.

"Better get back before my brush dries," Douglas said, tilting his head toward his own house. Paint fumes and submission emanated from his property.

"See ya later," Ollie said, engrossed again in his tools.

Douglas walked back across his lawn, resisting the urge to open the trash cans lined up on one side of the garage. Ollie had a clear view. He went inside and peeled the plastic off the new roll of tape and started again where he had left off. New line of thinking. Flowers? Who could have sent them? One of her clients or a coworker? Or maybe the college friend she sometimes talked about, Fitz? When Margaret saw his picture or his name in the newspaper, her mouth would tighten as if she were trying to suppress something, a frown or a smile, he didn't know which. It made him wonder.

An hour went by as he finished taping, always the longest part of the process. He pried open the can of trim paint, let loose the chemical vapors, and dipped his one-inch brush, beginning at the floor level, coating the yellowed and nicked baseboard trim with a slick white veneer. Isn't that what we all did? Covered up our insecurities and stray thoughts with a big white smile. Go along to get along. And before you know it, you've been married for almost two years to someone whose thoughts remained as opaque as the day you met.

The front door hinges squeaked. Margaret's keys rang into the ceramic bowl on the kitchen counter. Footsteps through the living room.

"Hey," she said, hands against the door frame. She looked tired. "You've made some progress."

"Coming along. How'd it go with the insurance?"

"Also progress, although Lauren can't be trusted to hang on to a piece of paper. I'll have to call the nursing home to reissue some of his statements."

Douglas kept painting. His brush transformed the baseboard. It shimmered like new, though in a few weeks the first dings and scratches would begin to show. It was like buying a new car. The freshness only lasted until the first drip of coffee on the new upholstery.

"Had a nice talk with Ollie today." He kept his eyes on the paintbrush.

"Still fixing that motorcycle?"

"Always," Douglas said. His mouth felt dry. "You know what he told me?"

"What?"

"He said he saw you throwing flowers into the trash. He asked me if I did something to piss you off."

Margaret stepped back, her face inscrutable. Douglas felt lightheaded from the paint fumes, hemmed in by the small room and the low ceiling and the clouds that kept intercepting the sunlight, his sunlight. Inside his chest, a weird syncopation began. Their marriage rested on her answer. This could be the moment where the screws came out of the wall and the packed shelf of their lives came down in a spectacular crash, or it could be nothing. He had no idea what Margaret would say.

"Oh, that," she said, digging in her jeans pocket and coming up with a Chapstick. "Geraldine came into work with all these hideous bouquets from a bridal shower, and she made everyone take one. Lilies smell like death to me. Way too many at my mother's funeral. I didn't want them in the house."

Douglas rested his paintbrush on the edge of the can. The pinging in his heart slowed. See, stupid. All worked up over nothing. You're painting your house, your beautiful and loyal wife is right there, smiling at you. Someday soon, maybe less than a year from now, you'll be rocking your firstborn to sleep right here in this very room. Stop looking for loose plaster, or you might find it.

"Ollie," he said. "What a loser."

"I picked up some chicken on the way home. I'm going to mix up some marinade. Seems like a grill night."

His wife made her own marinade. The chicken would be boneless and skinless because she cared about his health. She would be the mother with the bags of homemade trail mix and the grapes cut into quarters to prevent choking. With a sudden sweeping clarity, he saw that the other mothers would hate her. She would snap back after pregnancy, within months, into her smallest jeans. She would keep her hair long, slinging it up artfully into clips or buns that made her look vaguely European. She would find a second-hand diaper bag that mimicked an expensive purse. Yes, they would hate her with a passion.

Douglas finished the trim and washed out his brush in the garage sink, letting the water go warm to soothe his sore fingers. It was all okay. The screws had held, so they would put more and more on the shelf, testing its strength, shoring it up every now and again with do-it-yourself brackets from the hardware store. When he had cleaned up, he started to head inside but changed his mind. He opened the side door to the garage and stepped out, facing Ollie's house, half of it mildewed vinyl siding, the other half wood clapboards with peeling paint. Shabby as hell, which brought down the value of their house. He stood, hands in the pockets of his painting shorts, watching the sky, now the color of pumice, threatening rain. A cool breeze raised the hairs on his arms. Four metal garbage cans sat in a row like sentries to the underworld, guarding its secrets. Inside one of them were the flowers, and he didn't need to rummage around in case there was a card, because she had told him the whole story. From the backyard, he could smell the charcoal and lighter fluid. The humidity pressed down on his head. He picked up a stray leaf and opened the first garbage can. No flowers. He threw the leaf inside.

He picked up another leaf and opened the second can. Nothing. He stopped. He would not verify that the flowers were lilies or that they had a bridal shower look to them, that was beneath him. He turned toward the backyard, toward a clean conscience and a nice grilled chicken dinner, but then he turned back. He opened the third can and saw the flowers there, crushed beneath a coffee can. Nothing about them said bridal shower, although he wasn't sure what would. He moved the coffee can and turned the flowers over. There were white and coral-colored roses—could that be bridal?—and some other flowers he couldn't identify. Maybe lilies? He cursed his poor knowledge of botany and event planning and put the lid back on the can. He could ask her if she was telling the truth, but did he want an answer? Better to keep it to himself but heighten his vigilance and hope she got pregnant as soon as possible. Only then might he feel more confident that he had married the woman he was supposed to marry. Only then would he relax because a baby required total focus. Feeding schedules, diaper changes, teething, and sleep deprivation would push all this nonsense out of his brain and into the garbage, where it belonged.

—19—

Fitz

"You can't keep putting it off. You need to sit down with him and tell him you're leaving."

Fitz's mother, as usual, went right to the pulsing artery of the situation.

"You think so?" he said, one hand acting as a visor. The umbrella on the outdoor patio at the country club shaded only his mother.

"I know so."

He envied her ability to know things. He knew very little, except that he was miserable in his work. His father would retire at sixty-five, two years from now, and he fully expected Fitz to follow in his footsteps. In such a large publicly owned company, Fitz couldn't inherit the top job, but he would be expected to rise up through the ranks with his father's influence greasing the way. This had been the family narrative since he was a young child.

The accident he had witnessed in the park had changed all that, as if he had been the one to fly through the air and land with a bone-crushing thud on the pavement. It told him that his life didn't have to play out the way his parents had imagined it. It brought to mind a famous line from the Greek poet Pindar, whom he had studied in a class at Trinity: "Learn what you are and be such." So simple and so true. And yet, there would be consequences.

"He'll hate me for it."

Arlene shrugged. She picked up a slice of banana bread and spread a whisper of cream cheese on it with a butter knife. The club had its own bakery, and Fitz could attribute half the blubber he once had to its flaky and tender cheese Danish. His mother spent an hour a day in vigorous step and Jazzercise classes so that she could fit into her wardrobe of knit St. John pantsuits. "Life goes on." This was one of his mother's favorite phrases, often said in moments of extreme insensitivity, as when their longtime housekeeper lost her husband. Arlene moved through the world with a detachment he found enviable. Nothing seemed to rattle her, and yet, he could tell that she wasn't completely comfortable with his decision. This was her second piece of banana bread.

"It's not like I don't have a plan." The injured woman had never called him from the hospital, but he hadn't forgotten how the car connected with her slight body, her brief excursion through the air, how she had tried to hop away on one foot rather than incur the expense of riding in an ambulance and being admitted to the hospital. The business plan for his foundation would pool the insurance risk for the uninsured. People without insurance would be able to apply for coverage financed by the large donations he planned to acquire.

His mother opened her mouth to take a bite of banana bread. In the bleached light that reflected off the white stone patio deck, her teeth reminded him of chickpeas. Despite all the hush money she slipped to gravity and time, body parts were drooping and discoloring faster than she could keep up.

"I know you have a plan, sweetheart. Let's just make it the best plan."

Fitz could hear his stomach rumbling. He sipped his water. Hunger was familiar to him now, and he welcomed it. He had learned to eat only when he needed sustenance. The thirty-five or so pounds he had lost since college had become eighty, and for the first time in his adult life, he could walk into a store and buy a suit with only minor alterations. Inside him, though, the fat boy ate a hot fudge sundae with preternatural focus, each bite the proper ratio of ice cream, chocolate sauce, nuts, and whipped cream.

"Are you sure I can't bring you anything, Mr. Fitzhugh?" The bow-tied waiter stopped by again, seeming disturbed by Fitz's perspiring glass of water. It was August, the Sunday evening of summer, and the club had a listless and impatient atmosphere, ready for the cool industry of fall.

"I'm fine," Fitz said. "Just leaving."

He pushed his chair back, took one more sip of water.

"You know who I ran into the other day?" his mother said. She wasn't ready to release him.

"Who?"

"That lovely college friend of yours, Margaret. I was leaving Arturo's after having lunch with some friends, and she was there on the street. We practically knocked each other over."

Fitz slid his chair back toward the table. He had heard nothing from Margaret since the awkward phone call, some nine or ten months earlier, when they had made some vague comment about getting lunch. His mother knew that he and Margaret had been friends in college, nothing more.

"We haven't been in touch lately. How is she?" He tried to say this casually, but a note of distress crept into his voice.

"Oh, Billy," his mother said, her mouth turning down at the corners. She was the only person alive who still called him Billy. "I'm sorry, I didn't know."

"It doesn't matter. She's married now."

"She is, and still such a pretty girl. No little ones yet. I asked."

"Mother."

"In my day, most women had two or three before they turned twenty-five. I was already an old maid when I got married at thirty-two to a confirmed bachelor who wasn't even forty. No one could believe it when I had a child at thirty-seven. The doctor called me a geriatric mother."

The waiter had circled again, his shadow appearing across the table like the negative of a ghost. In silence, he refilled Fitz's water glass with a silver pitcher swaddled in a cloth napkin to absorb condensation. Fitz nodded his thanks.

"What else did she say?"

Fitz's mother brushed a few banana breadcrumbs from the table.

"Let me see. She's still at the same accounting firm, not loving it but fine for now. Her husband is a teacher, I think she said. They have a little house in West Hartford. Fixing it up and all that."

"What else?"

His mother crossed her arms, looked up toward the dark recesses of the umbrella and back at Fitz.

"What else, what else. Oh yes, her father's not well. Early Alzheimer's. In some nursing home. Terribly sad. Apparently, she spends a lot of time with him."

Was this what Margaret had been trying to tell him when she called? Last he knew, her father was still living with Margaret's sisters. What a complete shit he had been.

His mother had run out of things to say about Margaret and was now asking after his college friend, Paul the linebacker, who always flirted with her when he came around. Then she told Fitz about some redecorating she planned to do. He nodded along and sipped his water. Could he walk it all back? Margaret had not asked for anything more than his friendship, and he had pulled it away out of childish pique. It wasn't her fault that his love didn't match up with hers, that he had hidden it except for a confession that apparently didn't count because he was drunk, then a second only weeks before her wedding.

His mother's voice swam up into the umbrella. White spots floated in front of his eyes.

"If I can't get the fabric I want, we'll have to repaint the room, because, I'm sorry, teal does not go with eggplant, no matter how many so-called professionals try to tell me it does."

He couldn't call her; too much time had gone by. He would have to make some grand and anonymous gesture that somehow she would know came from him. If nothing else, at least they could once again be friends.

Fitz went back to his office with two action items: 1) Tell his father that his only child would not follow in his footsteps. 2) Make some grand and anonymous(ish) gesture that would tell Margaret how sorry he was for rejecting her friendship.

The second one was easier to knock off than the first.

"Brenda, would you come in?"

"Be right there."

Brenda slipped in the half-open office door without even moving it. She would make an excellent ninja, Fitz thought, if it weren't for that hair. The layered helmet she wore these days looked a little less stiff than it had before but still seemed doused in hairspray or shellac or some other substance that prevented it from moving. Brenda perched on the chair in front of his desk, the barest majority of her rear actually on the seat, as if she might have to spring into action at any moment. He hoped he could afford to take her with him when he left the company.

"I need your advice," he said, bouncing the eraser end of a pencil on his desk. "I have to send a mea culpa type gift to a friend."

"How big of a mea culpa?"

"Pretty big."

"Man or woman?"

"Woman."

Brenda glanced upward. She slightly altered the angle of her knees in a gesture that Fitz found unsettling, though he couldn't say why.

"More information might help."

As per company policy, Brenda was now called his administrative assistant instead of his secretary, and though her job hadn't changed, she affected a less subservient air.

"It's my college friend Margaret? I've told you about her."

"I remember," she said. She pushed back a little into the chair, crossed her legs.

"Her father's sick, early Alzheimer's, which I didn't know until recently."

"Didn't she get married? I thought I saw it in the paper."

"Yes, she's married. No kids, though."

Brenda bounced her crossed leg a few times. Her skirts had become significantly shorter recently, which seemed to be the trend. He sometime wondered what Brenda did in her off hours. She seemed like the type to quilt or crochet or create intricate mosaics out of broken shells or sea glass. She had never mentioned a boyfriend, but that didn't mean anything. Brenda was the soul of discretion. For all he knew, she spent her weekends at dance clubs wearing tight sequined dresses and four-inch heels, her hair infused with glitter. Maybe that was why it looked so stiff.

"Does she like New York?"

"She does like New York."

Fitz remembered the one time he and Margaret had been to New York together. He had organized a small group to see *Dreamgirls* while they were still in college. Before the show, they had all stopped at Rockefeller Center to skate, though in the end, he had stayed inside watching, too afraid he would fall on the ice and crack it.

"Maybe get her some tickets to a show, or the ballet? For her and her husband."

This struck Fitz as the perfect gift. He would make it three tickets.

To the ballet. That way she could take her sisters or a couple of friends. Her husband didn't need to go.

"Love that idea. New York City Ballet. Get three for a Saturday, the next show with great orchestra seats."

"Anything else?"

Many, many other things, Brenda. He wanted to tell her about his foundation plans, to seek her advice, but he had sworn himself to secrecy within the company. Everything had to be in place before he dropped the bomb.

"Nope, that's all."

"Should I have the tickets sent to you or to Margaret?"

"Directly to her. I'll give you the address."

"No note or anything?"

"No note."

Brenda stood and tugged her skirt down bit. She paused as though she had something to say but decided against it. Women he interacted with at NatCo seemed to do that a lot around him. It was the kind of issue he would have brought to Margaret and asked her to explain had they still been friends.

—20—

Brenda

Brenda had learned about the circulatory system in a college biology class during the year she had flirted with the idea of becoming a nurse. The diagrams in that class had fascinated her. In them, she could see that skin and bones were only the crude outlines. The circulatory system powered the production and told the true story. Bodies could recline, sit in a chair, be at rest; the heart could not.

Thus it was possible for her to act normally around Mr. Fitzhugh, to fetch his coffee and to remind him to call his mother back, even as the blood shot through her veins in a worrisome fashion. Her body kept its distance as her heart tapped the urgent Morse code of love in his direction. When he was heavier, she sometimes thought she might have a chance. With her alopecia, each of them had roughly equivalent physical deficiencies. But since he had lost weight, she had less hope. He was a catch now with his thick, dark hair and nice, even teeth, and now, a definable neck. She still wouldn't call him handsome by Hollywood standards, but his salary, which she knew from processing paperwork, permitted many women to see him through specialty glasses with green-tinted lenses.

Mr. Fitzhugh didn't know that Brenda was looking for other jobs, or that she had finally finished her bachelor's degree. She was twenty-six now. Time to shake the sand out of the beach towel of her pointless pining and fold it up, take it elsewhere. Maybe find a lake or a pond. She wasn't cut out for the ocean. Except that the ocean was where the breeze never died, where the salt air cleansed and renewed, where a barefoot walk was as good as a pedicure in exfoliating your feet, where a head wrapped in a silk scarf didn't look out of place. Where everyone wanted to be.

She was considering applying to a small computer company that was looking for someone to manage projects. Almost everyone had computers now. It made her wonder why she had wasted so much time learning to type a flawless eighty words per minute. If she got the job, she would walk into Mr. Fitzhugh's office and she would shake his hand, then grasp it with two hands, staring into his sad brown eyes. She would give him a long look, and he would know. He would know everything.

"Brenda, you in there?"

She and her mother were making pies for the church, which they did once a month. Four apple, three sweet potato, one pecan for the minister. Her mother found solace in a perfect crust: feed the congregation, feed the soul. For Brenda, chores like this one occupied her hands but not her mind, leaving too much time to moon over Mr. Fitzhugh. He would never see inside her in the way she needed to be seen, and yet, she could not seem to shut off the yearning. It was like a faucet with a faulty valve.

"Need something?"

"Pass the flour."

Brenda slid the metal canister toward her mother, whose deft hands worked a perfect disc of dough. Her mother never measured. She knew the ingredients by weight and feel, which meant that Brenda had no idea how to replicate the perfect, flaking crust even after all these years. She only dealt with the fillings, peeling dozens of apples and mashing the sweet potatoes. She sometimes envied the containment of her mother's world, which rarely stretched beyond the triangle that circumscribed her home, the church, and the grocery store. It was a world over which she had complete mastery, while Brenda had to venture out into places where anything could go wrong, where her wig might come off in public, for example, on a blustery day.

"Pastor Dan wants a word with you after the service tomorrow."

"What about?"

"He didn't say."

"You can guess, Ma."

"He's looking out for you, that's all."

"Another setup."

"Just keep an open mind."

Brenda picked up another apple and noticed the overhead kitchen light reflected on its smooth skin, much the way light reflected from her scalp when she wasn't wearing a wig.

"Does he warn them?"

"Who?"

"The men Pastor Dan tries to set me up with. Does he warn them about what they're getting into?"

Her mother shifted her hips and sighed, rubbing her nose with the back of her flour-coated hand.

"Hair isn't everything, Brenda."

"That doesn't answer my question."

"He doesn't warn them, because he doesn't know. He thinks you're shy. You need to get out there and give it a try."

Brenda placed her knife's blade against the apple and turned it, creating one long, continuous peel. This she was good at. This she could do for the rest of her life, left alone in a room with bushels and bushels of apples, no questions, no sideways glances, no fear of her wig sliding into the soup as she leaned over to eat it. That's why she stuck with the salad bar. She could bring the food up to her mouth.

"Okay."

"Okay, what?"

"Okay, I'll talk to Pastor Dan."

Her mother's kitchen was cluttered, countertops covered with rusting cookie cutters, an old electric can opener, shears, used wax paper folded into squares, rubber bands, empty canning jars and the like. In the future she liked to imagine, her own kitchen would be pristine: bare counters and curtain-free windows, Scandinavian-style cabinets and built-in appliances. She would cook adventurous foreign cuisines, not the same old recipes week in and week out. But this future required a partner. Someone who made more money than she did. Otherwise, she would be here until she was old, cleaning these same counters and washing these same dishes, including the plate with the crack in it.

"Now you're talking. Pass me the apples and let's get these pies in the oven."

Brenda slid the bowl of diced apples along the counter. In the future she liked to imagine, dessert would be anything but pie.

—21—

Margaret

Margaret walked from the parking lot to the New Haven train station, dodging the torrents of water that ran along the curb. She hated wearing rubber boots, country mouse wear, to New York, but Douglas had insisted. He was afraid she would slip. Above her, the troubled clouds in a dark November sky spat out fat raindrops that pierced the puddles on the sidewalk like buckshot. She hurried, tugging the belt on her raincoat tighter. A middle-aged man smiled and held the door for her as she entered the station. Inside, it felt only slightly less damp under the cavernous ceiling. It was the hour of the commute. The worn wooden benches held mostly men reading expertly folded newspapers, exposing their wrists at regular intervals to glance at their watches. An elderly man with a seeing-eye dog stood facing a wall.

She spotted Lauren, who was sitting on a bench, one foot jiggling.

"Finally," Lauren said when she approached.

"The traffic was horrendous. Where's Annabelle?"

"Getting coffee. Want one?"

"I'm good."

"Since when do you turn down coffee? Oh."

Dead giveaway. She had hoped it wouldn't come up until they were at least seated on the train.

"How far along?"

"Five and a half weeks. Not even vomiting yet."

"Feel okay?"

"Sore boobs, a little queasy, but not too bad. Douglas is a wreck, though. He didn't want me to come today."

Annabelle arrived with a large coffee in hand and gave Margaret a tepid hug. Light from the high, arched windows washed over Annabelle's face, and Margaret noticed how the skin below her eyebrows had begun a slow migration toward her eyelids, like two continents moving toward each other, the shifting of tectonic plates that happened as youth slid toward middle age.

"I'm not awake yet," she said, lips barely moving. "Need three more of these."

Lauren shook Annabelle's shoulder.

"Wake up. How often do we get to go to New York to see the ballet? And by the way, your little sister here is preggers."

"Back on the horse. Good for you!"

Annabelle seemed to wake up a bit at the news. She gave Margaret a hug.

"So is that why we're seeing the ballet? One last day of freedom?"

"Not exactly. I still don't know who sent the tickets."

They had come in the mail directly from the box office with no note or return address. Douglas claimed not to have bought them. Eventually, Margaret flipped through her address book of friends and acquaintances and came upon Fitz. It was the kind of gesture he would make if he were reaching out to repair their friendship. But she hadn't called him yet. She needed to know first if this pregnancy would hold.

They walked toward the escalator that would take them to a tunnel that led under the tracks, Lauren and Annabelle elbow to elbow and Margaret behind them. As they passed the last of the wooden benches in the station, Margaret noticed a man with long, dirty hair wearing fingerless gloves and holding a small cardboard box about the size of a toaster. He gave Margaret a long look as she walked by, scanning her from top to bottom.

"Yeah, baby," he said, just loud enough for the three of them to hear.

Bile came up in Margaret's throat along with a collective noun: men. She had wrongly assumed that marriage would form a protective barrier to their leering, their propositions, their invasions into her space, the threat they posed to her body. Lauren glanced back at her, opened her mouth, but then closed it again. Annabelle took a long sip of her coffee, staring straight ahead. Any reaction from the leer-ee almost always seemed to encourage the leer-er. They walked on.

The platform was crowded and pungent. A fine mist smelling faintly of urine and coffee settled on Margaret's skin as they waited, looking down the empty train tracks as if into the past. Something about train stations always reminded Margaret of London after the Blitz, not that she had ever been outside the country. Movies must have formed this impression. A man in motorcycle boots stepped on Margaret's foot as the train came into view and the jockeying for position began. Lauren nodded left, and Margaret and Annabelle followed her.

They stepped into a sparsely occupied car. Lauren and Annabelle sat down together, leaving Margaret to sit by herself behind them. She sighed, choosing the window seat. She loosened the belt on her raincoat, sat down and pushed her purse under the seat ahead with the toe of her rain boot, but the seat next to her seemed too inviting. She retrieved her purse and put it on the empty seat as though she were saving it.

Outside the window, the leering man with the cardboard box was striding down the platform, occasionally breaking into an odd hitching run. He looked directly at Margaret as he passed their car, then entered through the far door. Margaret moved to the aisle seat, putting her purse on the seat closest to the window. She bent down, tugging on her boots, so as not to make eye contact as Cardboard Box Man came down the aisle.

He placed the box in the luggage rack over Margaret's head.

"This seat taken?" he said, nodding to the seat in which Margaret had placed her sincere wish to be left alone. This wish took up almost the whole seat, with barely enough room for her purse. Margaret glanced around. She could see that two single seats in the rows behind them were still empty.

The conductor entered the train car and began punching tickets as the train pulled away from the platform. The man stood above Margaret, leaning into her, his jean jacket giving off the sharp odor of cigarettes. His baggy corduroy pants were stained around the hem. She moved her purse and slid back into the seat by the window. The man sat down and spread his knees so that one was touching Margaret's leg. She pulled her legs toward the wall of the train car, making herself as small as possible.

Lauren looked over the seat at Margaret, then up at the cardboard box, wordlessly asking Margaret if they should find a new car, and she wordlessly replied, *It's too late now.* As the train gained speed, the man reached into his pocket and pulled out a package of pistachios. He cracked them one by one, his fingers turning bright red with the dye. The empty shells fell on the floor.

"Want some?" he asked, holding the package toward Margaret.

She shook her head.

"C'mon, baby. Be nice. I won't hurt you."

She closed her eyes, holding back tears. The new grain of rice stirred, making itself known, and anger welled up in her, a mothering instinct. Why couldn't she get on a train and ride to New York without some stranger's leg pressing against her own?

"Excuse me," Margaret said. "I need to use the restroom."

The man sucked on his lower lip as if deciding whether or not he would let her out.

"Excuse me," she said more firmly.

Instead of standing up, he pulled his splayed legs together and turned them out into the aisle, which forced Margaret to decide if she wanted her backside or her front to brush up against him. She chose the back, and the man brazenly cupped her rear as she lurched into the aisle. If anyone saw it, they said nothing. The train rocked from side to side, mocking her. She fought her way up to the restroom, steadying herself on the headrests. Once there, she closed the sliding door and sat on the toilet for a few minutes, seething, whispering words of apology to the grain of rice for the sorry state of the world he or she would be entering.

She washed her hands in the tiny metal sink and dried them on several paper towels. When she left the restroom, she saw only one empty seat other than the one she had vacated, and it required her to pass the man and his cardboard box. She could have gone into the next car, but her sisters would have wondered what happened to her. She also didn't want to give Cardboard Box Man the satisfaction of chasing her away.

She made her way back down the aisle and kept her eyes aloft as she passed the row where she had been sitting.

"Bitch," the man said loudly, and every eye in the train car looked at Margaret, as if she were the one to blame for disturbing them from their train-induced comas.

She sat down, glaring at the back of the man's asinine head. Such men depended on women not to make a fuss. The thought of his hand on her rear brought back memories of Anders and how he had touched her that night as if she were a thing and not a person, just a vessel for his need. She pulled her purse tight to her stomach, hunching over it, arms and legs forming a neat package.

Not all men were like this, she reminded herself. Douglas was polite to a fault. Her father, when he had his faculties, had been the sort of man who held doors for women and called them *ladies*. It occurred to her suddenly that the grain of rice itself might one day be a man. If it were, she would teach him that women didn't need his protection. They simply needed his respect. Treat them as you yourself would want to be treated and keep your hands to yourself. That's what she would tell him.

And that's what she would tell the owner of a chain of liquor stores who had given her the flowers her neighbor Ollie had seen her throw in the garbage can. The liquor store mogul had been one of her biggest accounts, and she had been afraid to lose it. Already, she had lost two clients because she had rejected propositions, and her boss was beginning to think she couldn't do her job.

It wasn't as if she invited their interest. She took pains to dress professionally. Though her vision was twenty-twenty, she had purchased a pair of heavy black frames with clear lenses, but this had only seemed to inflame the interest of the liquor store mogul, who showed up at their appointments with bottles of champagne or boxes of chocolate that she would bring back to the office and leave anonymously in the break room. She had rejected his suggestion that they meet in a hotel bar after work to go over his accounts. She had told him she was married, held up the ring. He seemed not to care. The flowers had been delivered to her home, and she still wondered how he had gotten her address.

She hugged her purse tighter. Soon, the grain of rice would change everything. Her body would swell, and men would leave her alone for many months, at least she thought they would. She pulled a tissue out of her purse and blew her nose, then took out her paperback copy of *The Unbearable Lightness of Being*. When the train pulled into Grand Central, she left her seat a bit early and reached up to the overhead bin behind the Cardboard Box Man as if she were finding something she had placed there. Instead, she shoved the box behind a large shopping bag brimming with knitting yarn, then hustled ahead as the train slowed to a stop. She glanced back to see Cardboard Box Man looking for his namesake. When he couldn't immediately find it, he reached past another passenger and grabbed the sleeve of Margaret's raincoat.

"What'd you do with my box?"

Margaret yanked her sleeve out of his hand, her face aflame. She wanted to throw something at Carboard Box Man's head, but instantly, she was back in the borrowed Toyota Corolla with Anders, paralyzed with fear. She turned to her sisters, who were right in front of her, and mouthed the words: *He grabbed my ass.* Lauren and Annabelle threw themselves in front of Margaret as Cardboard Box Man was lunging toward her.

"Listen, you dirtbag, what you did was assault," Lauren yelled at him. "I'm going to call nine-one-one as soon as I get off the train."

Annabelle, who was closest, kicked a high-heeled boot toward him, and crouched into a defensive stance, blocking him from moving up the aisle.

"Crazy bitches," he said, turning around and hurrying to the exit at the back of the car.

"Damn right!" Lauren screamed after him. "You messed with the wrong sisters."

Margaret was shaking as they left the train. Lauren and Annabelle each took one of Margaret's arms and they walked down the concourse together. She was upset that she hadn't been able to confront him more directly. She had let Cardboard Box Man get away with the ass grab except for her passive aggressive hiding of his box. At the same time, she was proud of her sisters, who had stood up for her and scared him away. Maybe she wasn't the caboose who had ushered in tighter times anymore. Maybe they had suddenly realized she was just like them—a woman struggling to navigate the world of men.

"You saved me," she yelled, as they ran into the rain outside the station and found a taxi.

"Nobody picks on our pregnant little sister," Annabelle said, flicking her boot again before ducking into the taxi. "I was aiming for his crotch, by the way. He should be glad I missed."

After lunch and the ballet, the three of them squeezed into the back seat of a taxi that took them back to Grand Central Station. They checked the board for the next train to New Haven, then wandered through the food court for provisions. Margaret, who had had a salad for lunch, was suddenly faint with hunger. She bought an obscenely priced roast beef sandwich, craving iron, and a bottle of water. The platform smelled of the city (rotting cabbage, deep fryer oil, exhaust), and the people pressing in and around her emitted a peculiar urgency that would only dissipate when the train crossed into Connecticut.

As they boarded the train, Lauren kindly took a single seat so that Annabelle and Margaret could sit together. Pregnancy came with a fatigue unlike any other she had experienced. It made her seek out the horizontal in all things. Her head had drooped onto Lauren's shoulder even during the ballet, but Annabelle wanted to talk about Richard.

"The last time I went to see Dad, that imbecile at the front desk told me that he needed new pajamas. She said they couldn't *find* his pajamas, and the way she said it, it was like she blamed him—or us— for throwing them away or something. Like we would deliberately throw away his pajamas."

Annabelle's monologue fluttered over her. She chose to hear but not to listen, although she was thinking about her father as well.

Visiting him now meant steeling herself for the next shock. Somehow, he was aging in reverse, regressing almost to infancy. Once, she found him curled up into a tight ball on his bed, sucking his thumb. The nurses had given him a stuffed cat, and he would cry if he couldn't find it, or if they took it away to clean his frail body. In her heart of heart of heart of hearts, where language wasn't allowed to form thoughts, she wanted him to die. What purpose did it serve to keep his body alive, leaving his children's emotional and financial spigots wide open, when he didn't know his own name?

The last time they had met with his doctor, about a month before, Margaret had asked how much longer her father could live, given that he was now in a post-verbal state, emitting only animal-like sounds.

"He's already outlived most people with his diagnosis," the doctor had said, raising his eyebrows as if this were an admirable accomplishment. "It could be six months, three years, who knows?"

Modern medicine. In the next century, Margaret imagined, it would seem neither modern nor medicinal, more like witchcraft once they finally figured out how the human body and brain actually worked. As Annabelle's skein of aggravation unraveled next to her, she thought about the child inside her who would have no grandparents to buy it toys it didn't need or sneak it a cookie when she and Douglas weren't looking. How sad. Suddenly, she felt a cramp. A creeping dread began behind her knees and traveled upward. This was how her other miscarriages had started.

She took a deep breath and closed her eyes, gripping the seat cushion with both hands. Annabelle kept talking. The cramp subsided. She went to use the restroom, and all was fine. No spotting. It would be okay. She stood washing her hands in the tiny train sink, remembering that morning when she had been hiding from Cardboard Box Man. The days of her pregnancy stretched out before her like white stitches on a white quilt. She couldn't see the pattern. The thread might break or run out, clumsy knots might have to be tied, and despite that, she would have to create something beautiful, something perfect, something unique. Nothing to do but sew on.

—22—

Douglas

Their marriage had its own gravitational pull, and with Margaret passing the twelve-week milestone of her pregnancy, high tide swept in and splashed over the dunes. A new year—1987—and a new watermark. Douglas finally allowed himself to picture a future with a baby in it. His daughter. Or his son.

Christmas had been shrouded in fear. The tree had gone up, but they had never even put lights on it, only a few plain ornaments and a couple of candy canes that Douglas had received from his students. They had avoided the mall, or any place where they might see families, strollers, car seats, Santa Claus. Their hope was like a frozen lake. Each day, they inched out a little farther, the water below deeper and more deadly, never knowing whether the ice was thick and solid or about to crack.

Next Christmas would be different. The three of them, cheeks red with cold, would hunt for the perfect tree. The baby would ride in a carrier on Douglas's chest, and their hearts would beat in tandem, like the baby's heart was now beating inside Margaret. Douglas would buy ten strands of lights, and he would let the tree glow all night in their small living room, no matter what Margaret said about the electric bill.

154

Douglas could finally understand why his presence had saved his own parents' marriage, why having a child would bind them together in a way their vows never had. This was not just a baby inside Margaret. This was the two of them made new, reborn into unblemished skin and unlimited potential. More than that, this was the receptacle of their own never-achieved goals. This child might actually be good at baseball or French horn or public speaking. This child might change the world; at the very least, it would change theirs.

Once Margaret's morning sickness subsided, her head for numbers returned. She calculated the cost of supporting a child until college and the eventual cost of college itself and determined that she would not be able to stop working for more than the six-week maternity leave offered by her company. Douglas disagreed.

"But day care?" he said. "What if they leave the baby to cry in a crib all day? How will we know?"

"We'll find a good place. The numbers don't work otherwise."

Margaret tapped her adding machine rapid fire, turning the total toward him.

"See?"

The sum looked menacing, but it didn't take into account the number of gassy smiles they would miss, the miniature spoons heaped with pureed pears or peas airplaning into a waiting mouth, open, birdlike. The rattles shaken with no one but other oblivious babies as witness to his own baby's brilliance.

"This assumes we'll be paying for your dad forever."

Margaret's face turned hard. Douglas sometimes marveled at her ability to look like a classical marble sculpture while sitting at a dining room table strewn with newspapers, twist ties and paper napkins.

"We're still paying now, so we have to figure that in."

"Realistically, it can't be much longer. There's nothing left of him."

This wasn't exactly true. While his brain had checked out long ago,

Richard's other organs seemed to function independently, oblivious that their host no longer needed them. Douglas's own parents had died relatively quickly after falling ill, which he now saw as a blessing.

"I would have said that a year ago, but he's still here, isn't he? We can't push him off a cliff just because we're having a baby."

Tradeoffs. Life had become one big series of them, every day a distribution of limited resources into gaping holes of need that would never be filled. Maybe this accounted for the hollow feeling in his chest. The tide was in, and yet he still had a hard time taking a deep breath, as if he had swallowed sea water.

Margaret's face softened from marble into polished wood. This took effort, and he gave her credit for it.

"I give you that it might not be forever," she said. "Maybe one of us could work part-time. Eventually."

Douglas nodded, noticing that Margaret had a hand on her belly, which had swelled only slightly, as if she had eaten a large meal. He wanted her fat, bursting to ripeness. A pregnant Margaret would be a Margaret that no man could ravish with his eyes, as they often did when she walked down the street with him. He could feel onlookers peeling off her clothes, layer by layer, until she was completely naked, the curves of her lovely body stoking their unthinkable fantasies without even knowing it. If she ever knew what those men were thinking, she might never go out in public again.

The baby might be a girl, too, and part of him hoped that she didn't inherit Margaret's beauty. It was too much of a burden. With his genes in the mix, at least, they had a good chance of producing a child whose looks garnered no particular attention. Adequately attractive, that was a given, but within the spectrum that didn't cause undue disruption.

"We have some time to think about it," Douglas said. Staying home with a baby appealed to him greatly. He would buy one of those new jogging strollers and finally get some exercise. Stress had upped his candy consumption so that his own paunch was about the equivalent of a five-months-pregnant belly. He had advanced much farther along than Margaret.

Later that day, Douglas took out his supplies to paint the bedroom hallway. He had painted it right after they had moved in, when all the paint stores had been pushing bold choices—crimson, navy blue, aquamarine—but the brick color he had chosen seemed too dark for a home with a baby in it. A baby needed light, comfort, and positive energy. He had been reading about something called feng shui, an ancient Chinese tradition of creating a peaceful and fulfilling environment. Margaret would think it was hogwash, so he planned to make small but impactful changes on his own before the baby arrived.

The color he had chosen was called *foam*. It was almost white but had a trace of green-blue in it. He could picture the baby, learning to walk, her little hands running along the wall about two feet above the baseboards. He had gone with a satin finish, which would be easy to clean.

An hour into his painting, he found the zone. He had worked the paint into all the corners and cut in around the trim. Now he was rolling the blank canvases of the walls, and as he did, the sea water in his lungs subsided. Despite the fumes, he could breathe deeply again. Then he heard Margaret in the kitchen, picking up the phone.

The hum of the dishwasher and the buzz of Ollie's lawnmower next door made it hard to hear distinctly, but he thought he heard Margaret say "Fitz."

The name stirred up a hornet's nest inside Douglas. Though he had never met this Fitz, he knew enough. The man was rich. Margaret had been close friends with him in college and, therefore, he was gay or asexual or secretly in love with her. He put the roller down on the paint tray and edged closer to the kitchen, where the dishwasher had started a new and slightly quieter cycle.

"I knew it was you," she was saying. "Nobody else would think of sending me to the ballet."

A pause then, followed by a laugh that felt to Douglas slightly too girlish for a woman Margaret's age. A woman about to become a mother. His old paint-stained T-shirt suddenly felt tight across his belly. He pulled at it and strained again to hear.

"Let's have lunch, okay? It's been way too long."

Way too long for what? Where Douglas came from, male-female friendships did not extend past college. They could not exist in the airless vacuum of adult life, especially after marriage. Desire could not be pocketed like a disposable lighter.

"Great," Margaret was saying. "Tuesday at one sounds perfect. I'll meet you there."

Douglas walked back to his roller and picked it up as Margaret hung up the phone and went into the living room. Surely, she would tell him about her lunch, and they would laugh about how she lived in the small ranch with him instead of in a mansion with her old friend Fitz, but you couldn't choose with whom you fell in love, could you? The heart wanted what it wanted. Who said that? Some poet or philosopher. She would shrug, and they would laugh again.

He finished rolling the walls and came into the living room, where Margaret had turned on the television. She liked to watch tennis on weekends. Though she had never picked up a racket, she enjoyed the intensity of the competition.

"Almost done with the hallway," Douglas said, pulling again on his T-shirt. "This room is next."

"Is it?" she said. She was following a long volley that ended with a high lob out of bounds.

"I might start it Tuesday, after work."

"Sounds good," she said, taking a sip of water. The doctor had told her to stay hydrated, so she carried a large plastic cup with her around the house. The word Tuesday had not prompted her to mention lunch. He tried another approach.

"I may have to stay a little late next week to finish up my curriculum plan. What do you have going on?"

She murmured something, the cup of water at her lips. Her eyes were fixed on the television, another long rally.

"What was that?"

"Nothing."

"You said nothing, or you have nothing?"

"Both."

So lunch was nothing. Or it wasn't nothing, but she didn't want to tell him about it. The screws holding the shelf of their marriage to the wall loosened slightly. He looked at her again, the perfect profile composed, inscrutable. He thought of the flowers in the garbage can, and of the ballet tickets, which he now knew came from Fitz. If only he could twist off her ears and climb inside her head, squishing around in the muck of her thoughts until he figured out what she was really thinking. She put a hand on her stomach, rubbing it absently. Remember that? That was why the shelf would stay in place. That was why lunch was nothing.

"Look," she said, pointing. "My feet are already starting to swell."

They were. He could see her uncharacteristically fat toes pressing against each other, the once-delicate ankles inflated like water balloons. She had given her body to him, offered it freely, and now suffered the physical consequences of constructing a human being from the cells of her own body, and how did he thank her for it? Suspicion. Jealousy. Cold manipulation where there should be joy.

"Let me get you some more water," he said, and took the cup to the kitchen.

Mistrust. Nothing was more corrosive. Left to its own devices, it would eat through any barrier he might erect, and so he had to guard against it. He had to rinse it away with pure thoughts, with reassurances, with the knowledge that in a few short months, a baby would bind them together for all time.

—23—

Fitz

The time has come, the Walrus said, to talk of many things.
Fitz stood in the outer office waiting for his father to finish a meeting.

Of shoes and ships and sealing wax, of cabbages and kings.

If only they could talk of shoes (his were chafing at the heel) or sealing wax (as obsolete as that was). He buttoned his suit jacket then unbuttoned it and buttoned it again. He took a cone-shaped paper cup from the dispenser and filled it from the bubbler. Almost immediately, the thin cup turned soft in his perspiring hand. He gulped the water, then wiped the corners of his mouth with the folded handkerchief he had been trained since birth to keep in the back pocket of his trousers, the word his mother had always used. He had once said "trousers" around Margaret, and she had laughed. Even dry cleaners, she had said, called them "pants."

The door opened, and a woman in a black skirt, white blouse, and houndstooth suit jacket left his father's office. She was blinking rapidly, which Fitz took to mean she was trying not to cry. His father's administrative assistant, a briskly efficient woman with a severe mouth and close-cropped gray hair who had been recommended by his mother (why tempt fate?) nodded Fitz toward the door. He threw

the damp paper cup into the wastebasket on his way to the inner
sanctum.

His father's office was four times the size of his own. It had two
large windows on either side of the massive wood desk, but his father
usually kept the heavy drapes closed, preferring the dark, clubby
atmosphere of a smoking room or a library. On the wall to the left was
a floor-to-ceiling set of cherry built-in cabinets and shelves crammed
with books, framed certificates, photos, and awards. One shelf dis-
played his father's golf trophies. On another was the only trophy Fitz
had ever won in his life, second place in high school debate club. He
had thrown it away when he left for college, but his father had rescued
it from the garbage and given it a home where it could be compared
to his own bigger, shinier trophies.

"Sit down," his father said as he came in. He gestured toward a
small grouping of two black leather armchairs instead of the hot seat
in front of his desk, where the woman in the black skirt and houndstooth jacket had no doubt been sitting. The shame of her watering
eyes still hung in the room. "What can I do for you?"

Many things, Fitz wanted to say. *Treat me with kindness. Remember
what it's like to be young. Open a window and let some air in here.
Throw that damn debating trophy in the garbage where it belongs.*

"It concerns my future," Fitz said. He and his mother had agreed
on this opening line as one that would launch the conversation on
Fitz's terms. *My* future. Not the one you want for me.

A smirk began to play around the corners of his father's mouth,
but he covered it with his hand. Momentous decisions had been made
in this office: stock-market-rattling mergers, new lines of business,
top-level firings. The smirk said that Fitz's future, such as it was,
would not rank among them. His father straightened his mouth into
a line and nodded. "Go on," he said.

"Both of us know I'm not cut out for this business," Fitz said. "I
don't have your instincts. I never have."

This was the business logic piece of his argument, and Fitz internally applauded himself for uttering the words. He would have to be given some credit for being brave enough to face his father's disappointment, which was a sharp, jagged thing that had hung over Fitz's head from infancy.

"What are you trying to say? Out with it." Hamish's face had gone reddish-pink, approximately the same shade he liked the interior of his prime rib.

Fitz had expected this. He unbuttoned his suit jacket to give himself something to do. A second passed. Then two.

"It's like this, Dad. I'd like to start a foundation."

The red in Hamish's cheeks subsided a bit. He cleared his throat, preparing to make some pronouncement. As was his Pavlovian response to the throat clearing, Fitz arranged his face into an expression of attentive respect. This required that his eyes stay fixed on his father's face (*look at me, son*) and that he bend his mouth into an awkward half smile.

"Nothing wrong with that. I've been meaning to start a foundation myself. The Hartford muckety-mucks have been after me for years."

Fitz's eyes fell to the carpet, which he was somehow able to view with microscopic precision. The fibers in the soothing camel-colored Berber looked like little olive trees, their branches whirling upward. He had seen such trees on a family cruise through the Mediterranean when he had been in middle school, mortified to be seen in a bathing suit. The fat boy's fear of going hungry came back to him now, and he considered bolting out of his father's office straight to an all-you-can-eat strip mall buffet, where he would gorge himself on fried chicken and lasagna and cheesecake and creamed spinach and other foods that had no business being in anyone's stomach at the same time. But he wouldn't do that. Now a hair under two hundred pounds and almost fit, he wrestled the fat boy. Pinned him to the ground. Tore his eyes from the carpet.

"I don't think you understand. This foundation would require all my time. I would have to leave the company."

"Leave the company" was a phrase that had probably never been spoken in his father's presence in a voluntary way. Hamish came from the generation that joined for life, accumulating watches and fountain pens and mantel clocks for decades of service along the way.

"What kind of foundation are you talking about? And why would you have to leave the company?"

"So what I'm thinking is a foundation would cover the uninsured. It would pool the risk. I think it's a perfect—"

"I still don't see why—"

Fitz would have to say the words directly, and those words would detonate in this space, the inner sanctum, like tiny nuclear bombs, leaving a fallout that his father would never completely clear away. It was possible that Hamish didn't deserve this. He was a pushy man, no doubt, who had tried to dictate his son's every move for far too long, and yet, Fitz understood that these machinations came from a place of deep insecurity and fear. His father was terrified that Fitz would not be able to build a life as enviable as his own. Downward mobility inspired a special kind of disappointment.

"I can't stay here, Dad. This job is killing me."

Hamish leaned back and curled his upper lip, as if Fitz's statement were a bad smell. Then he leaned forward. "This job is killing you? This job that anyone your age would be lucky to have? This job that your parents devoted their lives to securing for you?"

"But you never asked if that was what I wanted, did you?"

His father's jaw emitted a cracking sound that Fitz had never heard before. Or had he? In an instant, he was back in his father's study as a young boy, no more than eight, holding a remote-controlled plane with a broken wing. The jaw crack had preceded the avalanche that poured down on his head, the "ungratefuls" and the "irresponsibles" and the "disappointed in yous." He braced for them now.

In the unexpected stillness that followed, his father let out a hoarse whisper.

"Get out."

"I'm not you, and I never will be you. I don't understand why you can't see that."

"I said, get out!"

Before Fitz could leave, Hamish walked over to his bookshelf and picked up Fitz's second place debate trophy.

"Do you know why I keep this?" he said, holding the trophy aloft.

Fitz knew he should leave without taking the bait, but he had been programmed to answer when his father asked him a question.

"I really don't."

"Because it's the only thing you ever accomplished on your own. The only thing."

Before he could think, Fitz was across the room taking the trophy out of his father's surprised hand. He couldn't leave it in that office, mocking him, any longer.

"I'll get this out of your way, so you don't have to be reminded of how little I've accomplished on my own. And I won't be back."

"You won't be back? Good!"

Fitz turned and left to the sound of his father's shouting. On the way to his car, he passed a small pond on the insurance company's property and heaved the trophy into the reedy middle, where it hit the water with a satisfying *plunk*.

In summer, the club had a nostalgic feel to it, as even the oldest members walked around with a kind of glow as their faces tanned to the color and texture of used paper bags. But in February, the whole enterprise seemed as fragile as a snowflake, a nursing home that happened to sit on a golf course. The younger members only came for the required monthly dinners, which left the retired executives roaming the halls in polyester track suits, looking as if they had lost their keys.

Fitz's mother had scheduled him for tea right after the meeting with his father. He brushed the snow from the shoulders of his overcoat before handing it to the attendant, a stout young woman who was dressed in a coat herself because of the draft that came through the lobby every time the door opened.

"I'm afraid it's a bit wet," he said. He tried to treat the club's employees as people, unlike his parents, who seemed not to notice them except when something wasn't to their liking. His mother had once sent a lemonade back to the kitchen because it had too much ice in it.

"I'll have it brushed while you're here," the woman said, and Fitz once again felt the gaping divide that separated the wealthy from the non-wealthy in almost all things. His efforts to cross it were often met with a kind of prideful disdain, and so he had learned to simply nod and smile politely. The staff of the club probably thought he was mentally impaired.

His mother was already seated in the formal dining room, but she had nothing in front of her except a table setting—no cup of tea, no glass of water. As Fitz approached, he could see that his mother had her eyes fixed on the kitchen door across the room, which occasionally swung open and revealed the prosaic scene inside: stainless steel counters littered with trays of finger sandwiches awaiting their radish roses or sprigs of parsley; dirty dishtowels strung up like Tibetan prayer flags; steam belching from the industrial dishwashers. Arlene had perfected the art of sitting alone with elegance, her face in perfect alignment—neither bored nor interested. "I simply observe the world around me," she had told him once when he had asked her what she was thinking as she waited for the valet to bring around her car.

She sighed sympathetically when he arrived at the table.

"I heard from Dad before I came down to the club," she said, waving to a waiter who had been lingering nearby in anticipation of her signal. "He's livid."

No sooner had Fitz unfurled his linen napkin than a multi-tiered tray of miniature sandwiches and pastries appeared on the table. The waiter, now with a white cloth draped over his forearm, leaned toward Fitz to pour hot tea into the gold-handled cup parked on the gold-rimmed saucer in front of him. So much gold. A hideous excess of gold. Fitz hated tea, too, would have much preferred coffee, but it was too late. The wretched stuff was there in front of him, and he could no more correct the waiter than throw one of his wing tips across the room.

"Tell me everything," his mother said, blowing on her tea before taking a delicate sip. "Is this chamomile?" she asked the waiter, who was still hovering. "I specifically asked for Earl Grey."

The response to this affront involved numerous staff whisking the teacups away and replacing them, bowing and scraping as if they had slapped his mother across the face, as Fitz wished to do in that very moment. He pulled on the knot of his tie to loosen it.

"Don't do that," his mother said, reaching over and tugging the knot toward his throat. She knew how to strangle him in more ways than one.

"At least it's done," Fitz said, picking up the new teacup, then setting it down again. The strong odor of fish wafted toward him from the tiered platter. Smoked salmon in there somewhere. The dining room could be wallpapered in the amount of smoked salmon the club consumed on an annual basis. Fitz pictured thin pink fillets covering the walls, plastered on with crème fraiche, seams studded with capers.

His mother sipped the replacement tea then served herself two crustless triangle-cut sandwiches with silver tongs. She bit into one.

"Eat something," she said, frowning. "You don't eat anymore."

Fitz obeyed, but he hardly tasted what he put into his mouth. Sweet or savory, he couldn't even say. Watery winter light flooded the room through a bank of windows out of which he could see enormous stalactites of icicles descending from the overhang of the roof. His whole world had been devoid of color, of taste, of meaning since his lunch with Margaret the week before. Maybe that was why he had been willing, finally, to face his father.

"He'll get over it," his mother was saying. "Eventually."

Even as he felt the chair beneath him, he was also outside, balancing on a high wire strung between tall trees, the wind stuffing his ears like cotton. He would have to reach the platform on the other side before he could think properly. His mother's monologue was like so much bird chatter in the distance.

"So exciting, really," he heard around the wind. "Running your own nonprofit. I've already thought of a few friends for your board of trustees. You'll need some deep pockets."

"Margaret's pregnant."

His mother put down her teacup and gave him a stern look. How he wished to rewind time, to relive Margaret entering the restaurant, her exquisite face beaming, the quick catch of his own breath upon seeing her, the blue flash where he nearly lost consciousness as she grasped his hand and then leaned forward to press her cheek to his, almost a kiss. But something was different, he had seen it almost immediately. Oh, to edit the scene and remove the fullness from her face, the slight press of belly against her dress. He knew. He knew before she even said the words. As much as he wanted to regain her friendship and as much as he'd prepared himself to hear about her happy marriage, he wasn't prepared for the disappointment of finding out she was pregnant. Bound to Douglas for all time.

His mother was frowning again, coral lipstick creeping into the vertical crevices around her lips.

"Now, look here," she said. "I don't care if she's having triplets. We need to talk about your board of trustees. If you don't have that together, you'll get sucked right back in. You'll be back to work on Monday."

"Why do you even care?"

His mother answered by picking up her linen napkin, placing half a dozen tiny sandwiches and scones in its center, tying the ends like a hobo's bandana, then dropping the whole package into her black leather Prada purse.

"When you're ready to be civil, you know how to reach me." She walked out of the dining room without looking back.

Fitz nodded to the waiter, who made the tea things vanish and brought him the cup of coffee he requested. He sat there, recalling his conversation with Margaret, during which she had patted his hand and told him how happy she was to be "reconnecting." She had missed him. She had thought of him often. She wanted him to be part of this new chapter in her life. The light went dim in the dining room, granting Fitz entry into the no man's land between tea and dinner. He looked around and saw a light in the window of the kitchen door that told him someone had been asked to stay until the sad man left.

—24—

Margaret

Maternity. The word had a flat and clinical quality to it. The clothes associated with it had unfamiliar shapes and secret flaps and panels that Margaret found distasteful, but she could not escape their necessity. At fourteen weeks, she lived in fear of a gust of winter wind that would lift up her oversized shirt and reveal a gaping zipper. The distorted shape of her belly surprised her every morning in the shower.

Lauren, unmistakably gleeful at Margaret's need to size up, had agreed to come along on her first foray into a maternity store. A leech in shapeless black clothing and a nametag had suckered herself to Margaret's side the moment they came in the door.

"How far along are we?" the saleswoman asked Margaret after Lauren pointed directly at her sister's belly.

"We are fourteen, almost fifteen weeks," Margaret said, surprising herself with the pride she took in being plural. Without even knowing how it was done, she had coaxed the new grain of rice into a small potato. According to the books, the baby could already squint and frown. She pictured it looking suspiciously at its own tiny hands and feet, wondering what they were for. It would also be covered in a fine down called lanugo, a word Margaret had never heard before. She looked down and placed a protective hand over the spot where she guessed the downy potato to be.

"Let me show you some of the basics," the saleswoman was saying, and Margaret followed along at a remove. She still had a hard time imagining the body—soon to be her body—for which these clothes were constructed. Poster-size pictures around the room gave her some idea of the shape and size of the protrusion, but it hardly seemed possible. Her skin and muscles were already taut over the new swelling. How would they stretch and expand to such absurd proportions in a few months' time?

Lauren gathered an armload of jeans, tops, and dresses for her to try on. The saleswoman led her to a large dressing room, and Margaret closed the door. She sat down on a padded bench looking into the full-length mirror on the opposite wall. She was wearing the same dress she had worn when she had lunched with Fitz the week before. This, more or less, was how he had seen her when she walked into the restaurant he had suggested, a small but elegant place that favored pink linen on the tables and crushed velvet on the chairs and banquettes. It had smelled of fresh basil and garlic.

Even pregnant, she had changed less than Fitz had. The weight loss had altered more than the shape of his body. The proportions of his face had found the balance that had eluded him for so many years. The beautiful smile was no longer hidden in pillowy recesses, his nose looked less off-center, his eyes more appropriately sized.

"Wow," she had said upon seeing him. "You look . . . different."

"In a good way?"

"Absolutely."

"Sit down, you look shocked."

Margaret had descended slowly into the chair, absently accepting a menu from the waiter.

"I don't know, I mean, I've seen pictures, but in real life, it's hard to take in."

This was Fitz, but not her Fitz. He was altered, tucked, and pinned as if someone had let the air out of him and folded back the excess. She felt shy, unsure of how he would see her now that she was swollen with new life. She was more and he was less, but in the circles in which he moved, less was always more.

"I have some news," she said, because she could see in his eyes that he already knew.

"Let me guess," he said, smiling. "You're having a baby."

"I wanted to tell you in person. I'm fourteen weeks along. Does it show?"

It did show, at least she could see the changes as she sat in the dressing room, suddenly weak at the thought of taking off her clothes and putting strange stretchy fabrics on her once-lean body. Fitz, though, had waved his hand, shaken his head. "You look stunning. As always."

He had always been able to sense what she needed to hear. He opened his menu, somehow knowing she would be hungry and eager to place an order.

"You should get the pasta," Fitz said. "They make it from scratch. It's fantastic."

It had been fantastic. She had eaten every bite, even as Fitz poked at his spinach salad and took short sips from his water glass as he laughed at the stories Margaret told about her mold spore of a boss, who kept passing her over for promotions. She had started missing Fitz, the ease of being in his presence, before they even finished lunch. When the waiter returned with the check, she reached for it, but Fitz shook his head.

"I'm so happy for you," he said, reaching for his wallet. "Things seem to be going so well."

"Let me get this. You gave me the ballet tickets. This should be on me."

"I insist."

Fitz's body had changed dramatically, but the eyes with which he insisted on paying the check were the same eyes she knew from her college days. Sympathetic eyes. Sadness there, too. Outside the restaurant, she hugged him for a little too long as a cold rain began to fall, and he had been the one to pull away.

"I'm so glad we can be friends again," Margaret said. "So glad you found someone."

A momentary look of confusion passed over Fitz's face.

"The anchorwoman? The one you take to all the charity events?"

"Of course, Madeleine. Yes, she's wonderful."

Margaret was surprised at her own reaction to hearing that "Madeleine" was "wonderful." She had no right be envious. She was the one who got married after Fitz told her he loved her. She was the one having a baby with another man.

She bent down now in the dressing room to take off her shoes, which were much farther away than they had ever been before. The light in the dressing room had a sickly yellow wash to it, like the sky before a violent summer thunderstorm.

She had almost finished untying the laces on one of her short, low-heeled boots when she felt the first cramp, which was low, right above her pelvis. She sat upright and gripped the padded bench with one hand, rubbing her belly with the other. The cramp faded, and she bent down again to her boot laces.

The second cramp was stronger than the first. She sat up and bit the knuckle of her forefinger, clenched her Kegel muscles. A few cramps were normal. She'd had them before, and they'd gone away. She looked up. The fear was there in the mirror, in the narrow space between her eyebrows. She tried to breathe deeply, but the oxygen seemed to have vanished from the dressing room.

"Okay in there?" Lauren said, sticking her head inside the flimsy curtain.

Pressure on her pelvic floor, then a tight, sharp pain.

"Something's wrong. Get me to the hospital."

The heap of clothes that Margaret had intended to try on fell to the floor. Lauren held Margaret's upper arm and elbow and led her out to the car. The cramps were getting stronger, closer together. In between them, Margaret sent messages to her womb. *Stay inside, inside, inside, where it's warm, cushioned, rich with nutrients. Outside is a horrible place, all cracked sidewalks and cigarette butts, all low, threatening clouds, exhaust, and exhaustion.* She squeezed her legs together as Lauren drove to the hospital as if she were driving an ambulance, running lights, gunning it on the straightaways, jumping the curb at the emergency room doors. The sharpest cramp came as they lifted her onto a stretcher, and she knew. Dearest potato. Disconnected now. All alone in the harsh, strange world.

Miss Carriage. That was how she had first heard the word in middle school when a friend had whispered something to do with their music teacher and why they had a substitute, but Margaret had pictured a beauty pageant with sashes, toothy young women in evening gowns vying to be queen of all the carriages.

Now, in the hospital bed, the doctor palpated her abandoned uterus, pressing deeply even when she winced. No obvious medical reason, he said. Sometimes these things happen. Yes, fairly unusual at fourteen, almost fifteen weeks, no doubt about that. Still, the body is imperfect. It sometimes forgets what it's supposed to do.

When Douglas arrived, Margaret turned her face toward the wall. She couldn't bear to see his disappointment.

"It'll be okay," he whispered, lips against her ear. "I promise."

Her stomach felt slack and empty. When she had passed the twelve-week mark, they had announced her pregnancy to everyone they knew, and now everyone they knew would find out that her body didn't work the way it should, that she was damaged on the inside, unable to sustain life. Though she had little actual pain, narcotics seemed like a good idea, something to let her drift off for a week or two while Douglas explained what had happened.

A nurse came in with the clothes Douglas had brought in for her. Margaret rolled toward the wall, pulled her knees up toward her chest. She heard Douglas ask if the baby was a boy or a girl.

"A boy," the nurse said quietly. "It was a boy."

Margaret pulled her knees up higher. She had somehow known it was a boy.

"It's time to send you home now," the nurse said. "You'll be able to rest there."

Home. Where a butter-colored room waited for a baby that no longer existed. Where a drawer in her dresser already housed two stuffed animals and three onesies she had purchased the week before. Where the freezer was packed with the pistachio ice cream she had already started to crave. Why had her body fooled her this way? Warm womb cushioning and cradling its occupant only to reject it. Again, she wondered if Anders had somehow damaged her permanently. She wondered if she would ever be able to have a baby, even though the doctors told her they could find nothing wrong.

"Why," she said, an indictment more than a question. Douglas helped her into a seated position as the nurse left the room so she could change. "I don't understand."

Douglas nodded.

"I know."

"I tried to hold it in, I did. What happened?"

Douglas's shoulders sloped at an odd, dislocated angle. She could see that he was wrung out, twisted and limp as an old mop, but she needed someone to give her a reason, any reason.

"Tell me what happened."

"I don't know."

"Douglas, please. Tell me something."

Douglas cast his eyes to the door, as if looking for someone to enter and save him.

"I don't know what to say. I guess it wasn't meant to be."

She had forced the words out of him, only to reject them, shaking her head. No. It was meant to be. It existed. Every element of her body—her hair, her skin, her muscles, her digestive system—had changed to accommodate her quiet little potato, and therefore, it was meant to have existed. She said nothing, though. As if moving through deep water, she dressed herself and let Douglas lead her from the overly warm hospital room through a maze of carpeted halls, then a glassed-in pedestrian walkway, then a cold elevator and finally a rooftop parking spot in the hospital garage. She shivered in the thin coat she had worn to the maternity store.

Before she opened the car door, she glanced in the back seat at a large box. It had a picture on the side of it, and she turned her head to see it. An infant car seat.

"I bought it when you were out with Lauren," Douglas said quietly. "It was on sale."

—25—

Douglas

Douglas woke, stumbled to the kitchen, and opened the refrigerator. He took out a half-gallon of orange juice, popped off the cap and swigged the juice with the door open, wiping his mouth with his sleeve. Whenever Margaret was away, he turned feral within a day, forgetting that people used glasses and plates, and swept floors, and made beds. None of it seemed necessary, and yet this backward slide scared him a little. Where would he end up if left to his own devices for too long?

Margaret's sisters had taken her to a friend's house on Cape Cod for the weekend, where she could stay all day in her pajamas and drink hot tea and walk the cold beach at dawn wrapped in a down sleeping bag. He had not been invited, which left him to assume that Margaret needed time away from him. Both of them had been extensively probed and their various fluids and emissions examined under microscopes. Neither had any obvious deficiencies. Sometimes, the doctors repeated, miscarriages just happen. They used the word *just*, when all Douglas could think was *unjust, unfair, unacceptable.* But these words stayed inside him, rattling around like dried kidney beans in a paper cup, the kind that kindergartners in his school used to practice counting; the kind his child, this one anyway, would never get to count.

Douglas went to work, then came home directly after his classes and sat on his front porch steps drinking a beer. A sudden thaw had melted most of the snow on the lawn, leaving lumps and patches that looked like miniature striated glaciers.

Ollie, who had been laid off from his delivery service job months earlier, spotted him and sauntered over, hitching up the cargo shorts he wore even in winter.

"Doug-O," he said, eyeing the beer. "Got one for me?"

Douglas nodded and went inside, returning with a bottle. Ollie sat on his left, where Margaret usually sat on fine summer nights when they would take turns speculating about the causes of the shouting heard from nearby homes.

"Where's that gorgeous wife of yours?" Ollie said, downing half the beer in one swig.

"Away with her sisters."

"Sure, she is."

This kind of comic assholery bonded most men, but Douglas had never properly learned how to engage in it. Probably, he was supposed to respond with some crack about Ollie's wife, but he had nothing in the tank. He decided to tell Ollie the truth.

"She had a miscarriage. We're pretty broken up about it. It's her second."

"Shit," Ollie said, looking down at his unlaced, oil-stained work boots. "How far along?"

"Fourteen weeks. Almost fifteen."

"Tiffany had one a couple years back. Tore her all to pieces. I'm sorry, man."

Douglas swiveled his head to look at Ollie's dilapidated house. He didn't even know how many children Ollie had, though it seemed like a swarm, a gaggle, a flock, too many to count. He also hadn't known that Ollie's wife was named Tiffany. He put his beer down on the step and clapped a hand on Ollie's shoulder.

"Thank you, man."

Ollie's unexpected sympathy lifted him out of a dark place, giving him surprising hope. A miscarriage had happened at the house next door, yet children spilled out of its doors and windows. The house was lousy with children, stuffed to the brim.

"How many kids do you have anyway?"

Ollie paused and looked back toward his house.

"Well, depends on how you look at it, but Tiffany had three before we got married, one with her shithead boyfriend from high school, then two with her shithead supervisor from Burger King. So they're here most of the time, but they go off with their dads on weekends. Then me and her have three little ones. She says they're mine, but who can fucking tell? All of 'em look like her."

Douglas let this information hang in the air, unsure of how to respond to it. They drank from their beers.

"Women," Ollie said. "They know, but we don't. Unless you get a DNA test. And try bringing that up. It don't go over well."

Douglas nodded. It had never occurred to him to doubt that Margaret had been carrying his child. But there were the flowers thrown in the trash. And the ballet tickets. And Margaret refusing to tell him about her lunch with Fitz. He stopped himself. Unlike the thousands of other random thoughts in his head, this kind of doubt would not be absorbed. Like water falling on the hard ground before him, it would stay on the surface and pool, and then it would freeze, and then he would slip on the ice on his way to work, and then his hip would need replacing, and then the surgeon would botch the job, and then his life would be over. He saw no other possible scenarios.

Ollie, who had already finished his beer, sat next to him in silence. What would a life without Margaret even look like? Douglas imagined a spare one-bedroom in a shoddily constructed apartment complex where the family overhead would stomp around like Clydesdales day and night. He pictured coming home from work alone, heating up a frozen dinner. Then he pictured watching television with his feet on the coffee table, switching channels whenever he wanted. Briefly, he speculated about having sex with the new fourth-grade teacher whose inappropriate lacy black bras could almost always be detected underneath her thin tops and sweaters. But then he thought about Margaret again, wan and afraid in the hospital room. What an ass he was.

The sun had gone down, and now it was suddenly frigid on the hard cement step. He stood up, and Ollie took his cue, handing him the empty beer bottle and scuttling home. It was too soon to talk to Margaret now, but when a little time had passed, he would tell her about his conversation with Ollie. How Tiffany had had a miscarriage but managed to give birth to six kids. And maybe one day, if they were patient, he would see his own children at Harwood, wearing their own tiny green blazers.

—26—

Fitz

Fitz's mother gave him a tight smile.

"So nice of you to join us. I'd almost forgotten what you looked like."

Fitz had indeed been scarce around his parents' house for a few months. First there had been the announcement that he was leaving the company. After that, the awkward sale of his beautiful West End house in which he had lost money, and his move across the city to a humble condo in the South End where his neighbors were a plumber married to a dental hygienist and a couple who owned an Indian restaurant at the end of the block.

His parents would come around, though. He had to give them time to adjust, to grieve the unrealized future. The silver platter had to be encased in layers of bubble wrap and stored for the next generation, which might be more grateful to have it handed to them.

"Holding up?" he asked.

It was early April, when his parents were usually in Boca Raton, but they had delayed their trip to attend the wedding of one of Hamish's close friends (third marriage). His mother looked pale and on edge. By this time of the year, she needed to be on the beach soaking up vitamin D or she wilted like an orchid in a cold draft.

"Miserable," she said. "Does this surprise you?"

Hamish came down the stairs as Fitz and his mother stood in the foyer. In Hamish's brief nod, Fitz sensed a softening. Perhaps he had read *The Hartford Courant* article on Fitz's foundation. It was getting some nice press and had attracted some powerhouse donors. It made sense for the Insurance Capital of the World to back a charity geared toward the uninsured.

"Let me get my jacket," Fitz's mother said, giving them a moment. "I'll be right back."

The foyer, never Fitz's favorite room, was hub of the house. To the left, the formal dining room. To the right, the formal living room. Next to the grand staircase, a hallway to Hamish's library, the kitchen, the butler's pantry, the family room. Up the staircase, the bedrooms and their en suite bathrooms. As a child, he had used the back, kitchen door because the foyer's marble floor was so slippery. Falling down was frowned upon, tears greeted with heavy sighs as if they were a sign of bad breeding.

"So," Fitz said, his words echoing off the polished stone. "How goes it?"

Hamish fingered the Windsor knot in his tie.

"Not bad," he said. "How goes it with you?"

"All good."

This was how they would forgive each other, in awkward small talk. Even in this innocuous exchange, his father was acknowledging that Fitz had chosen a different sort of life for himself. He smiled with relief.

"Happy birthday, by the way," Fitz said. He took a small wrapped gift out of his jacket pocket. "I got you something."

Hamish looked surprised. He took the package and pulled at the tape with fingers that looked as thick as tree roots. After some time, he opened the box inside the wrapping paper and pulled out a small silver key.

"Safety deposit box?"

"Exactly," Fitz said.

Fitz's mother came back with her jacket. Her cheeks looked more sunken than they had during their aborted tea at the club. She looked at the key, which dangled from the tree roots of Hamish's fingers like a cheap trinket, and Fitz looked at them both with emotion, his parents, pillars of the community and pillars of salt, dissolving with time.

"I had my lawyer draw up some papers. It turns the William Fitzhugh Foundation into the Fitzhugh Family Foundation. All you have to do is sign."

Only in breaking away had Fitz discovered that he loved his parents, as annoying as they could be. Without their constant meddling, he found himself slightly adrift, disconnected. Setting up the foundation had kept him completely absorbed for several months, but last Sunday morning, he had wandered around his new condo in his pajamas wondering what his parents were doing that day. He missed them.

Hamish raised his left eyebrow.

"Why would you do such a thing?"

Fitz scanned the foyer again. This is what money meant to them. Impervious surfaces. Spindle-legged antiques that had no practical purpose except to gain value over time. Hired help that meant they never had to lift a broom or clean a toilet. Not that his parents hadn't given generously to charity over the years—they had—but it was sporadic. Big checks written with shaking heads as if the money would disappear into the quicksand of irresponsible behavior they saw all around them. This would give them a greater purpose.

"You said you always wanted to start a foundation. Now you can have one. Nothing needs to change operationally. You'll be on the letterhead, though. And frankly, your name means something to the donors."

Hamish looked at Arlene, who smiled in open-mouthed surprise as if she had been given a new car. Fitz hadn't given much thought to how his decision would affect his mother, but now he realized she would have her own ideas about how to run a foundation.

"How wonderful!" she said, hugging Fitz. "When's the next board meeting?"

After brunch with his parents, Fitz went to visit Margaret's father in the nursing home. Margaret had called to tell him about her miscarriage in a quavering voice, and later to tell him that she couldn't make the foundation launch event to which he had invited her. "I'm sorry," she had said in a message left on his answering machine. "My father's not doing well, and I'm not good company right now."

He had two motives: one, to leave a set of rosary beads he had purchased when in New York on foundation business; and two, to run into Margaret should she happen to be there. He missed her. Not only the lurch of his heart whenever he saw her, but the ease of their conversation, the delight he took in listening to her stories, though indeed he was often only half listening as he watched her face and reflected back her own delight in the telling. He felt unsteady on his feet at the thought of seeing her again.

Ordinary attraction was not like this. Fitz knew because he had been dating a woman for several months now, though not Madeleine the anchorwoman, who was not his girlfriend but his charity circuit companion. This woman's name was Sharon. She was a tall redhead with skin the color of buttermilk sprinkled with cinnamon. He loved her smile and the way she tucked herself under his arm after athletic sex and then fell asleep snoring. Her parents owned a real estate development company in Boston, which meant his parents might call it a good match. And yet with Sharon, his heart stayed inside his chest. Only Margaret unleashed it from the cage of his ribs, took it for high-altitude rides that left him breathless. Only Margaret could elicit euphoria by waving to him from across the street. Sometimes he felt that Margaret was inside him like an addiction or an incurable virus corrupting the mitochondria in his very cells. He tried to manage the symptoms, but every once in a while, he succumbed to these cellular urges, reaching out to see what kind of reaction he might get. Good or bad, these interactions still meant time in her presence.

He drove into the nursing home's parking lot, looking for Margaret's car, an older model dark gray Honda Civic. It wasn't there. Inside the unstaffed entry hall, he dashed off an illegible scribble in a guest book that lay open on a small table and pushed through a set of swinging doors into the patient wing, into overly warm air, into the astringent smell of urine and ammonia. His pulse beat in his neck as he scanned the doors for signs of Margaret's father. What was his name again? Yes, Richard. There it was.

The door to the room was open, and Fitz knocked on it lightly before walking past a bathroom with an extra wide door for wheelchairs. The bed was a scramble of white sheets, metal railings, a profusion of wires and tubing whose purpose he didn't want to know. Margaret's father was in there somewhere, curled onto his side. His eyes were closed.

An aide entered the room with a tray as Fitz stood over Margaret's father wondering if he should pat a shoulder or pull up one of the thin blankets pooling at the base of the bed. The aide had acne on her chin and forehead and seemed no older than a teenager, and Fitz knew she went home from each shift with the stink of the place in her nostrils. That's why they call it work, Fitz's mother would have said.

"Am I interrupting?" Fitz said, glancing at the tray.

"Oh, no," the girl said. "Mr. Carlyle doesn't eat much anymore. We just bring some mashed potatoes to help him take his meds."

On the tray were an elementary-school-style half-pint of milk with a straw inserted, a glass of cranberry juice covered by a paper lid with fluted edges, and a heavy plastic plate with a metal lid. Nothing, not even the cranberry juice, seemed to have any color to it.

"I was hoping to see some of Mr. Carlyle's family. I'm a friend."

"His two older daughters sit with him on Tuesday and Thursday evenings after they close their candy store. His youngest daughter and her husband come on different days during the week, but they never miss a Sunday," she said.

Fitz nodded. The old familiar lurch and sway of his heart. He would see her, even if her hack husband were here, too.

"Except today. They had a funeral. Margaret's boss, I think. She called and said they'd be in tomorrow."

He kept his face neutral, but inside, a dirge began. No Margaret today. How appropriate that a funeral had kept her away, death interfering with life as it always seemed to do.

He placed the gift bag with the rosary on a window ledge. He imagined Margaret entering the room, spotting the bag, and examining the tag, wondering where it came from. She would reach inside, through the carefully arranged tissue paper, and find the long, hinged box. She would open it slowly, looking around to see if the gift giver might suddenly appear. She would lift the strand of beads fashioned from Murano glass, feel the surprising coolness in her fingers.

Margaret was Catholic, so the beads would mean something to her. He had been moved by their beauty when he picked them up in a museum gift shop. A sense of comfort had descended on him when he ran them through his fingers to test their effectiveness. Ancient societies called them worry beads, and these were no different except for the silver crucifix. Margaret would know they were from him in the same way she had known about the ballet tickets.

As he walked out, though, he felt ashamed. All this mooning over Margaret had gotten him nowhere. Sharon was lovely, uncomplicated. Built for having babies. He could simply turn the ship around and embark upon a different sort of existence. He would never make a mint at the foundation, but he wasn't poor either. Together, he and Sharon (a real estate agent!) could put together a decent mortgage, buy a house in the suburbs, slip into jocular parenthood. A half-dozen of his friends were already there, raising children who would attend Montessori preschool and begin reading before their parents even knew they could. Precocious little monsters all.

The whole notion of choosing a particular sort of life gave him pause. He could also choose not to have that life. He could decide to give Sharon the heave-ho and see what happened on the next spin of the one-armed bandit. Eventually, someone hit the jackpot. Why not him?

—27—

Margaret

She stood in front of her closet, pulled out an old dress, and put it back. Nothing there she wanted to wear, only tired old jackets and dresses with shoulder pads that had slipped from their moorings and needed to be safety-pinned into place.

Douglas came into the room whistling, of all things. His ability to unfold his sadness, wear it around for a few days, and then store it with the off-season clothes both astounded and troubled her. Douglas stopped whistling as soon as he saw her.

"Why don't you buy something new? It might make you feel a little better. At least temporarily."

She shrugged, and he left the room. Buy something new, as if that would change anything. She pulled out the same old dress again. Maybe with a scarf.

Decisions loomed. Her father was in his last days. She and her sisters would meet with the doctors this morning and sign a paper missing from his file to relieve the nursing home of taking extraordinary measures. They would sit with him, witness the last, slow movements of his wasted body. She tried to recall him as he once was, young and vital, but those memories were dated and drained, the color faded.

When her father was gone, Douglas might ask if she were willing to try again for a baby. It was not an unreasonable request a few months after the last miscarriage, and yet, it was. His body didn't have to swell with hope only to be emptied of it. She put on the rejected dress, tied the belt in a new way, and came downstairs. Douglas handed her a cup of coffee, as he did most every morning. He always put too much cream in it, but she had failed to correct him early on, and now it was too late.

She took the cup, sipped. No one had ever told her about the crushing repetition of marriage. Of how her husband would press his forehead to the kitchen window every morning and comment on the state of the weather. "Looks frigid out there," or "Hot one today," or this morning, "It's sunny now, but I guarantee it'll rain before noon. April showers." Or how he would crowd her every night at the bathroom sink, brushing his teeth as she brushed hers, spitting on her spit, leaving her to rinse the bowl. Or the mechanical nature of two bodies fitting together in the same way, over and over again.

Margaret opened the back door and sat in the sun in a plastic chair on the small deck they had installed the year before. She surveyed their kingdom and found it wanting. Nothing but a square patch of lawn with a tiny vegetable garden. No swing set. No tricycles. Nothing but a swath of grass and a chain-link fence they had sworn to replace right after they moved in.

In the next yard over, Tiffany was picking up paper napkins and party hats from the lawn after a birthday bash the night before for one of the older kids, who might have been eight. The music had gone on late into the night, well past the time when eight-year-olds should have been in bed. The crux of it: She knew when eight-year-olds should be in bed, but Tiffany was the one with all the kids.

Tiffany caught her staring.

"Hey, neighbor," she said, bending to cram something into an already strained white plastic trash bag. "Think it might rain?"

Tiffany, from a distance, was both soft and hard. Her shoulders swelled like rising dough around the straps of a blue tank top, and her middle pooched out, round and innocuous. Her long, thin legs, though, poked out like breadsticks from the tight denim miniskirt she had also been wearing the night before. She had good legs, no denying that. Something sexy about them, and she knew it, too, wearing her short skirts no matter how cold it was. Her face was hard under the white-blond hair she shared with all her children. Even from a distance, Margaret could see the smudges of black eyeliner circling Tiffany's eyes, the traces of red lipstick on her mouth.

"Feels like it might," Margaret said, regretting the wasted words, pellets of stupidity. She had read once that the average person speaks about 860 million words in a lifetime. How many of those were banalities? She would have guessed about ninety percent, and most of that about the weather.

"Hope we weren't too loud last night."

"Not at all." Though they had been loud, and Margaret had berated their carelessness, wondering why an eight-year-old's birthday was an excuse to drink beer and play Mötley Crüe at maximum volume. Tiffany reached for an empty cup. She tied the straining bag tight, then went back inside with a nod, leaving half the lawn still strewn with garbage.

Margaret took a final sip of her coffee, savoring the bitterness on her tongue. The hot weather was months away, but if she closed her eyes, she could imagine it, collapsing her summers into one memory: the sun on her face, bones soft in the heat, at peace with herself, alone.

Lauren and Annabelle were waiting for her in the doctor's office at the nursing home. They turned toward her, their faces crumpled and wet, their mouths identically frozen with grief.

"The doctor called the house this morning," Lauren said. "We tried to call you, but Douglas said you were already on the way."

The doctor nodded. "We just need you to sign. Then you can sit with him. It shouldn't be more than a few hours."

Margaret scrawled her name. No extraordinary measures. She wasn't sure she wanted ordinary measures either, except to preclude any pain. He had died years ago, as far as she was concerned. This was nothing more than his stubborn heart finally admitting defeat. And yet, her sisters' tears reminded her that something was ending. As old as they were, it was still a shock to think of themselves as orphans.

"Let's go," Margaret said, and they followed her, sniffling into tissues.

Though Richard had not attended church since Caroline died, a priest was waiting for them inside the room, his stiff white collar cutting into a thick neck red with bumps from shaving. His broad ruddy hand was on Richard's brow. Margaret saw the priest first, then saw a gift bag sitting on the windowsill. She walked over and picked up the bag as her sisters shook the priest's hand, waterworks again. What was wrong with them? They had been waiting for this day forever. It was time. It was beyond time.

The tag on the gift bag said "Margaret." Nothing else. She opened the bag and pulled out an elegant black box, long and thin, the kind that contained jewelry. The hinges creaked as she opened the box. Inside, a rosary, nestled on a bed of satin. She lifted it out of the box, dangled it in the light coming in from the window. It was exquisite. Clear glass beads with tiny pink glass roses inside each one. A silver crucifix, meticulously detailed. Who would give her such a thing? She coiled the rosary in her hand. It felt cool, substantial. Its weight made her think of the necklace her father had given her on her seventeenth birthday.

"Wish they could be real pearls," he had said. The dry-cleaning business was already teetering then with the strain of her mother's treatments. The hospital bills were never discussed, but Margaret had seen her father hunching over them at night when he thought every-one else was asleep.

"I love them, Dad."

He had placed the necklace ceremoniously around her neck, fas-tened the clasp.

"Now you're all grown up," he had said. Tears leaking. Smile faltering.

Then it all rushed back in, sweeping her into the waves, a deluge of colors, scents, love, all of it. This was the man who had bought her a professional adding machine after seeing how much she loved playing with the one at the store. This was the man who sat in the passenger seat as she learned to drive, pretending not to flinch. This was the man who had told his wife how beautiful she was even after she had lost her hair, her eyebrows, her eyelashes.

She put a hand over her mouth, muffled a gasp.

She wrapped the rosary beads around one hand and approached the hospital bed. For months now, years maybe, she had seen only the loose skin and the unkempt eyebrows, the liver-spotted lips, the limp muscles. She had forgotten that what lay underneath was still there. Kindness, patience, fortitude, generosity. All still there in the blood that flowed through her father's narrowing veins.

"This should not be happening," Lauren said, her voice raw from crying. "He should be playing golf and spending the winter in Florida. It's not fair."

Annabelle had folded herself into the shape of a snail in an arm-chair next to the bed, her head coming up only to breathe. Margaret took her father's hand, pressing down on the thick blue veins, the rosary between them. The glass beads grew warm. The hard land-scape of his emaciated hand in hers became, at once, all the memories of his once-strong hand in hers as they sat at her mother's bedside.

Whatever had caused her emotional amnesia, the rosary reversed it. The beads belonged in her hands. Their rightness astonished her.

Then she remembered. She and Douglas had just attended the funeral of her boss, who had lost a battle he didn't know he was waging to heart disease and dropped dead in the office break room. They had seen his wife holding a set of rosary beads, and Margaret had remarked on her calm demeanor. "Maybe it helps to pray," Douglas had said, shrugging. "Some people say it does."

So he had bought them for her. She imagined him searching through some strange religious gift shop crowded with statues of saints, terrifying crosses, crowns of thorns. He had driven to the nursing home yesterday, or the day before, and placed the bag here where she would see it. Goodness there. Kindness, too. And she had been too tangled in her own sadness to let him comfort her.

She put her ear down close to her father's mouth and listened to his stuttering breath. How many breaths did one person get in a lifetime, more than words? Fewer? It didn't matter, really. She looked at her sisters, who were hugging. They had always been closer to each other than they were to her, but in that moment, she was glad for them. Glad each one had the other.

Douglas had wanted to give the three of them time, but he would be here soon, and she could thank him for the rosary, for the dam it had broken, for the subsequent flood that had washed the tar and gravel from inside her. She felt flushed and raw, her anger scoured away. Her father coughed, and all three of them moved closer.

"How will we know?" Annabelle asked.

The priest, who was still in the room, said gently, "You'll know."

Douglas slipped through the door just then and stood quietly in one corner.

"Come over here," Margaret said, and when he did, she put one arm around his waist and rested her head on his shoulder.

Douglas looked slightly surprised, but then folded around Margaret, his chin on her hair. Lauren and Annabelle stood on the other side of the bed, dabbing their dripping eyes and noses with their tissues. In this way, they watched the minute motions of Richard's face in the way that Margaret had seen parents watching the faces of their newborns, every eye flutter or pursing of the lips a small miracle. Margaret couldn't have said how long they stood there, but then the movements ceased, and the priest called in the doctor, who checked for vital signs and then firmly pressed on Richard's eyelids until the top lashes touched the bottom lashes. Margaret half-expected them to open again, but they didn't.

She squeezed the rosary. Stop wallowing, it told her. One precious and unpredictable life is all you get. Don't waste it wondering why it can't be the story you would have written for yourself.

—28—

Douglas

"You need a hobby, man."

Ollie delivered these sage words as Douglas sorted through the painting supplies on the worktable inside his garage. The odors of motor oil, paint, and turpentine challenged each other for dominance and made Douglas light-headed, though the bay door was open.

"Just touching up the trim in the living room," he said, as though he owed Ollie an explanation. "Margaret's relatives are coming this weekend."

"Oh, yeah, sorry about her dad. Tiffany told me he passed."

Douglas wasn't sure how Tiffany could have known. Richard's obituary had been printed in *The Hartford Courant*, but Tiffany didn't seem like the sort who would read the newspaper, much less slog through the paid death notices. She seemed instead like the sort who painted her toenails on the front steps while wearing a skirt the size of a handkerchief. He wondered if he could tell Ollie to keep her inside when the cars rolled up after the funeral.

Minor point, though. What mattered was that Margaret had come back to him. Some seismic shift had happened in the room where her father had died. Either that, or someone had replaced his wife with someone who looked exactly like her. A meat mallet thumped in the kitchen where Margaret was preparing veal parmesan. The veal had to be pounded thin, dipped in egg and coated with breadcrumbs, pan fried, layered with cheese and sauce, and finally baked and served with pasta. She hated to make it because of all the steps involved, but there she was in the kitchen getting veal under her fingernails, and he had no idea why. When they had returned from the nursing home after her father died, she had undressed and crawled into bed, pale and shaking, looking as if she had the flu. On the nightstand, she had placed the set of rosary beads he had seen her carrying earlier that day.

Before closing her eyes, she had looked at him.

"You," she said. Soft kiss of a smile.

He looked at her quizzically.

"The rosary," she said, picking up the string of beads. "I swear it saved me. I don't know if I can explain it, but I was able to see my father again. The way he used to be. I'm so grateful."

Douglas had assumed the beads came from the nursing home staff or from the priest or from Margaret's coworkers. In that instant, seeing Margaret so fragile and sweet, he couldn't tell her it wasn't him.

The next morning, she had made him coffee, when it had been his ritual to make hers. She had found the energy to rake the garden, which had grown feral with neglect in the same way he did when Margaret was away. Then she had gone grocery shopping, and now, she was making veal parmesan. The meat mallet thumped again.

"What's going on in there?" Ollie said.

"Margaret's cooking."

"You like her in the kitchen, huh? Is that how you keep her in line?"

Douglas felt the hair rise on the back of his neck.

"How do you keep your wife in line? Cattle prod?"

Douglas thought he had gone too far, but Ollie laughed and even bounced on his stocky little legs like a boxer, as if Douglas were finally giving him what he wanted. Ollie found energy in combat, no matter what form it took.

"Shit, man. Maybe I better get me one of those. But what you need is a—"

Margaret opened the garage door, her beautiful face leaning into the fouled air where it floated like a butterfly over a landfill.

"Honey, where do we keep the cast iron skillet?" she said, looking as if she needed Douglas desperately. He wasn't sure she had ever looked at him that way before. There was a little smudge of red sauce on her chin, and he had the urge to lick it off and see what happened, but Ollie was standing in his garage like a bulldog that had wandered away from its owners. Margaret suddenly noticed him. "Hi, Ollie."

"Hey, there," Ollie said, looking down. Margaret had a strange effect on him, as though he were a mischievous young boy in the presence of a teacher.

"I'm pretty sure it's in that drawer at the bottom of the stove."

"Of course," Margaret said, smiling. "I always forget about that drawer."

The door closed, the butterfly was gone, and the garage smells once again assaulted Douglas's brain. He still couldn't fathom what Margaret was thinking as she labored away on his favorite meal.

"Looks like you got work to do," Ollie said, the sparring over, the charged air neutralized. "And I gotta go shopping for a cattle prod."

Douglas laughed, watching Ollie half-jog back to his toy-strewn lawn, the magical land of towheads. Was that where the joy was? In hunks of molded plastic from Toys-R-Us? In the light those flimsy racetracks and doll strollers and miniature lawnmowers brought into the eyes of a toddler? He wanted to find out, but it wouldn't be easy. His thoughts slid past Margaret's in the dark. Uneasy bodies side by side, six inches or six miles between them, it didn't matter. The gulf was unassailable. Maybe tonight would be different. Maybe, after the veal parmesan and a glass or two of red wine, one of them might throw out a line and tow the other to shore, and they would linger in the warm tide pool of their bargain sheets from Sears, back into primordial bliss. Back to when their bodies knew how to circumvent their brains and block out the consequences of their actions.

Douglas had appointed himself the cup collector. It gave him something to do as Margaret, Lauren, and Annabelle received the dozens of friends and neighbors and clients from the days when Richard presided over the business. He would start on one end of the kitchen and eventually make his way across the living room, gathering the empty plastic party cups that covered every available horizontal surface, then return to the trash can in the kitchen and start again. Their small house had never held so many people. The floorboards groaned under the strain.

Margaret had not expected such a turnout, since Richard had been absent from the business for years. Very few of his old friends had visited him in the nursing home, and yet, here they were, telling stories of how he had cleaned the bedding and drapes of families caught in floods or fires for free. Of how he had delivered bag after bag of abandoned coats and suits and dress shirts that were never picked up to Goodwill. Of how he had employed their directionless children or their boozy aunts when no one else would. No wonder he'd found it hard to make any money.

Margaret kept looking out the window, though. Fitz had been at the funeral, sitting in a back row, slipping in after the service started. Douglas had never met him in person, but he recognized him right away from the pictures he had seen in the newspaper. The guy had abandoned a high-paying job to start a nonprofit, and within months, that nonprofit already had a high profile. You couldn't open the paper without reading about it, which reinforced Douglas's view that it was all a marketing ploy for the insurance company Fitz's father ran.

Margaret had a glass of water in one hand and those rosary beads she had somehow acquired in the other. She hadn't let them out of her sight, even on the night of the veal parmesan and the red wine, when they had gone to bed, and she had slipped her hand under his T-shirt. "Are you sure?" he had whispered into the darkness, and she had responded by pulling her nightgown over her head.

That Fitz would be arriving soon made Douglas nervous. The soap bubble around them since the arrival of the mysterious rosary beads could be punctured at any time, and Fitz seemed like the kind of ham-fisted guy who couldn't be trusted around a soap bubble. Margaret moved toward the window as Douglas swept the living room once more for stray cups. In the next moment, she was at the door.

"You made it," she said, and all at once, the crowd in the living room seemed to part to allow the man space as if he were royalty.

Douglas sized Fitz up from the kitchen, where he had retreated with his empty cups. He certainly still shopped in the Big and Tall Man department, though he used to be much bigger. He had the look of a man who wanted everyone to like him but feared they wouldn't, a glad-hander with a big shy smile. He moved as if he were still fat, checking around his hips and legs for furniture and pets and small children. In no way was he handsome. But the guy wasn't hideous either. He reminded Douglas of Harwood's headmaster, who had an inexplicably young and beautiful wife.

Margaret gave Fitz a long hug, and Douglas could almost sense it himself, knowing the pressure of her body and how it made him feel. Fitz would be warm now, too warm. There, he could see the red creeping up Fitz's neck above the collar of his white dress shirt. Now Fitz would find some excuse to touch her a second time. Right again. He took her hand, patted it like she was an invalid. Transparent as Saran Wrap.

Margaret beckoned Douglas from the kitchen, and he came to her, drying his hands on an embroidered tea towel, one of the many common household objects that he and Margaret jointly owned. It also showed that he was comfortable enough with his masculinity to be seen with something feminine. Fitz, he knew, would take the point.

"It's about time you two met," Margaret said, waving them toward each other. "Fitz, this is Douglas"—not "my husband Douglas." "Douglas, this is Fitz, my very, very good friend from college." One too many "verys."

Margaret seemed a little giddy for a funeral. Douglas shook Fitz's sweaty hand with the grip of a longshoreman, and then stood back, folding his arms, rocking back a little on his heels.

"Thanks for comin'." Instinctively, he left the "g" off his gerund, as if that somehow made him sound tougher.

"Of course," Fitz said. He looked around but seemed not to notice that the conversation had dropped to a whisper since he came in. "Are your sisters here? I heard they opened a candy store."

"They are," Margaret said, pointing with the hand that held the rosary.

The glass beads caught the sun. Pinpoints of light scattered across the ceiling.

"Glad you have those," Fitz said, nodding toward the beads.

Douglas was glad she had them, too. The glass talisman of reconciliation. Somehow, that cheap string of beads had brought them back together. Margaret was looking at him now, and in her eyes, he could see a tincture of tears, love even. And if he could see it, Fitz could see it too.

"Douglas got them for me. So thoughtful," she said, her voice thickening. "I swear, they saved me."

Douglas got them? Douglas looked at Margaret, who was still looking at him, the tears still visible. Then Douglas stole a glance at Fitz, who was looking at Margaret as if she had kicked him in the throat. That's when he knew. Idiot. Dope. Loser. The rosary beads had

come from Fitz. Why hadn't he realized that before? The screws holding up the shelf of their marriage loosened again, plaster dust coating
the floor. They had never been properly bolted to the wall studs, and
they would pull away once Margaret realized Douglas had not given
her the rosary, leaving a heap of household goods that would have to
be appraised and divided between them. God knows they didn't have
enough insurance to put it all back together.

But Fitz chose a different path. He looked at each of them in turn
and slowly nodded his big head.

"Beautiful gift," he mumbled. "Very thoughtful." And then he
moved toward Lauren and Annabelle, who had not stopped crying
all day. Both of them fell onto Fitz as if he were a long-lost relative.

Douglas wiped his hands, now sweating, on the tea towel. Fitz,
whom he had despised from the moment he heard his stupid nick-
name, had rescued him. Fitz had seen the love in Margaret's eyes and
had chosen to let it be. He had put her first, which surely meant that
he was in love with her. Douglas was both jealous and grateful. Had
he been in Fitz's shoes, he doubted he would have done the same.

When the mourners started to leave, Douglas stood near the door,
helping elderly women find their wool overcoats. Fitz was still there,
sitting in a corner, speaking to a man in a dark pin-striped suit,
maybe a former customer of Richard's, probably the kind of guy who
wrote checks with six digits to foundations like Fitz's. So here he was,
soliciting at a funeral. At least he could hate him for that.

No more than ten people were still in the room when Fitz got up
to leave. Douglas watched from the door as Margaret sobbed into
his shoulder. She had been too busy that day to cry, but now it all
came flooding out, absorbed into Fitz's perfectly tailored jacket. Fitz's
long arms were around Margaret's small back, and Douglas fought
the urge to cut in as if they were dancing a little too closely at a bar
mitzvah or a wedding. His wife loved Fitz, that was clear, though the
nature of that love was unknowable to him.

Margaret pulled back, wiping her eyes, trying to smile.

"I'm so sorry," he heard her say. "I don't know where that came from."

"Don't apologize," Fitz told her. "You have to let it out."

She walked Fitz to the door, then unexpectedly took Douglas's hand as Fitz stepped out to the front porch and turned to wave again.

"Don't be a stranger," she said, slipping an arm around Douglas so that they were a couple gesturing from the top of a wedding cake. Why did that surprise him? Margaret had chosen him. Fitz was a guest in their marital home, and when he left, they would go on with their lives together, in part because Fitz had chosen to let them.

Fitz gave them one last glance. Margaret had already turned to go, but Douglas saw the hurt in Fitz's eyes. It was so plain that he had to look away.

—29—

Fitz

Why should it surprise him that Margaret's husband was a liar? Fitz prodded the New York strip steak smothered in a greasy mushroom sauce with his fork. If Brenda hadn't gone on vacation, he would have something healthier in front of him, seafood or the vegetarian option. She always took care of those things when he had to attend a fundraiser or a gala, and these days, he couldn't seem to get out of them. The deep pockets expected him to show up with his four-color brochures and his embossed business cards and his elevator speech, which he had twice already that night delivered in an actual elevator. The cost of soliciting donations, he had learned, was three-quarters pride and one-quarter room-temperature crème brulée.

This Douglas person, Margaret's chosen partner in life, had taken credit for giving her the rosary that he, Fitz, her "very, very good friend from college" (the second "very" had pleased him immensely) had so carefully chosen from the museum gift shop. What kind of a person did that? It wasn't like lying about who ate the last piece of cake. Granted, it was a lie of omission, but still. Douglas knowingly let her believe he had been the thoughtful one.

He cut a small piece of meat, chewed it slowly, feeling the marbled texture on his tongue. He had loved fat once, had sought it out on bacon and pork chops and chicken skin. Now, it disgusted him. He put down his steak knife and investigated the butter-laced mashed potatoes with his fork. He would rather go home hungry than eat the caloric nightmare on the plate in front of him. He lived in constant fear of waking up with the body he used to have, all his fat cells restored by one weak moment at an airport Dunkin Donuts. The cruelty of crullers.

"Have the rest of my salad," his mother said. Now that she was an active member of the Fitzhugh Family Foundation, she often attended these events with him.

"I'm not hungry." He was seven again, although then he would have begged for seconds.

"What's wrong? You've been off your game tonight."

The truth of it stung him. In the hour since they had walked into the hotel ballroom, he had spilled a gin and tonic, called an important donor by the wrong name, and forgotten the politics of another donor while talking about the next election.

"I met Margaret's husband last week, at her father's funeral." He picked at the cucumbers in his mother's leftover salad.

"And?"

"He's a schmuck. A liar."

His mother dabbed at the corners of her mouth with the silvery napkin that matched the theme of the night: Reach for the Stars. Every charity he had ever encountered used this theme at least once every three years.

"So what? Look around. You could have your pick."

Cascades of purple and silver material hung from the ceiling of the hotel ballroom, turning the vast space into a medieval tent of sorts, adding a pointless layer between the people inside and the stars they were being urged to reach. What Fitz saw were women stuffed into strapless gowns in unflattering jelly bean colors, little bratwursts of fat bulging on their backs; French twists straining against a riot line of bobby pins; pores clogged with foundation; lips either a sticky, glossy pink or dry, flaking red; feet straining against thin, painful straps like pork loins tied with string; cheeks blotchy with wine. Not a Margaret among them.

For the first time, he wished he had never seen Margaret, that she had never crossed his path on that Trinity College quad, because perhaps then he could have paired up with one of these women, some of whom no doubt were lovely and intelligent people outside of their ridiculous black-tie getups. Perhaps then his heart would have stayed inside his chest, protected from the violent strafing it endured in Margaret's presence. Why hadn't he told her the truth about the rosary? There had been a moment there, a beat, a pause no longer than a breath, when he could have flipped the well-laid table of Margaret's marriage, but he had let it pass out of pure shock. He took another bite of his mother's salad. He had to at least sit through dessert because they were giving him an award that would be presented after everyone was properly soused and ready to pull out their checkbooks.

This wasn't how he had imagined running a foundation. He had pictured himself meeting with desperate families who couldn't afford dialysis or hospice care as they died from AIDS and who, through the Fitzhugh Family Foundation, would suddenly find themselves "covered" in the best sense of the word. It meant they would be protected, sheltered, the egregious hospital bills sent to some other address and not garnisheed from their meager paychecks for decades. And those meetings did happen, occasionally, but mostly Fitz was needed on the development side, which was a fancy term for asking for money. If he didn't bring in the money, it couldn't be given away. At his father's insistence, these next few years were all about building an endowment so the foundation would generate an income of its own.

"Why don't you come down to the club tomorrow?" his mother said. "Take a class with me. Sweat out your frustration."

"I might just do that."

Exercise had become his sanctuary, the only time he could completely tune out the low-frequency thrum of his yearning for Margaret. He had been running more and more, and after the recent encounter with Margaret's husband, he might have to train for a marathon.

His mother rose out of her chair.

"Sharon!" she said, waving furiously. "Look, sweetheart, it's Sharon."

Sharon was wearing a light blue gown with crystals on the bodice that seemed to emphasize the paleness of her freckled skin. Sharon looked around as if searching for someone to rescue her before conceding she had no choice but to acknowledge Fitz and his mother.

"So nice to see you, Mrs. Fitzhugh," Sharon said, showing her teeth in something between a grimace and a smile.

"Please call me Arlene."

"Of course," Sharon said, then nodding to Fitz. "Hello."

"Nice to see you. You look great."

Thus would begin the one-act play wherein Fitz would stand stage right like an idiot while his mother and ex-girlfriend exchanged pleasantries with such obvious subtexts that Fitz heard only this:

ARLENE: I've brought you over here to make my son feel terrible about breaking up with such a lovely girl, who might have given me grandchildren.

SHARON: I concur that your son should feel terrible, so aside from my initial nod, I will treat him as though he's a plant or a piece of furniture.

ARLENE: I will ignore his presence as well so that he might repent and beg your forgiveness.

SHARON: So kind of you to cooperate.

Fitz stood there, taking it, because he had nowhere else to go. And what could he say? They were right, but that didn't change his heart. Nothing they said could make him fall in love with Sharon, who was a delightful person in every respect except that she wasn't Margaret.

As the waiter came by with the requisite crème brulée and coffee, Sharon went back to her table and Fitz gave his mother a withering look.

"What?"

"Did you invite her?"

"Who?

"Don't play dumb."

"I might have sent her a few tickets. Anonymously."

"For God's sake, why?"

"I thought maybe she'd bring a date and make you jealous, but she's here with a friend. She does look darling, though. That skin. I love the freckles."

"Please don't get involved in my love life."

"What love life?"

Fitz excused himself to use the bathroom before the awards, both to get away from his mother and to check his teeth for bits of salad, which he had learned to do after his first such event and the subsequent photo his mother later dubbed the Spinach Disaster. In the mirror, he saw a man who, despite his tuxedo and good grooming, would never be handsome; a man whose eyes could only be described as sad. Yet, on a sliding scale of sadness, he shouldn't even register. He had every advantage, every opportunity, had even convinced his father that running a foundation was a noble endeavor. Not that it was equivalent to running a multinational corporation, but it was far from an embarrassment. He checked his teeth. All clear. Even as he smiled, the sadness lingered there in the mirror, seeming to come from someplace behind his eyes, some deep cranial well.

Buck up. Be a man. That's what his father might have said to him had he been standing at his shoulder. Though what did that even mean? Was he not allowed to be sad? Was he not allowed to mourn the life he wanted but could never have, even if he still had a privileged existence? He turned on the tap in the sink and worked the soap into a lather as if that might wash away the stain of his self-imposed loneliness.

A few minutes later, he was on the dais, collecting a heavy etched-glass award, charming the room with his anecdotes and his pitch, watching the wallets and the checkbooks open. It felt good to see the effect he could have on people, even if the only person he truly wanted to affect was not in the room.

The band that had played during the cocktail hour returned, and those who hadn't overindulged at the open bar made their way to the dance floor to bump awkwardly against those who had. Fitz, who limited himself to one drink at these events, told his mother he was going outside for some fresh air, but instead, he sought out Sharon, who was seated alone at a table strewn with half-empty glasses and crumpled silver napkins.

"May I join you?"

She shrugged as he sat down. Her face was the picture of indifference except for two bright circular spots on her cheeks, which could have been makeup.

"I owe you an apology. My mother is a piece of work."

"Then you're a chip off the old block."

He deserved that, and yet, it hurt him to the core. Surely, she didn't want him to pretend to love her if he didn't. That would be cruel.

She fiddled with a small beaded clutch on the table in front of her, clasping and unclasping it. Fitz gazed at her strong, capable hands and remembered how they'd felt gripping his hair as they wrestled around in the center of his king-sized bed. He missed that.

"Would you like to dance?" he said, because she was there, and

Margaret wasn't. Because they knew each other's bodies, and maybe they would slip back into comforting each other. Because in dancing with Sharon he might be able to pretend he was dancing with Margaret.

"You don't get it, do you?"

"Get what?"

She stood up, towering over him in her heels, the spots in her cheeks even brighter, two glowing pieces of charcoal.

"I was in love with you," she said, the *love* so fraught with emotion that it sounded as if she were gargling. "How could you not know that?"

"Sharon, I'm sorry."

Fitz caught her final stinging glance but then turned his head, pretending to watch the band. He hadn't wanted to hurt Sharon, but his heart wouldn't listen to reason. It went its own way, and it seemed not to care that its quest was futile. It seemed not to acknowledge that it was leading its host down a path strewn with bitterness, weeds, and thorns. It seemed to have only one mission, and that was to keep him in Margaret's unintentional thrall.

He returned to his table to find his mother deep in conversation with Marshall Samuelson, the board chairman of the Fitzhugh Family Foundation. Both were on the committee to plan the foundation's first gala, and they had every intention of making it bigger and better than the one they were attending.

"Billy, dear, Marshall has had the most wonderful idea. Tell him, Marshall."

Marshall was a Churchillian man given to clearing his throat, which irritated Fitz no end.

"Ahem," Marshall said. "I was just saying to your mother that I'd like to get a celebrity for the gala. Everyone loves it when a celebrity shows up."

"And he's come up with a name. Someone we're hoping you know."

Fitz looked around. The room was emptying, which meant that the stains on the carpet from spilled wine could be seen more clearly. His run-in with Sharon had exhausted him. All he wanted to do was sleep.

Marshall nodded his big, balding head.

"Anders Salisbury. Do you know him? He's quite the movie star now. My wife goes bonkers every time she sees him on television. You went to Trinity with him, didn't you?"

Fitz suppressed an urge to sock Marshall in the mouth just for saying Anders's name.

"Nobody I know."

"Anders Salisbury," his mother said, enunciating each syllable. "Oh, come on, everyone knows who he is."

"I don't."

"What about your friend Paul? He knows everyone. Or what about Margaret? You could ask her."

Fitz would not be asking Margaret. He tried to put them off with a smile.

"Great idea to have a celebrity, but I'm sure we can find someone better than some B-list movie star."

"So, you do know him!" Marshall turned with a smile toward Arlene. "He does know him."

"I don't know him personally, and as I said, we can find someone better. Anders is not a good choice, trust me. Mom, I'm not feeling well. Heading home."

Arlene put a hand on Fitz's forehead.

"You're not warm."

"It's a migraine."

She sighed, saving her sympathy for real pain, which she associated with bullet wounds or severed limbs.

"All right then. Get on home."

The auras began just as Fitz reached his car, his fake migraine now a real one. He thought of Margaret as he had seen her the day she told him about Anders. So young, so afraid. So sure that all she had to do was hold her tongue to make the whole agonizing thing go away.

—30—

Brenda

The kitchen in Brenda's one-bedroom apartment had only enough space for one stool at the counter. In front of her were two scrambled eggs, half a toasted English muffin with butter, orange juice, coffee. Eating alone was a relief. *Pas de* small talk. No one waiting for the section of the newspaper they hadn't read yet. She stretched the broadsheet of the comics out on the counter, leaning over it while she finished her eggs.

To her parents' great surprise, she had been the one to dismantle the family tableau. When Mr. Fitzhugh opened his foundation, he made up a title—Senior Vice President for Community Relations—and gave her a significant raise. In practice, she functioned much as she had before, keeping Mr. Fitzhugh's schedule and managing his correspondence, but she also represented the foundation at city council meetings and any other meetings Mr. Fitzhugh couldn't personally attend. She had purchased three skirted suits with matching low-heeled pumps.

She was also dating. Pastor Dan had fixed her up with an older man, a dentist, who took her to restaurants and gallery openings and movies. She liked his company, though he seemed oddly content with a peck on the cheek or a hug. It occurred to her once, when she saw him glance at a waiter's backside as he cleared their plates, that he might be gay. She didn't love him, so it didn't much matter. At least her mother was off her back.

Her favorite pastime now was inviting her family over for dinner. She would spend a Saturday at one of the discount department stores buying inexpensive placemats and cloth napkins and then setting the table according to some theme she had seen in one of the many home-and-lifestyle magazines to which she subscribed. Autumn Jubilee. Citrus Celebration. Say It with Gingham. They would all squeeze around the card table she had disguised with a folded-over tablecloth, balancing on the flimsy wooden chairs she had rescued from a church tag sale. She had a dining room set on layaway.

Brenda would serve them some new recipe that required making stock from scratch or contained some ingredient they had never tasted before, like phyllo dough or won-ton wrappers.

"Not bad," her father would say, nodding his big head. "Not bad at all."

Her mother would take small bites, bringing the fork to her nose to sniff at foods she didn't recognize. Each time, she brought a pie with her, even when Brenda told her she was making dessert. Often, these dinners would end with Brenda's soufflé or berry compote or homemade ice cream pushed off to the side while her father and brother tucked into the pie they'd been eating all their lives. It didn't matter. This place was her own, and she could cook whatever she wanted. They didn't have to eat it.

"Aren't you lonely here all by yourself?" her mother said one night as Brenda served a mushroom risotto that had taken hours to make.

"Not really."

"I guess your gentleman friend keeps you company," her mother said, winking at Brenda's father. "You should bring him over sometime. Let me cook for him."

"I'm not ready for that, Ma. We're still getting to know each other."

"Well, don't take too long. He's not getting any younger. Neither are you."

Nodding, Brenda served herself another spoonful of mushroom risotto. Let her mother think what she wanted. She would bring him over when she was good and ready. Having her own place had allowed Brenda to regrow the spine her mother had weakened with her insidiously delicious pies.

Having her own place had also put a loose bandage on the open wound that was Mr. Fitzhugh. (With her promotion, he had asked her to call him Fitz, but she couldn't do it.) She still loved him: his beautiful ties and his white teeth and his deference to anyone required to serve him. She had once seen him sneak a wad of cash into the apron pocket of a waitress who told him she was retiring because her feet hurt too much. Most people in his economic bracket, even the one to which he had lowered himself after leaving the insurance company, took the ticket takers and the valets and the janitors for granted. Not Mr. Fitzhugh. He saw humanity in the grease-smeared hands that changed his tires and in the missing teeth of the homeless woman who haunted the church doorway two doors down from the foundation offices.

If only he saw her the way she wanted him to.

What troubled her most these days was Mr. Fitzhugh's father, who had taken to showing up at the foundation offices unannounced, lingering, and asking Brenda for coffee. "I'm a vice president now," she wanted to tell him. "I don't make coffee except for myself." But she said nothing and poured him a brimming cup. Once, in her own private rebellion, she had pulled an old coffee filter out of the garbage and made a pot just for him.

It wasn't only the coffee. Mr. Fitzhugh too often let his eyes settle on Brenda in a way that felt like he was watching her in the shower. She had also caught him once flipping through the papers on her desk.

"Can I help you find something?" she said.

"Just checking to see who's giving us money. You know how it is. You ask your friends to donate, and they say they will, but they don't always follow through."

"I'll ask Mr. Fitzhugh to give you a summary."

"Don't bother. I'm sure you have better things to do."

"Whatever you say."

Deference was bred in her bones, yet something about this man left her chafed and unsettled. What kept her in check was his generosity, or rather, the generosity of the insurance company. The checks coming from its charity arm seemed to get larger every few months, but then again, so did the balances on the senior Mr. Fitzhugh's foundation credit card. Lately, he had been to Hawaii and Prague to solicit donations. Two breakfasts, two lunches, two glasses of wine delivered by room service. The credit card statements told a story, but when she asked how Mrs. Fitzhugh had enjoyed Prague, he pretended not to hear.

—31—

Margaret

Starting in kindergarten, Margaret had noticed that people always seemed to want something more from her than it felt natural to give. "Where's your smile?" her elementary school principal asked every time he saw her in the hallway, and she would force her face into a joyless approximation of what he wanted to see. This need to please was something all girls learned when she was growing up, but she had always resented it. Why should she smile if she didn't feel like smiling? Why should she let the slower boys catch her in Duck, Duck, Goose? Why should she pretend that she didn't know the answers to all the math problems? Why should a boy force his body into hers after she told him to stop?

The tiny seeds of resentment planted over her lifetime had lately matured into a full-size tree as she was passed over repeatedly for work promotions in favor of men with growing families, men who didn't have to fend off their own clients. She was angry at the Cardboard Box Man for grabbing her ass. She was angry that she couldn't pass an alley or walk through a parking garage without lacing her car keys through her fingers like a dagger. She took a shower one Sunday morning in May, feeling the slow burn inside her. As she dried herself, her clavicle felt warm to the touch.

"Is everything okay?" Douglas asked her when she entered the living room, where he was watching the news and mindlessly plowing through a large bag of M&Ms. He turned down the volume.

"What do you mean?"

"You're scowling."

"Maybe I have a reason to scowl."

They were drifting apart again. His raft ran closer to the safe, flat rocks along the shore while hers was headed toward the rapids, maybe the falls, and yet, they were still connected. All she had to do was remember the rosary beads, which she kept on her bedside table. They reminded her that Douglas loved her, that he was steady and kind and thoughtful. They reminded her that she had chosen him for a reason. She tried to soften her tone.

"Sorry, I'm just tired."

Douglas had already turned back to the television.

"Hey, do you know this guy?"

"What guy?" She had picked up a stack of mail piled on the small side table next to the couch and was flipping through it.

"His name is Anders something. He went to Trinity, just a few years ahead of you. He's an actor. Big right now."

Margaret looked at the television, where Anders was sitting on a stool being interviewed by an attractive young anchor. By now she had seen his photo countless times in magazines and newspapers, but she had not seen him like this, in motion. The same hands that had lifted her dress were now gesturing to make a point, touching the anchor lightly on her shoulder, rubbing his own perfectly square chin. He looked buffed and polished, his hair—there was no other word for it—coiffed. She had to stop herself from throwing the potted plant on the side table at the TV screen.

"Yes, I've seen him before," she said in a low voice.

Douglas shrugged, and turned the volume back up. "He seems to think pretty highly of himself."

This, of course, had been Fitz's assessment, and she had ignored him at her own peril. The humiliation she had felt that night, her knees tucked under her chin beneath her nightgown, came flooding back. The light in the living room grew as pixilated as the television screen. She began to feel herself disintegrating, as if she were no more than Anders was on the box in front of her, a gathering of electrons with no depth or substance. She swallowed her panic, just as she had with Fitz on the morning after the rape, keeping her voice calm. In the last few months, she had come close to telling Douglas what had happened to her, but she could never get the words out. She was afraid he would wonder why she couldn't or didn't stop it from happening. She sometimes wondered that herself, why she hadn't fought harder, yelled louder.

"I don't doubt it," she said. She needed to get out of the room. "Hey, I'm thinking I'll go to church this morning."

"Really?"

"I haven't been in a while. I thought I'd try that new one by the rec center."

"Want company?"

"That's okay."

It would be a relief to sit alone in a quiet pew toward the back, gluteal muscles pressing hard against the wood. There, she could look around her and see all the pain that wasn't hers: the old Italian widow sobbing into a lace handkerchief, the veteran without legs, the gay couple forcing themselves not to hold hands. It did her good, those reminders. They made her focus on what she did have, rather than what she had lost. This would also allow her to bargain with God in a place where she felt more likely to be heard. She would offer to go to church every Sunday for the rest of her life if God let her carry a baby to term. In a related sub-bargain, she would pledge to say the rosary every day if God stopped rewarding Anders, who seemed to skate along, collecting awards and accolades, mocking her with his success. He had recently been cast in a film version of *A Midsummer Night's Dream.*

"Shakespeare's such a challenge," Margaret heard Anders tell the interviewer. "I'm afraid I don't do him justice."

Without another word to Douglas, she turned on her heel, left the house, and drove to the new church, which looked oddly like a spaceship. She sat in her car watching a group of boys playing basketball at the rec center, thinking not of the night when everything changed, but of the night before that, when she was still oblivious and pristine and had only the one deep sadness, that of her mother's death, instead of the others she had curated in her collection since then.

She opened the car door to go into Mass, which had already started, but hesitated. If she went in, the regular parishioners would look at her when she came in the door, wondering who she was and why she was alone. She closed the door again, unable to bear their scrutiny. Instead, she stayed in the car and quietly made her offers to God, hoping she was still inside the radius of his awareness.

—32—

Douglas

If Douglas had known his blood sugar was dangerously high, he might have done something to stop the black curtain from descending after his final class of the day. The assistant headmaster had been the one to find him sprawled on the floor still clutching his grade book and his half-empty bottle of Pepsi.

The symptoms had crept up on him. First was the excessive thirst, which he had attributed to the new forced-air heating and air-conditioning system that had been installed at Harwood. The second was the frequent urination, which he attributed to the larger amount of juice, soda, and water he was consuming due to his excessive thirst. When the nerve-splitting bell rang in between each period, he would dash down the hall to the teacher's lounge and pee like a farm animal, dashing back before the bell rang again.

The third was his sudden weight loss, which had delighted him since he was always trying to lose a few pounds. The belly he had acquired over the last few years made it necessary for him to buckle his belt below the protrusion or risk looking like an egg.

He had ignored all these symptoms to the point where his blood sugar spiked and left him unconscious, or so the doctor told him when he woke up in the emergency room to the sound of a staticky intercom calling a surgeon with an unintelligible name to the operating room. He thought at first that he had fallen asleep while watching a medical drama on television.

"Off the charts," the doctor said, shaking his head with an amused expression that Douglas found inappropriate to the situation. "It's a miracle you didn't go into a coma."

Outside the crookedly hung curtain of the small antiseptic bay, Douglas could see Margaret on a plastic molded chair in the hallway paging through a thick binder from home where she kept their insurance information. The doctor called her in.

"He's awake!" the doctor said, still sounding far more jocular than the situation warranted. "Gave us a good scare, though."

Margaret took Douglas's hand and into it pressed many things: fear, frustration, regret, hope. The last year had been difficult, which was probably why he had turned to Little Debbie, who was always there for him, offering a Zebra Cake or a Cosmic Brownie or a Cinnamon Bun. Little Debbie never turned him away.

"Thank God you're all right," Margaret said, releasing his hand and tapping on the binder. "I have a list of diabetes specialists inside the network. We just have to get a referral from your primary care doctor."

He was exhausted, barely able to keep his eyes open, and yet these words triggered a resentment so profound he thought he might retch. *Specialists inside the network. Referral from your primary care doctor.* In other words, his health crisis had caused an avalanche of paperwork that he and Margaret would now have to sort out. It wasn't enough to have insurance anymore. It wasn't enough to see the doctor when you were sick. Now everyone had to navigate the maze of preferred and non-preferred "providers" who might or might not *provide* medical treatment. This may have had something to do with why he had ignored the warning signs in the first place. It seemed like too much of a headache to even make an appointment.

Margaret put a hand on his shoulder, which felt cold. He looked down and realized he was wearing a thin hospital gown. Where had they put his clothes?

"This is all my fault," Margaret said. "I should have recognized the signs. You told me you were feeling thirsty all the time, remember? When we were at the bank. That was weeks ago."

Guilt talking. Douglas closed his eyes. Petulance suited him right now.

"Douglas?" Her voice was high and tight, swooping up on the second syllable of his name. He let his eyelids flutter, milking it. The shelf wouldn't fall suddenly, he now realized. In fact, their marriage wasn't a shelf at all. It was more like a sweater that would pill and fray around the edges, and eventually, a moth would eat a hole in it. When they gave it up as unwearable was anyone's guess.

But here she was, leaning over him, holding her binder as if it could shield them from catastrophe. So much paperwork bound them together. Utility bills, mortgage, car payments, and a whole raft of insurance policies: car, homeowners, umbrella, health, long-term disability, short-term disability. Life insurance was the cruelest one. Sudden death at an early age was the only way to win that gamble.

His eyelids felt like sandpaper, but he forced them open. Did she even love him anymore? Had she ever truly loved him? These questions seemed important in the cold emergency room with his bare feet sticking out from the thin blanket they had draped over him. He let his eyes close again.

"Douglas!"

"I'm okay," he said, mumbling. "Sleepy."

"Don't scare me like that."

Actual tears were sliding down her face, dripping from her nose. Maybe she did love him. Maybe something could be salvaged of the worn sweater. Maybe it could be repaired. What did they call that?

Darning came to mind, although that seemed to be associated exclusively with socks.

The doctor was handing Margaret a whole stack of papers and pamphlets that she would no doubt pore through line by line with a highlighter, outlining how Douglas would have to change his life. No more takeout food, pizza, ice cream, beer. Nice knowing you, Little Debbie. He would have to exercise as well, something he always intended to do but usually managed to avoid by convincing himself that painting and yard work were aerobic enough.

Margaret had a tissue up to her eyes. Now she was blowing her nose. Her head loomed close to his, her eyes red, tears running down her exquisite face, though whether they were for him or herself, he didn't know.

Two weeks later, Douglas left the house with Margaret's blessing to buy a new bicycle. It was less than a gym membership, he had argued, and she had agreed, "as long as it doesn't gather dust in the garage."

He had already lost five pounds after giving up his pre-lunch, post-lunch, post-dinner and pre-bedtime treats. The doctors had told him he could try diet and exercise as a means to avoid injecting himself with insulin, and his fear of needles was so profound that he was a changed man.

Though the doctor had said sugar alone wasn't to blame for his diagnosis, he would have to cut back on it to lose weight, and sugar had been his daily companion, sweetening his day from the first cup of coffee in the morning to the Jolly Ranchers he kept in his school desk to reward his students for good behavior but often ate himself. Boring movie on the Renaissance he had seen twenty times before? Pop a watermelon and drift off to a summer picnic. Standardized tests? For those, he chose something tart, lemon or lime, since he had to stay alert for possible cheating. His favorite activity was oral reports, where he could sit in the back of the classroom and watch.

The choice there was root beer, which was almost as good as an actual beer.

Most of his sugar consumption happened almost without his awareness, as in standing in line at Blockbuster and consuming an entire movie-theater-sized package of Goobers before he reached the register. It simply gave him something to do. On other occasions, he planned his day around a trip to the bakery or his favorite ice cream shop. But these calories were indeed empty, soulless, and they had betrayed him. Little Debbie had not had his best interests at heart. She was a cruel mistress, stringing him along only to sabotage his health, destroying her own host. It was not a healthy relationship. He realized that now.

He walked into the bike store sucking on one of the sugar free lollipops Margaret had bought him to step down from his habit. It took a moment for his eyes to adjust to the riot of colors and chrome. A line of bicycles from smallest to largest ran down the center of the store, front tires all turned to the same thirty-degree angle. To his left was a small alcove with a single recumbent bicycle, which seemed to be sitting on its haunches waiting like a patient dog.

The first salesman Douglas spotted was a wiry man in a polo shirt and khakis who was staring out the window, arms crossed and shoulders down, chewing on the cap of a pen. He straightened up and took the pen cap out of his mouth as Douglas approached.

"What can I do you for?" He stuck his hands in his pockets and leaned forward, placing his weight on his toes. He had the high and tight haircut of an ex-military man or a gym teacher.

"I'm in the market for a new bike. I've been told I need to exercise."

"You came to the right place."

"Looks that way."

"So what type of bike are we thinking about?"

Most of the bikes in the long line looked technically complicated and intimidating. He had never had particularly good balance. The recumbent had a squat solidity that made it seem less threatening. He nodded toward it.

"I've never seen one of those up close. What's it like to ride?"

Douglas guessed the recumbent was more of a conversation piece than legitimate merchandise, but the salesman surprised him with his enthusiasm.

"It's a totally different experience. It's a more natural position, so you can ride all day without getting tired. On a traditional bike, you have to hunch over the handlebars, so there's strain on your neck from looking straight ahead. On a recumbent, you can see what's ahead of you without craning your neck, but you can also see the sky. Take it for a spin."

The salesman wrestled the bike through the door and set it down on the parking lot. Douglas wedged himself into the seat and rode about twenty yards, then turned around awkwardly, gaining confidence as he trundled back. Aesthetically, the recumbent bike couldn't compare with the sexy European touring bikes that had tires as narrow as the ties and shoes that only Europeans could pull off, or with the new muscular American mountain bikes that emulated their huskier owners. But something about the recumbent, with its elevated pedals and its seat reclined to the angle of a beach chair, spoke to him. He took a deep breath of early spring air, which filled his lungs in a way that indoor air never did. Clearly, he didn't get outside enough. That would have to change.

"What do these cost?"

"Seriously?"

"Yeah."

"Everybody likes to try it out, but I haven't sold one yet."

"How much?"

"Let me check."

The salesman disappeared into a back room, and Douglas wandered among the shining fenders and spokes and handlebars. When he was a kid in Pittsburgh, a bicycle was freedom. It meant he could leave his mother to her ironing after school and cruise through the neighborhood, maybe head over to the corner store for a Coke or a couple of Airheads (he had loved sugar even as a child). In those days, kids rode their bikes everywhere, but the kids in his West Hartford neighborhood did nothing but loop the block as if they were tethered to their homes by an invisible rope. Ollie's kids all had bikes, but mostly they stayed tipped over on the front lawn like strangely compelling modern sculptures.

He touched the fat, corrugated tire of a mountain bike. In adulthood, a bicycle wasn't freedom, it was work. Or it was exercise, which was also work. He found himself back in front of the recumbent bike, which seemed to be waiting for him.

The salesman returned from the back room, pen cap back in his mouth.

"Good news."

"Okay."

"This recumbent sells full retail at six hundred ninety-nine, but my boss is willing to sell you the floor model, if you're interested, half price. So three fifty."

Margaret had given him a budget of two fifty. He gave the recumbent a look of apology.

"No can do. The wife—" he used that term only in the company of other men—"would not be happy. What can you show me for two fifty or less?"

For the next hour, Douglas tried out different models, at one point getting the hem of his khakis stuck in an oily chain. He could feel himself getting light-headed, maybe his blood sugar dropping. He looked again toward the recumbent, and the salesman, who had chewed the pen cap until it was flat and pocked with tooth marks, chucked him on the shoulder.

"That's the one you want, huh."

Douglas nodded, exhausted.

"Can you come up a little?"

Margaret's budget was like barbed wire around a castle he wanted to reach. He would get scratched if he went over it, but a few scratches might be worth it if he actually rode the bike. She'd be even more upset if he bought one and let it sit in the garage.

"I think so."

The salesman disappeared again. Douglas sat down on the recumbent and closed his eyes. He was barely thirty, and yet, he felt like an old man with special dietary needs and pill boxes and fragile bones. His marriage had reached a certain tipping point, where it would either go on for several more stuttering years and then fizzle like butter in a hot pan, or he and Margaret would come together—succeeding with another pregnancy or even an adoption—and turn all their energy and focus and frustration toward an unsuspecting child. He felt a chill and a crushing sense of loneliness that was at once shocking and familiar. The years went by so quickly, and yet each day—this day in particular—had no foreseeable end.

The salesman came back with his portly manager, who looked annoyed that he had been asked to move. He ran a thumb along one corner of his mouth.

"Benny here tells me you're looking for a deal. Best I can do is three twenty-five." He hitched up his pants in a way that suggested this was his final and only offer.

Douglas weighed his options. On the one hand, Margaret would be upset if he went over the budget. On the other hand, she had been so encouraging lately with her meal plans and her research and her late-night paperwork sessions. She wanted him to exercise, and shouldn't he give himself every incentive to do it?

"I'll take it."

Once the transaction was complete, the salesman helped Douglas load the recumbent into his hatchback.

"You two were meant for each other."

"You think so?"

"What can I say, I'm a matchmaker."

Douglas drove home, anticipating an argument. Margaret would hate the bike, its awkward, triangular shape, the fact that Douglas would practically be lying down while riding it, but most of all, its price. And yet, he felt a little less lonely, knowing that he would have an excuse to get out of the house whenever he wanted. People might even notice him. He imagined himself on a Saturday morning, parked outside the drugstore or the library, spreading the Gospel of Recumbency.

"She took the kids?"

Douglas had planned to ride his recumbent bike all morning, but before he could reach the end of his driveway, Ollie had waved him down. Now they were perched on Douglas's front steps, Ollie with a beer, Douglas with a bottle of water. Beer had too many carbohydrates, so he had given it up except on special occasions. Ollie had a hand over his eyes, shading them from the sun.

"All six of 'em. Back to her mother's in Naugatuck. Left me a note."

Douglas was not surprised. Tiffany seemed like the kind of woman who drove a powerboat through the small lake of her life, leaving a trail of drama in her foamy wake. She would have the kind of mother who opened the door and sighed and made a stack of peanut butter and jelly sandwiches, forgetting that one of the kids was allergic to peanuts. If Tiffany were not already on a first-name basis with the emergency room staff at the children's hospital, she would be.

"Did she say why?"

"Does it even fucking matter?" Ollie's voice traveled to an octave Douglas had never heard him visit before. "I love those kids, man, even the ones that aren't mine."

Douglas had always wanted to know paternal love, that gut-level attachment to a small, innocent person in his care, but he didn't. He could only guess at it. Next to him, Ollie stank of beer and sweat and anxiety, with the ever-present undertone of motor oil, as though he dabbed it each morning behind his ears.

"She'll come back. Don't you think she'll come back?"

"I don't know. We haven't been good lately. I caught her talking to that shitbag from Burger King, Petey and Nickie's dad. He's been sniffing around when I have the late shift at the warehouse."

Douglas had seen the shitbag from Burger King the week before. He was dropping off two of the kids, Petey and Nickie presumably, hauling their unrolled sleeping bags and their fraying backpacks from his ancient, low-slung Datsun to the front door. Tiffany had slouched against the doorframe after the kids went into the house. Douglas remembered thinking she'd looked ready to hitch up her postage-stamp-sized skirt right there, in plain sight of the outdoor cats and the elderly neighbors across the street parked in their plastic Adirondack chairs. Poor Ollie.

"I love her, but I fucking hate her," Ollie said, draining his beer. "Know what I mean?"

This was a rhetorical question, but he did know. Margaret had been so careful with him lately, so attentive to his nutritional needs. But for some reason, the more she did for him, the more he resented her. Ollie set his beer on the step next to his untied work boots. His head hung down almost to his splayed knees. This is what love did. It pulled you apart from the inside, infiltrated your cells, gave you strength or made you weak in turns. It was the only disease that people craved no matter how much it hurt.

Douglas unclasped his bike helmet, the straps of which were cutting into this throat. His leg muscles twitched, having been primed for the ride before being asked to stand down.

"Hey, I'm keeping you, man. I know you want to get on that bike."

"It's okay. I have all weekend to ride."

"You really like that thing, huh? Looks strange as hell."

"That it does."

It was pointless to explain to Ollie how the recumbent had given him new perspective. The experience brought him back to childhood, riding so low and slow that everything seemed more majestic and certain and significant than it did from a car. Though his family had attended a Congregational church, at least on holidays, he saw evidence of God only when he was riding down a sun-dappled road with the wind streaming across his bare arms and the trees rustling overhead. In his car, he was agnostic, or on certain perennially troublesome Hartford-area highways, an atheist.

"You go ahead. I'll be okay."

"Maybe she'll call."

"I fucking hope not. Because I'd let her have it. Those kids need some stability."

"You're right. They do."

Maybe Ollie had never gone to college, but he knew what was what. Margaret called him the knucklehead next door, but she couldn't be more wrong. Douglas had learned that Ollie had a heart. He also had the welfare of six white-blond children foremost in his mind. For that, Douglas had to admire him. Ollie stood up and looked toward his empty house. The lawn erupted with bikes and toy trucks and Nerf guns. Douglas clattered down the front steps in his biking shoes and climbed on his bike as Ollie stood to one side, looking like he might stand there until Douglas returned.

"Get outta here, man. I'm good."

Douglas pedaled down the driveway, knowing in the core of his being that Ollie was not good. Then again, no one was truly good or fine for more than a half-minute anyway. He and Margaret were far from fine, yet they got up every day and went to work and paid their bills and tried new restaurants and talked about the weather.

He turned right toward Newington, where he could ride for a long

stretch without crossing too many intersections. His now-strong legs
carried him away from the tiny, tidy ranch. As he left the neighborhood canopy of maples and white ashes, the sky opened like a movie
screen. His throat ached, and he swigged from his water bottle, steering with one hand. Now that he could think, he turned his attention
to an idea that had been nagging him for months, that Margaret
might leave him for Fitz, who had somehow known how much she
would need the rosary beads. She would come back from work one
day, and she would tell him it was over. Fitz, who had money and
status and went to charity galas, could give Margaret a different kind
of life. Maybe with Fitz, her pregnancies wouldn't end in miscarriages. Maybe they would go off into the sunset and have a beautiful
life, leaving Douglas with nothing to keep him company except his
strange recumbent bike.

Then again, he could be completely wrong. Douglas had never
imagined that married life would be so full of uncertainty. He had
assumed that he and Margaret would settle into it like other couples
he had seen, becoming more alike and finding comfortable patterns.
Instead, he had no idea if they were a good, stable couple who were
having some temporary interfertility problems or a pair so mis-
matched it was a miracle they had been together this long.

He pedaled along, glancing at the movie screen of sky overhead as
if it might reveal something he needed to know about the future, but
for some reason, he could only think of the past.

When Douglas was nine, his father decided to paint the exterior of
their small, clapboard house, mainly to stop Douglas's mother from
complaining about the cold drafts that had given her chilblains
the previous winter. Douglas was his father's assistant, holding the
ladder, scraping the lowest boards, and opening cans of paint with a
flathead screwdriver.

He was shy around his father, who worked intermittently in a

Gothic-looking factory on the outskirts of Pittsburgh that spewed smoke through towering brick cylinders like a gigantic, sentient pipe organ. He didn't know what his father did inside the factory, and he didn't know how to ask him about it. They spoke only about whatever repair or maintenance task was at hand. The silence in between was a comfort to them both, whereas silence in his mother's presence meant that he had somehow disappointed her.

"Pass me that putty knife," his father said as they worked on the clapboards at the back of the house, where direct sunlight had dried the wood to the point where Douglas could fit his fattest finger into the gaps. He lifted the putty knife toward his father on the ladder, squinting into the sun.

As his father worked above him, Douglas scraped long flakes of white paint from the dry, graying boards, occasionally gouging out bits of wood in the process. It was a messy job, but he liked helping his father, who had a mastery of all things mechanical that Douglas envied: the way he held a crescent wrench or a hammer as if it were an extension of his hand; the expert flick of his paintbrush into hard-to-reach corners; his casual use of the word "joist." His mother did everything for Douglas—made his lunch, cut his meat, folded his laundry after ironing every piece of it—but his father saw his utility and treated him as a smaller, less experienced version of himself.

His father stepped down the ladder and pulled a pack of Marlboros out of his flannel shirt pocket. He tapped out a cigarette and let it rest on his lower lip, stuck there with saliva, as he dug around in his pants pocket for a lighter.

"Don't ever smoke, you hear me?" he said, lighting up and pulling on the cigarette so hard that Douglas worried he might inhale it.

"Why?"

"It ain't good for you."

Douglas didn't remember noticing the irony in that moment. He recalled only the sense of connection, his body feet away from his father and yet bonded to him by some invisible force akin to gravity. He was vaguely aware of a war happening in Vietnam, of protests playing out across the country, of assassinations and upheaval relayed by serious voices through the radio and television, but none of it was real in the same way that his parents were real. They told him what he needed to worry about: get good grades, do your chores, don't ever smoke. Those were the things that mattered in the enclosed world of his family, which only intermittently intersected with the more frightening, outer world.

Now, as he cycled along, he found himself adrift in the outer world, neither parents nor children, nothing to identify his place in the universe. He felt like an astronaut floating around outside the capsule, connected only by a single rope. That rope had a name: Margaret. She could relieve the angst of the only child only by giving him his own child. She could reel him back to the prepackaged meals and the recirculated air, and then both of them could return to Earth. Feet on solid ground.

—33—

Fitz

Anders was a hot commodity. One movie in which he starred was playing in art house theaters to critical raves while he simultaneously promoted an action flick that, if successful, would put him on the short list of actors who could guarantee big box office. Rumors were rampant, as they were with any famous actor, but Fitz caught wind of some particularly troubling reports when his college friend Paul invited him out for a beer.

"Apparently he's slept with every costar he's had," Paul said. "And a few have been underage. The last one was fifteen."

"Where'd you hear that?"

"His old roommate is on my touch football team. He's been out to visit him in Hollywood."

He thought about Margaret, who possessed the knowledge to stop Anders, or at least slow him down. He couldn't bear seeing her unhappy, but what about those young girls? Should what happened to Margaret happen to them? Where would it end? As he drove in the general direction of Hartford, he reminded himself that Anders was the root of all this pain. What he had done to Margaret years ago—a moment so unimportant to him, a moment he'd probably forgotten—had fractured her in a way that couldn't be mended. She had counted on time to heal her, but time was not reliable that way. It ticked along, appearing to be impartial, but Fitz wasn't sure. Maybe time had its own agenda, spreading healing here and suffering there. It certainly seemed that way.

As much as it pained him, Fitz decided he needed to make one last effort to convince Margaret to report her rape. Otherwise he would be complicit in the apparent unchecked crime spree that was Anders Salisbury. Around noon the next Saturday, he stood at the door of Margaret's small ranch house, reliving his one previous visit: the rawness of Margaret's grief after losing her father, the clean smell of her hair as she hugged him, the smug face of her husband drying dishes as if he owned the place (goddammit, he did), the shock of her husband taking credit for giving Margaret the rosary beads. He put his hands in the pockets of his jeans, stepping forward, then back, then forward again. Next door, he noticed, was a house that had seen better days. A gnomish man wearing cargo shorts, a tank top, and work boots puttered around the open door of the garage muttering to himself.

Fitz knocked, then inclined his head toward the door and heard nothing but the change of seasons as spring eased into summer: the hum of flies; the whine of a chainsaw a street or two over clearing downed limbs after a thunderstorm; the restless chirp of birds around a feeder suction-cupped to a side window. He should have called first.

"They ain't home," the gnome yelled across the driveway.

Fitz backed down the concrete steps, his hand on the wrought-iron railing, still looking up as if the door might open at any second. He turned to respond and found the gnome, to his surprise, right next to him, hands in two of the many cargo shorts' pockets.

"You a friend?" The gnome lifted one hand out of his pocket and pulled on a small goatee.

"I know Margaret from college."

"Reason I ask is we've had a bunch of salesmen showing up around here, pushing cable packages or vinyl siding or whatnot. They fucking ring the doorbell all hours. Freaks out my kids."

"I'm glad you're looking out for them."

"They didn't know you were coming?"

"I should have called first."

The gnome nodded.

"Used to be people just stopped by. Bell rang and your mother put out the coffee cake before she even opened the door, but that don't happen anymore. Now you have to make an appointment."

"Do you know when they'll be back?"

The gnome looked down the road, then back to Fitz. His neck was a plumber's nightmare of grease and hair. He barely came up to Fitz's shoulder and yet there was a raw masculinity about him that Fitz had to respect. In a fight, this little man likely would kick his ass. Then again, a nine-year-old girl with an attitude would probably kick his ass. His size always meant he had never had to fight.

"Douglas went off on his bike—he's got one of those weird ones, you know, low to the ground—and Margaret drove out a little while after he left. Maybe getting groceries. Hey, you're in luck. There's her car."

As Margaret's Honda pulled into the driveway, the gnome slipped back to his yard with an awkward wave. Margaret's car door opened, and her face came into the light. She smiled as if she were genuinely happy to see him.

"Fitz? What are you doing here?"

What was he doing there? Why hadn't he called? His motives now seemed suspect, even to himself. In Margaret's presence, he was back on the Trinity green, on another spring day, the air similarly fragrant with tulips and daffodils displacing the dirt, spiraling skyward. He was a boy again, a large and lonely boy despite his many friends, a boy whose heart betrayed him by longing for a girl he could never have.

Margaret was wearing Saturday clothes, jeans and a T-shirt with a light blue hooded sweatshirt that zipped up the front. Running shoes.

No makeup. Hair in a ponytail. And yet, she had never been more lovely, more open, less guarded.

"I was heading over to the post office, and I thought I'd stop by."

As he spoke, his voice rang in his own ears, sounding foreign and high-pitched. Margaret opened the trunk, and Fitz dutifully grabbed every bag he could reach, leaving her with one.

"Well, come on in. It's nice to see you. Sorry I look like such a slob."

"You look fine. Great. I should have called."

"Don't be silly. You're always welcome."

He followed her up the steps and waited as she unlocked the door. The gnome next door was back outside, watching them even as he lifted a white-haired child onto a bicycle with training wheels. Once inside, Fitz deposited the groceries on the kitchen table and began to unpack one of the bags: spinach, red peppers, a container of Greek olives.

"Leave all that." She pulled on the bottom of her sweatshirt. "I'll get it later. Can I get you anything? Water? Coffee?"

"No, I'm fine."

"Well, how are you? How's it going with the foundation?" She sat down at the small kitchen table and nodded toward a chair for him. He pulled it out and gave it a little shake to make sure it wasn't wobbly, a habit from when he was heavy and worried about finding himself on the floor.

"It's going well, actually," he said, telling her a story about a family the foundation had helped after a cancer diagnosis. The words felt pointless in Fitz's mouth, but he said them with a smile.

Margaret rested her elbows on the table and listened quietly.

"And your girlfriend, the anchorwoman? Also going well?"

Fitz shook his head. He didn't want to let Margaret continue believing that fiction, especially since he was hoping she'd be persuaded of telling the truth no matter how difficult it might be.

"She was never my girlfriend, Margaret. People sometimes pair up out of convenience. It sucks going to those events alone."

"Is that true?" Margaret said. "I didn't know."

"I was dating someone for a while. A very nice girl named Sharon, but it didn't work out."

"I'm so sorry." She put her hand briefly on Fitz's forearm, which was resting on the table, and he wanted to put his own hand on top of hers, but he resisted.

"None of that is why I'm here," he said.

Margaret looked down at the table.

"Okay, then. Why are you here?"

He hesitated. "To talk about our, um, mutual acquaintance."

Though she barely moved, Fitz could see Margaret folding inward, her chest caving as her shoulders moved forward, though her face stayed neutral. "I just saw his face on another magazine cover in the grocery store."

"Yeah, he's everywhere. Unfortunately, that's not the worst of it. I'm hearing things."

Margaret stood up and left the table, leaning back against the sink. She folded her arms across her body, holding each shoulder with the opposite hand.

"What things?"

Fitz took a deep breath.

"That he's sleeping around, no surprise. But also that he's going after girls that are under age. Remember my friend Paul, the football player from Trinity? He knows Anders' old roommate. It's thirdhand information, of course, but I have no trouble believing it."

Margaret put her chin to her chest. She seemed to have gotten smaller while standing in front of him.

"I'm so sorry. I know this must be hard to hear."

The light was dim in the small kitchen, even on a sunny Saturday. When Margaret spoke, her voice was low and strained.

"I want it *not* to have happened. I don't understand why it did."

"I don't understand either."

"I thought I could forget, but I can't. I think about it every day."

Fitz took a deep breath.

"He'll keep doing this until someone speaks up. You know that."

"It was a long time ago."

"It doesn't matter. The police can still look into it. I don't think the statute of limitations has run out, though I could check if you want me to."

"So, I could talk to them confidentially?"

He rubbed his forehead.

"I mean, eventually, if you pressed charges . . ."

Margaret's knees swayed, and Fitz led her back to the kitchen table. Her hands were shaking.

"You don't deserve this, Margaret. You never did, but neither does anyone else."

Margaret stared at a blue-and-green carved candle sitting in the center of the table, the kind of gift teachers get from their students at the end of the year.

"I can't open this all up again. I know it's hard to understand, but the thought of him even thinking of me, the idea that I would be resurrected inside his sick little brain, is too much."

Fitz heard the garage door opening and then the door into the kitchen creaking as Douglas came in wearing shorts and a T-shirt with strange hard shoes that clattered on the wood floor. He seemed startled to see Fitz standing in his house with his wife wiping away tears with the heels of her hands.

"So sorry to interrupt," he said toward Douglas. "I was just leaving."

Douglas opened his mouth to say something, but Fitz didn't wait to hear it.

He turned back to Margaret, "I'll call you, okay?"

Fitz ran down the front steps, got into his car and backed down the driveway, dazed and depleted, regretting his decision to talk to Margaret. It was clear that he had only managed to deepen her wounds. She wasn't ready, or she wasn't strong enough, or he was wrong to ask. Whatever the case, he had made a terrible mistake.

After driving around aimlessly, he found himself turning into a Wendy's, remembering how fast food used to comfort him. He sat in his car debating whether or not he should go inside. Finally, the thick smell of hamburgers and French fries in the parking lot was too much for him, and he joined the line, his mouth watering. Maybe a double burger, fries, and a chocolate shake, more calories than he usually ate in a day, would distract him from his regrets. But once at the counter, he asked for a cup of ice water and a plain baked potato, which he took to a small empty table and ate methodically, scraping the soft insides out of the brown shell and then folding it in two, consuming every bit of it without even salt to relieve its terrible blandness.

Through the restaurant's glass walls, he watched a minivan pull up: doors opening, children and empty snack wrappers spilling out, a young mother exiting the front passenger door, rubbing her lower back, herding the children inside like a sheepdog, father bringing up the rear. They would have no idea how much he envied them their messy lives. He felt trapped, not only by his circumstances but by his inability to walk away from Margaret, even though she was married to someone else.

Oh, the liability of love. It warped the senses, bent time, obliterated brain cells, and yet, there was no way to be held harmless. No waiver one could sign, no release forms. It was a risk few people had any control over taking.

Margaret wasn't the most selfless woman he had ever met. She was beautiful, of course, but that didn't explain it. He had seen many beautiful women in his day, some up close, some even available to him, and they failed to move him the way Margaret did. No, it was something else. Margaret was like an elegant porcelain vase with a chip in it, the damaged side turned toward the wall. It was pride that drove her concealment, as if she had been raised in another time, another place. Stiff upper lip and all that. It troubled him, and it drew him to her. Beyond that, his bond to her could not be explained.

He stuffed his garbage into the trash bin and watched the young mother and father herd their fed and watered children back into the overstuffed minivan, completely unaware of how he wished he could trundle back on the road with them in all their mundane glory.

—34—

Brenda

*G*ood *morning, Mr. Fitzhugh. I hate to start your day with bad news, but it's my duty to inform you that the foundation's business account has been used for personal expenses of a questionable nature. I encourage you to review the attached statements and take action.*

Brenda

She balled up the note, which had the potential to destroy a family and a foundation. Homes might have to be sold, time shares liquidated, critical insurance policies lost, marriages (at least one) decimated. The only winners would be the lawyers. She would have to tell Mr. Fitzhugh in person. Better not to leave a paper trail.

Really, she should have known. Hamish Fitzhugh had been too friendly, too present, too free with his time and attention, dropping by the office with expensive trays of sushi for lunch. Charities were supposed to scrape by. Her skin should have been oily with the consumption of cheap mayonnaise from Subway.

It had been Mr. Fitzhugh's idea to give his father a credit card for foundation expenses since he was expected to wine and dine prospective donors. But she was the one to review the statements.

The first one she questioned was six months ago, an exorbitant bill for a hotel room in Atlantic City. She called the hotel and asked for a detailed invoice, which told her that a room service order had included a bottle of expensive champagne and two lobster dinners. Extra butter—a six-dollar charge. When she had gotten up the courage to ask Hamish Fitzhugh about it, he gave her some story about a high-roller donor who had invited him for a night at the craps table. "It's called priming the pump," he said, as if she were stupid.

Then other hotels rooms. Other dinners, always for two. But now, more recently, cash withdrawals. Most for a thousand or two thousand, but last week one for ten thousand dollars. Embezzlement. That's what it was properly called. She pictured Hamish Fitzhugh's mugshot on the front page of *The Hartford Courant*, pleading eyes distracting from the massive jowls that could pocket enough foie gras to keep him fat in prison for a half-dozen years. *Quelle horreur.*

She couldn't bear to see Mr. Fitzhugh unhappy, and yet, she had to tell him about the credit card charges and the cash advances. He hadn't been himself lately, which worried her. Too often, she found him brooding in his office when he should have been out meeting with donors, and this news wouldn't help. But it was more than that. He had also retreated from Brenda, closing his door when he used to keep it open. Forgetting to ask her about her weekend. And just a few days ago, she had overheard him on the phone with his college friend Margaret, insisting that she come to the foundation gala, pressing free tickets on her and her husband. "I'm so sorry I upset you," he had said. "Please say you'll come." Brenda had been jealous to hear the raw emotion, the intimacy, in his voice.

She didn't blame Mr. Fitzhugh, though, for disappointing her. This was what happened when you had a relationship that existed almost exclusively in your head. She was a woman battered emotionally by a man who didn't know, and would have been appalled to know, that he inflicted any pain.

In a way she had not expected, the dentist she had been dating had become a close friend. One night after two glasses of Chardonnay, she had told him about her alopecia and removed her wig, and he had clapped in delight. "That's you," he said, turning her toward the mirror. "That's the real you."

They had taken turns trying on her wigs, regressing through the years. Modern Brenda, bobbed and angled. Mid-eighties Brenda, curled bangs and long layers. Earlier eighties Brenda, unfortunate helmet, a Raquel Welch poof on special. Teenage Brenda, curly and wide, hair the texture of a poodle. Then the dentist had insisted on helping her shop for a new wig. This latest was a little darker and had more movement to it. It framed her face better and brought out the deep brown of her eyes.

Her mother had noticed the change in her, assuming an engagement was imminent.

"Hint around a little," she told Brenda one Friday night as they washed dishes after a family dinner of lasagna and garlic bread. The dentist sat at the dining room table drinking coffee and digesting pie with her father and brother. "Tell him how much you like rings."

He likes rings, too, Brenda almost said, but held her tongue. A change was on its way. She could feel it in her fingertips as they traced the corners of the soapy lasagna pan, checking for baked-on residue. Life would not continue as it always had, and that might be good or bad. She couldn't yet tell which.

—35—

Margaret

Douglas placed another log on the inferno in the stone firepit he had constructed in the backyard. The early June nights were still cool. In the last week, Ollie had helped Douglas build four low benches made from planks and notched tree stumps, and this would be the grand unveiling of their handiwork.

"Enough with the wood," Margaret said. "You'll set the neighborhood on fire."

Men and fire. They always had to make it bigger and more forceful than it needed to be. Margaret wondered how the history of the world might be different if women had been left in charge of something so destructive.

"Ho! Intruder on the premises!" Ollie jumped the fence between their two houses and made a beeline for the cooler. "Tiffany's doing some shit with her hair. She'll be over in a minute."

Ollie sat down on one of the benches and opened a beer. He bounced up and down a few times.

"We do good work, man," he said. "This ain't going nowhere."

"You get all the credit. All I did was pound some nails."

"Nonsense. You, sir, are a goddamned treasure."

Margaret hadn't wanted to invite the neighbors over, but Douglas had insisted they make an effort to get to know them better. So here she was with a little-used wedding shower platter brimming with tortilla chips and salsa, and a pitcher of margaritas and a false smile, ready to make the smallest of talk with Tiffany as Douglas and Ollie reminisced about their Herculean efforts to build these sad little benches. Ollie, strangely, had grown on her, but Tiffany remained an empty husk with corn silk hair. As far as Margaret could tell, she spent most of her time wiping runny noses and instructing her children on the proper slamming of a screen door, sending them back to do it again if it wasn't loud enough.

Margaret had returned to the house to fetch a plate of cheese and crackers when she heard Tiffany tap on the door into the kitchen from the garage. Douglas must have left the bay open, as he often did.

"Yoo-hoo."

"C'mon in."

Tiffany seemed to have trouble lifting her feet over the transom. She stumbled and righted herself, then held a bag of opened potato chips in Margaret's direction.

"The kids got to them," Tiffany said, wine on her breath. "Nothing is safe in my house."

"Don't worry about it, I've got plenty."

"So nice of you to have us over." Tiffany sounded as if she had rehearsed this line, and Margaret felt sorry for her. In some prehistoric version of this interaction, Tiffany would be much higher in the social order, head of a powerful clan that had produced six young laborers, but in this century, Margaret had the upper hand by virtue of her education. In this world, their lives barely intersected except for their adjacent yards.

Margaret was about to open the door to the back yard when Tiffany touched her left arm, which was balancing the cheese and cracker platter.

"Give them a few minutes," she said. "You know, for guy talk."

That Tiffany knew this reminded Margaret of something she had learned in a college psychology class. There are different kinds of intelligence. She put the platter back down as Tiffany propped herself up by her elbows on the counter, bending at the hips, knees locked on the long tan legs emanating from white shorts that barely covered her rear.

"Did you know that Ollie and I aren't together anymore?" she said. "I mean, we live together, but we don't, you know, sleep together anymore. I wasn't sure if you knew that."

Margaret took a block of cheddar out of the refrigerator and began cutting, though she had more than enough already arranged on a plate. The cheese allowed her to avoid Tiffany's eyes, which were slightly bloodshot, red-rimmed, and hollow. In them, Margaret saw Tiffany's fatigue and unhappiness. A trace of recklessness. The eyes of a bobcat pacing its cage at the zoo.

"I'm sorry, I didn't know."

"A while ago, I actually left him, but the kids wanted to come back. It was too cramped at my mom's."

"I'm sure they missed him." Margaret took a damp sponge from the sink and began wiping down the already clean counters.

"He's a good dad, but we just don't have much in common. Actually, it's kind of a relief to admit that we're staying together for the kids and not for anything else."

Margaret swept invisible detritus into her hand. Tiffany's hollow eyes followed her, then turned to the full margarita pitcher, stopping there. Margaret poured Tiffany a margarita and handed it to her. She took a long sip.

"I'm so jealous of you. You have no idea."

"Who, me?" Margaret picked up a cracker and placed a piece of cheddar on top. This was the longest conversation she had ever had with Tiffany.

"I see you go off to work every day in your nice clothes and your heels. I don't get to wear heels unless I can find a babysitter for six, and let me tell you, that's not easy."

Tiffany watched her go off to work every day? Tiffany thought about her life and wished she could trade places? Tiffany *wanted* to wear the pumps that tortured her feet? The idea seemed absurd. She was the one who watched Tiffany carrying a little one on her hip as if the baby were part of her body.

"We're only here now because Ollie's mom came over. And she hates my guts."

"I'm sure she doesn't—"

"No, she does. She fucking hates me." Tiffany pushed away from the counter and propped herself against the wall. She put her chin down to her chest, looking directly at the small pooch of her stomach, a miraculous part of her body that had ferried six different children who now strutted around outside of it, demanding juice boxes.

"My life is shit," she said, the words directed toward herself more than Margaret.

"Don't say that."

Tiffany's mouth turned hard. She closed her bloodshot eyes and pulled in a defeated breath, then slowly let it out. Margaret had the sense that she was unnecessary, that Tiffany had often said the same words in front of a mirror or a wall.

"You don't know. You don't know what I wanted to do. You don't know what I wanted to be."

Margaret had no idea what to say. That Tiffany had these existential thoughts just yards away inside a house full of boisterous children took her by surprise. She asked the only question that came to mind.

"What did you want to do?"

She wiped the back of her hand across her nose.

"Not—" the word caught in her throat—"this."

Margaret put a hand on Tiffany's soft shoulder. Poor girl. Her days were no doubt filled with bodily emissions and fights over what to watch on TV and the crises caused when one shoe of a pair went missing, and that was the good part. In a few years, she would have to worry about unplanned pregnancies and illicit drugs and children missing in the middle of the night. They weren't so different, really. Both of them wanting what they didn't have.

Margaret glanced out the window where Douglas was tossing another log onto the already roaring fire and laughing at something Ollie had said. This was her husband. This was her life. And as she stood there in her small, dim kitchen, a cosmic cleaver split her in two. Often, she was grateful for what she did have with Douglas, which was a respectable life, a good life, a life that her neighbor envied, a marriage that might yet become a family. Other times, she barely kept it together, aware that she had married Douglas, in part, because he was the safe alternative to navigating a world that harbored and rewarded men like Anders, who seemed good until they weren't. For a while, she had been able to avoid these thoughts, but now that Anders's face was everywhere she turned, it was impossible.

Tiffany nudged her out of her reverie.

"We should go out there before they burn down the neighborhood."

Tiffany shook her hair toward the front of her face and ran her fingers through it, lifting the white-blond strands so that they fell just so around her face. It was a gesture Margaret had seen her use before, a gesture Margaret had assumed was left over from her flirtatious high school days. Now she could see that Tiffany's hair was her talisman. It was the locus of her power in a world where a mother of six could feel almost powerless.

"Men and fire," she said. Her breath was so drenched with alcohol that Margaret hoped she didn't get too close to the flames. "Not a good combination."

"You took the words right out of my mouth."

—36—

Fitz

Fitz shut off the lights in his office and pulled the shades. He could see his migraine like a distant freight train, the vibrations already bouncing the pebbles on the tracks. His headaches had become more frequent, even as he tried to avoid the usual triggers: processed foods, caffeine, alcohol, his father, Anders's smug face on the cover of a magazine. Beyond that, the gala was a day away. His mother had become far too involved with all the details, second-guessing him on his choices: flowers, music, table assignments, speakers, microphone placement. He would never agree to it again.

He tilted his head from side to side, trying to work out the clerical-collar stiffness. Pressure was beginning to build in his skull, so he tried massaging his jaw, his mouth yawing open like a lion's. He looked toward his computer screen, hoping to get a little more work done, but the aura had already started: a jagged staircase of bright light that flashed in the lower left of his field of vision. He felt weak, but the pain was not upon him yet. The aura was like a raised dagger catching the light, and the pain would arrive suddenly. He didn't know when. Sometimes it liked to tease him with a half-day of nausea before hitting him across the head like a tire iron. Medicine helped but only enough to keep him from fainting.

He heard a gentle rapping on the door. Brenda always seemed to know when he was about to succumb and spoke even more softly than usual. God bless her.

"Come in." His own voice scraped the inside of his head like a butter knife on burnt toast.

She opened the door a crack. The light flooded in around her silhouette, piercing his eyes.

"I'm so sorry to disturb you."

"Do you mind sitting in the dark?"

"Not at all."

Fitz nodded toward the chair in front of his desk. As Brenda sat down, he noticed that her hair was different again, a little softer and more natural. It was also noticeably longer than it had been yesterday, which wasn't possible unless it was some kind of . . .

Brenda pushed up on her new bangs as if she were wearing a hat that had slipped down too low on her forehead.

"I'm not sure how to say this."

"What is it?" He could tell that she had argued with herself about telling him whatever it was she was about to tell him. The freight train grew louder.

"It's about your father."

"What about him?"

Brenda kneaded one hand with the other. Fitz could feel the tension in her body as if it were his own. She was sweating, too, little beads of water springing forth on her forehead where the bangs had parted. He couldn't remember ever seeing her perspire.

"I'll just come out with it. He's been using the credit card for personal expenses. And recently, cash withdrawals. It's not good."

Fitz closed his eyes and swam into a bright blankness. The migraine was teasing him, putting words into Brenda's mouth that made no sense. He opened his eyes, almost surprised to see her still sitting there, still tense and perspiring. Still wearing a hat made of hair disconnected from her body.

"Wait, what?"

"Your father. He's been spending foundation money on hotels and expensive dinners, wine, champagne. Which is bad enough, but the cash withdrawals can't be designated as donor recruitment. I have no idea what to do with those."

"How long has this been going on?"

Brenda's head bent forward as if she were studying an intricate pattern on her shoes. When she finally spoke, he almost couldn't hear her.

"I started noticing about six months ago, but he said he was taking prospective donors out to dinner. I thought that was okay. But the cash withdrawals are new. Just this past month."

"You should have said something."

"I was trying to find the right time."

The freight train had accelerated, and it was upon him now, smothering him as he tried to flatten his back against the railroad ties.

Brenda placed a stack of papers on his desk.

"It's all there."

He nodded.

"I'm glad you told me."

"What happens next?"

"I'll have to talk to him. Maybe there's some explanation."

"I hope so."

"Me, too."

As Brenda left, Fitz let his head rest sideways on the desk. The cool of the polished wood against his flattened ear and the side of his cheek mitigated the pain. Despite this revelation about his father, he could think only of Brenda and her ill-fitting wig. So many things made sense now: the stiff texture and her reluctance to go outside on windy days. In his experience, women younger than seventy didn't wear wigs, but then again, maybe they did—maybe every other woman he passed on the street had a fake head of hair—and he hadn't been astute enough to notice.

After an indeterminate amount of time with his cheek mashed against his desk, the weird tangle of Fitz's pain and bewilderment eased enough to allow him to lift his head. Brenda had gone home. He left his office and passed by Brenda's neat desk in the outer office, unsuccessfully pushing aside thoughts of what lay underneath her wig: A shaved head that appeared only on weekends while she played in a punk band? A skull that was flat on one side and needed padding? A hairless dome, smooth as an egg?

A warm rain began falling as he walked to his car, bringing forth the memory of an unforgettable fat camp all-nighter during which Pudge had led them to a fire pit in the woods with all the ingredients for s'mores but no matches. Fitz and Arnie had tried striking rocks and rubbing sticks as the same sort of rain falling on him now, with the same womb-like warmth, stirred up the scent of pine from the bed of needles on which they had kneeled as Pudge sat on a fallen tree and ate an entire bag of untoasted marshmallows. He sometimes wondered what Pudge and Arnie were up to these days, but they were in the category of people who popped up and influenced and left lasting memories only to recede back into the unknown. He had never learned their last names.

In this wistful state, he drove to his parents' house and parked outside in the semicircle of the driveway. His mother had insisted on crushed white stones for it, ordinary asphalt seeming gauche, even as she railed against the pebbles that got stuck in pant cuffs and sneaker treads and soft soles and dragged into the house. The wood floors in the foyer had to be refinished every other year.

He turned off his older model Subaru and listened to the *tick, tick, tick* of the engine as it cooled. His parents had wanted to buy him a new car for his birthday, but he couldn't drive around in a BMW or an Audi while his clients wondered whether they could afford the ultrasound that was ordered after a sketchy mammogram. Money. It was nothing if you had it, everything if you didn't.

While he sat and observed the sky go from dark to darker and contemplated the born-on-third-base-but-ran-back-to-second arc of his life, his father came out the front door in his pajamas and a pair of the shearling-lined leather slippers he favored for late evenings and early mornings. He crunched around the car through the damp crushed stone—the rain had stopped—and rapped sharply on the driver's side window.

Fitz opened the window.

"To what do we owe this visit?" His father's tone was jovial, and yet Fitz sensed he wasn't happy to see him sitting there.

"Get in."

"You get out. Your mother's in bed with a book. I'll get Cassandra to make you some waffles. She's here late working on the centerpieces for the gala."

He hadn't eaten Cassandra's waffles since he left home for college, but he had often dreamed of them, crisp rectangles of goodness drenched in maple syrup. The insides soft and light as eiderdown.

"We need to talk. In private."

Hamish crunched back around the car and opened the passenger-side door. He struggled his way into the Subaru's bucket seat, his plaid cotton pajama top riding up to reveal a white stripe of belly, a belly that had never known a day—perhaps not an hour—of hunger. A belly whose very cells had been fueled by prawns and high-butter-fat-content ice cream and prime rib and oysters Rockefeller and his father's favorite, tiramisu. Platinum level cells.

Now that Hamish was close enough that he could smell the scotch on his breath, Fitz had no idea what to say.

"Out with it," Hamish said. "I've got an early fitting tomorrow for my tux."

Fitz looked at his hands, still on the steering wheel.

"You've been taking cash withdrawals from the foundation account."

In the moment, he decided to frame it as a statement of fact rather than a question.

"Excuse me?"

"I've seen your credit card statements—" he wanted to leave Brenda out of it— "and it's clear that you've been using the foundation as your own private little bank account."

His father sat quietly, then his shoulders dropped, which told Fitz that this was not a misunderstanding. Any hope he had of leaving with his father's dignity intact evaporated.

Hamish pinched the bridge of his nose, which meant that Fitz couldn't see the expression on his face. When he spoke, it was a mumble through his hand.

"I'll pay back the advances. I always intended to pay them back."

"Bad investments? Gambling? What?"

Hamish slowly shook his big head. The backs of Fitz's thighs began to twitch. None of this made sense.

"You have to know, son, I didn't mean for it to happen."

"For what to happen?"

Hamish took in a long breath and let out a deep, mournful sigh.

"I was faithful to your mother for the vast majority of our marriage."

"Oh, God."

"It wasn't anything I asked for. I didn't go looking for it."

"Wait, you don't have to—"

"I fell in love. I didn't want to, but I did. And I couldn't be with her—I couldn't take care of her—unless I used an account your mother or my accountants wouldn't see. It was urgent, and I thought I could pay it back before anyone noticed. I just have to move some funds around."

"So you put the foundation at risk to support your mistress?"

"Don't say it that way."

"It's the truth, isn't it?"

Hamish spoke in the direction of the glove compartment, his voice low.

"You want the truth? I never loved your mother. I thought I did when we first got married, but I didn't love her the way I love Meredith. I didn't know that kind of love even existed."

"Who the hell is Meredith?"

It was humid in the car now, the air saturated with his father's heated breath. Fitz stifled an urge to reach across his father's belly (now almost as mountainous as his own once was), open the passenger side door, and push him out onto the driveway.

Hamish sighed again. His hands went to his splayed knees.

"You met her at the club. I introduced you."

"She belongs to the club?"

This would kill his mother. Some bleached socialite who wore too much eyeliner, someone younger than his mother, married to a man less rich or maybe older than his father. Someone trading up. Someone who wore chunky gold earrings and skirts too short for a woman her age.

"She works there. In the front office. Membership coordinator. I think that's her title."

Fitz had a brief flash of memory, his father touching the elbow of a sharp-eyed fortyish woman with a delicate vine tattoo circling her upper arm. She would handle the paperwork, Hamish had said, so that Fitz could finally end his membership. Blow of blows. His mother would disintegrate, leaving nothing but a smudge on the pavement, if she knew she was losing her husband to a woman with a tattoo.

"So you wined and dined her on the foundation credit card."

"You don't understand. Her life is a living hell. She makes

eight-fifty an hour, and she's got two kids to support. Her husband left her. She's got nothing."

"And the cash withdrawals?"

"Her landlord wouldn't fix the washing machine, so she was going to the laundromat and leaving her kids at home. For Christ's sake, I had to help her move. It wasn't safe."

Hamish almost shouted the last part of this, but he didn't need to. Fitz knew better than anyone that love could have that outcome. Faulty synapses. Rash decisions. Phone calls made in the middle of the night when reason was asleep. He tried to keep his voice from rising.

"Does Mom know?"

His father turned abruptly, putting his hand on the steering wheel as if to stop Fitz's car from veering of the road.

"God, no. And she doesn't have to find out."

"So you're not planning to leave her?"

Hamish put his hand back on his knee. His head dropped and rested on the chins that rested on his chest.

"I don't know. Not yet anyway."

No matter what the outcome, the puzzle of his parents' lives had been broken apart and dumped back in the box. How they would, or could, piece it back together was a mystery. His father sat there, drained and pale, looking older than he had when he entered the car. Fitz ran a shaking hand over his head.

"Is that why you and Mom only had one child? You didn't love her enough to have more?"

Hamish looked at him, eyes red.

"We tried and it didn't happen. And then after a while, we stopped trying."

Fitz put his forehead on the pebbled plastic of the steering wheel. He wanted to find his mother and have her tell him a different story, a story that would make their family less pathetic. His mother always knew how to reframe the picture so that Hamish wasn't in the center but off to one side.

"Go back inside."

"You won't say any—"

"I won't. But you'll pay every dime back to the foundation."

"I'll take care of it this week." Hamish opened the car door and put one foot on the ground. He turned toward Fitz.

"I'm sorry. If I could change any of this, I would."

The car door closed, and Fitz remained where he was for several minutes as the echoes of his father's confession further polluted the stagnant, scotch-heavy air. He thought about his mother again, her avian wrists bracing a heavy book propped up with pillows. She didn't deserve to be treated this way, just as Margaret hadn't asked him to treat her like something precious. She had asked for nothing but his friendship, while his love, compressed through years of secrecy, had evolved from a sweet, shining star into a sucking black hole, its density pulling everything inside it.

After the gala, he would take a step back, reevaluate, maybe look at moving the foundation to a different part of the country where his family's reputation didn't walk in the door before he did. It might do him good to try the West Coast or Chicago. Without Margaret in the next town, he might, one day, forget her, or forget her enough to find love with someone else. The cement had not yet dried on his path, nor, he wanted to remind Margaret, had it dried on hers. She could choose a different sort of life as well. Now she was young and beautiful, but one day she would be more history than potential. One day she would have to grow up and face the circumstances life had handed her and the decisions she'd made. For a moment, he allowed himself to be disappointed with Margaret, and it occurred to him finally that she was not only flawed, a porcelain vase with a chip turned toward the wall, she was human.

—37—

Brenda

The dentist had convinced Brenda to buy an entire wardrobe of wigs and to wear them according to her mood. Most days she wore a short, chic one, but on the day of the gala, she arrived at the office in a shoulder-length wig the dentist had helped her buy for special occasions. Alopecia, she told Mr. Fitzhugh when he looked confused.

"Ah," he had said, tapping his lips with a finger. "I didn't know."

Brenda nodded. She would miss his gentle sense of humor, his sensitivity. She would miss the way he greeted a new client, pressing his other hand on top of their handshake, saying what they needed to hear: *You are covered.*

"Can we talk for a minute?"

Fitz said "sure" and led the way into his office, which was filled with boxes of silent auction program books for the gala. Fitz sat down and gestured to a chair in front of his desk, but Brenda chose to remain standing. She took in a long breath.

"I want you to know I appreciate everything you've done for me, taught me, and I know this might come as a shock, but I'm taking a new job."

His face fell, as she knew it would. He sat back in his chair.

"What?"

"I'm taking a new job. Executive director at that refugee resettlement place where we sometimes get clients."

"In Wallingford?"

"That's it."

"Brenda, I thought we'd be working together until we were old and gray. You never said . . . is it too late to talk you out of it?"

Working together. It occurred to her for the first time that she was his work wife, and that this was, in some sense, a divorce.

"You've been very good to me. It's just time to move on."

The tears in his eyes were genuine, but the raw emotion, on his end, had nothing to do with love. Only work love, if that were a thing.

"When are you leaving?"

"Two weeks."

He nodded slowly, and she realized that this separation would be harder for him than for her. Lately, her pulse no longer raced in Mr. Fitzhugh's presence. Her fantasies were fewer and further between and more out of habit than anything else. She would always love him, but his innate sadness was beginning to trouble her. He nurtured it like a beloved pet, stroking and feeding it until it became his defining characteristic, but why? The clock ticks on love, even the kind of desperate longing she had had for Mr. Fitzhugh. It had a shelf life, and to her great surprise, it had expired.

"What if I match the salary? Would you stay then?"

It was tempting. She could do the same job she'd always done for higher pay, but what was she really to Mr. Fitzhugh? A glorified secretary.

"It's not about the pay. I need a new challenge."

"I understand."

Brenda turned to leave but changed her mind.

"Did you know that I loved you?" she said. It surprised her that the words came out so easily after rattling around in her brain for so long. "I had fantasies about us being together. Ridiculous, I know, and I'm over it now. But I thought you should know that you were loved."

Mr. Fitzhugh gave her a crooked, broken little smile, then got up from his chair and came around the desk.

"It's not ridiculous at all," he said. "I wish you had told me."

He pulled her into his arms and held her for a long time, a time in which she allowed herself to remember how for years and years she had craved a moment like this.

Brenda had always presented herself so carefully, like a piece of expertly crafted origami. Now she was unfolding, presenting angles and surfaces that had yet to be seen by the general public. To this end, she and the gay dentist mutually decided that she could be his girlfriend but not his *girlfriend*.

Her mother didn't understand at first when Brenda had told her as they peeled potatoes before a family dinner. Her mother's right hand dropped to the counter, knuckles resting in a bed of long, curved peels. Her left hand gripped a half-peeled potato.

"But you've been dating for such a long time. Why now?"

"Maybe you haven't figured it out, Mom, but he's gay."

Her mother sat down hard on a kitchen chair, the potato still in her hand.

"He's what now?"

"He's gay. That means he prefers to sleep with men."

"I know what it means, Brenda. When did you find this out?"

"I've known for a while. But, you know, we got along, and we liked a lot of the same things, so it was okay. But I'm done with that. I want a real relationship. I deserve it."

"Of course, you do."

Strangely, what her mother had told her from the beginning turned out to be true. Hair wasn't everything. She had every right to expect that someone would love her despite her condition. Confidence had always been the sticking point, but a few months before, she had seen Grace Jones on a movie poster with her hair shaved down to the skin. She looked indestructible. And all Brenda had to do was whip off her wig to join her.

The first place she tried was the grocery store. She sat in her car tying a gauzy scarf in different ways, but this made her look too much like a cancer patient. Instead, she went full Grace Jones, striding through the aisles in her short skirt and heels, picking up olives and hard cheeses and crackers, which she didn't need but wouldn't spoil. She stood at the checkout, certain that every eye in the store was on her but determined to hold her head high.

The clerk, a young man in his early twenties, gave her a smile.

"Having a party?"

She looked at the groceries as he scanned them and laughed.

"I am. A big one."

He gave her the thumbs up as she took her bag and left, feeling for the first time in a long time, like she had something to celebrate.

—38—

Douglas

Douglas took the tuxedo and shirt he had rented for the Fitzhugh Family Foundation gala out of the closet and hung it on the knob of his top dresser drawer. He wasn't looking forward to the event itself, but he would enjoy wearing the tux now that he had lost a little weight.

"I'm getting in the shower," he called to Margaret, who was at the dining room table paying some bills.

"Go ahead."

He turned on the water and stripped down, his clothes filthy from the two hours he had spent in the garden that morning. He let the water run over his chest, then turning around, put his head under the stream and felt a sudden pain that ran through his body into the soles of his feet. He ran a hand over his scalp but couldn't feel any lumps or scratches. He washed his hair gently, but the pain persisted. Had he bumped his head so hard that he couldn't remember having done it?

Head still throbbing, he finished showering and shaving, then trooped into the dining room in his towel. Margaret hated to be interrupted while paying bills, but he couldn't see the top of his own head.

"Hey, will you take a look," he said. "I did something to my head, and it's killing me."

Douglas turned around and bent his knees, tilting the back of his head toward Margaret, who laughed. It was a short but emphatic laugh, the kind of laugh married people forget how to keep to themselves.

"Looks like you got a terrible sunburn on your bald spot. I guess you should wear a hat while you're gardening."

Oof. Punch to the solar plexus. *Your bald spot.* She referred to it so casually, which meant it had been there for some time. Jesus, why hadn't she told him?

He went back upstairs more slowly, feeling a new and unwelcome heaviness in his leg muscles with each step. Shit. He had a bald spot. Women never had to worry about their hair falling out. It seemed unfair. He found a hand mirror on Margaret's dressing table and took it into the bathroom, angling it so that he could see the angry red patch of skin, about an inch and a half in diameter, at the top of his crown. The only kind of hat appropriate for a man his age was a baseball hat, and he couldn't wear that to a gala. He would have to walk around all evening with this screaming billboard on top of his head: Old Man Coming Through.

He could hear Margaret rummaging around in the hall closet where they kept their sunscreen and bug spray.

"Won't help now," he said.

"Try this." She handed him a spray bottle of aloe vera. "That should calm it down."

He took the bottle and spritzed. A cooling sensation spread over his scalp as he watched Margaret undress to get into the shower. How nice of her to think of the aloe vera. Maybe she wasn't ribbing him after all. His head was throbbing again. He touched it, wincing.

"Take some aspirin," she said on her way to the shower. "That'll help."

He took his time dressing as Margaret showered. Ollie's kids were in their backyard on the used trampoline Tiffany had somehow acquired. He could hear them screaming, though it sounded like cheerful screaming rather than the screaming that would pierce his heart when a couple of their hard, little skulls cracked together. An ambulance would be tearing into the neighborhood any day now.

Strangely enough, Ollie and Tiffany had reconciled. From his yard, he saw them making out one night on an old lounge chair in the backyard. The next day Ollie told him what happened.

"She was bitching about how she never gets out of the house, and I told her to sign up for some classes. 'Like what?' she said, and I was like, 'Whatever you want—yoga, pole dancing, photography, whatever.' And she said, 'You would watch the kids?' and I said, 'Fuck, yeah,' and she practically jumped me. So that's all it took."

"Unbelievable."

"Marriage, man. It's like a fucking roller coaster."

"You said it."

Douglas was, in fact, at the bottom of a particularly steep fall. He and Margaret had argued after he came home to find Fitz in his kitchen. She couldn't or wouldn't adequately explain what he was doing there.

"It's not important," she had said. "It's all in the past."

When he had pressed her on why she had been crying, she had given him a sad smile.

"I'm fine. Really. It's something I have to work out for myself."

He had let it go, but now they were going to some idiotic fund-raising event where he would have to watch Fitz ogling his beautiful wife and no doubt be coerced into writing a check for the privilege. He threw his wet towel on the bed and put on his boxers and undershirt, then his tuxedo shirt and pants. He would leave the cuff links, bow tie, cummerbund and jacket until Margaret was just about ready to go.

She returned from the shower wearing her bathrobe, her hair

wrapped in a towel. He liked to see her that way, no makeup, no hair-spray, no perfume. Without armor. Only the sweet symmetry of her face and the smell of shampoo. But there was something else there, some secret that hid in the corners of her eyes.

"Tell me again why we're going to this thing."

"Because Fitz asked us to go. It's a big deal for him. And the tickets were free."

Margaret took the wet towel from her head and hung it on the doorknob. She glanced at the one Douglas had thrown on the bed.

"What is it about Fitz that you like so much?"

The slip she would wear under her dress was halfway over her head when she spoke.

"He's been my friend for a long time. Do you have a problem with that?"

The slip was down now, her face revealed, twisted and pained, as if she were going to cry again. It was too much. The venom he had stored up in tiny pockets inside himself pooled up and formed words he couldn't prevent, words that had almost wrestled free from his defenses before. He had always stopped them, the little beasts, too afraid to see them unleashed into the world where they would alter the shape of his life.

"Goddammit, Margaret, what is going on? Are you having an affair with him? Just tell me."

"Of course not. Why on earth would you think that?"

"Because you're keeping secrets from me. And he's always there with the ballet tickets and the rosary beads, and the other day I find him in my kitchen—"

"The rosary beads? I thought you gave me the rosary beads."

She staggered to the bed and sat down on it.

"No, Margaret, those were from Fitz. I tried to tell you but—"

"You didn't try very hard. How many times did I thank you?"

"Forget the rosary beads. What is going on?"

She looked paler than he'd ever seen her, as if she might faint. She clutched the fabric of her slip with both hands.

"I can't talk about it."

"I'm your husband, Margaret. If you can't talk to me about it, who can you talk to?"

She gave him a look that he would later understand was one of pity. Then he said what needed to be said, what had weighed on him since the day he had proposed.

"You don't love me, Margaret."

"What are you talking about?"

"Whatever you think you feel for me, it's not love. I just came along when you felt like getting married."

"You're losing your mind, Douglas."

"Am I? Then tell me you love me and that you want us to have a family and that you're willing to do whatever it takes to keep us together."

When he had put this ultimatum out into the room, it floated all alone, abandoned. Margaret put her hands up to her face. Douglas turned and left.

He stalked into the garage, shoved his feet into his biking shoes, opened the bay door and boarded his recumbent bike in his dress pants and tuxedo shirt. Without knowing where he was headed, he coasted down the driveway, then looked back. Margaret stood at the front door in her slip, her mouth agape, distinctly fishlike. He had never seen her look so unattractive. All that mattered was putting distance between them, but as he turned at the end of the driveway toward Ollie's house, he saw Margaret run over to Ollie's lawn and grab one of the many bikes abandoned in the grass. The one she took was too small for her, but she pedaled gamely, trying to catch him as her voice cut through the neighborhood din.

"Douglaaaaaas! Waaaait!"

She followed him all the way to the peak of the long downhill into

Newington, where Douglas always paused. Everything seemed to move in slow motion. On his recumbent bike, his torso hovered close to the earth. If he chose to move forward, the road's imperfections would vibrate through him: every divot, every loose patch of gravel, every dismal, flattened bit of roadkill that would look like an odd, discarded carpet fragment until he bumped over it. He sat with his feet on the pedals, debating his next move. Behind him he could hear Margaret's voice slicing through the wind.

"Doug-laaaaaaas. Wait for me."

He glanced behind him. Margaret was making up for the bike's lack of wheel circumference with her relentless energy. With his progress halted, she had almost erased the distance between them, her legs pumping like pistons. Persistent little pistons. A smudge of light in the distance marked the bottom of the hill. If he stayed where he was, he could smooth things over with some monumental groveling, make up some excuse about why he said what he did. He could choose to file this fight in the ever-expanding accordion folder labeled, "The Things on Which Margaret and Douglas Will Never Agree." Their marriage might endure it, just as it had endured many other slights, misunderstandings, and outright lies. Or he could allow his greater weight to carry him down the hill at a speed Margaret could never match on that toy she was riding. The drop would be heart-stopping. The wind would roar in his ears, and his tuxedo shirt would all but laminate his chest. He would, if he chose to go forward, shed his old life, leaving it on the side of the road like a snakeskin among the carpet-fragment squirrels.

He could hear Margaret's panting. The wind whipped around him and lifted a cloud of dust into the air, forcing him to cover his eyes. Then the wind died down, seeming to take a breath, and Douglas grabbed the handlebars with both hands. He inched forward. The crunch of Margaret's tires on the road's gravel-strewn shoulder grew louder.

He took one more look down the hill, sucked in a lungful of air, and gave a mighty push. The bike tipped into the void.

As he hurtled downward, he forced himself to open his eyes and peer through slits. The dense air shuddered against him but failed to slow him down. He tried to turn his head to see if Margaret had followed him, but when he lifted it slightly, the air thudded against his cheek. On his left, the road became not a ribbon of highway, as the old song said, but a bristling rope of macadam that would tear the skin from his body if he hit a pothole or a crack in the pavement. On his right, a smear of dark green, pine trees in the distance. Closer was the no-man's-land just off the paved shoulder, the four-foot-wide trail of dirt and detritus that would grind into his skin if he tumbled off in that direction. He tightened his grip on the handlebars, veering around sudden breaks in the road surface into the travel lane without checking for cars. His lungs expanded and contracted in double time. His heart pummeled the inside of his chest, and he feared that it might break through.

Then the road leveled out, and time suddenly snapped back to its normal pace. The bike began to decelerate of its own accord. The wind subsided until it was nothing but a soft breeze and then completely still. He came to a stop near a local farm stand selling tomatoes. The punishing punch of his heart slowed to an intermittent jab as the fragrant air folded around him like a warm blanket. Silence. It meant Margaret had turned around.

Douglas gazed back at the hill, picturing the snakeskin of his old life nestled among the weeds. His marriage was up there, too, scattered like the shards of a broken bottle along the side of the road.

—39—
Fitz

In his fat years, Fitz had assumed that his life would improve in every way if he could lose weight, and in some respects, it had. No longer did he have to bear furtive, hostile glances when he walked into a restaurant or sat down on an airplane. No longer did he have to wedge himself into hotel showers and mop up the floor afterward. No longer did he stand at the mirror with a hand over all but one of his chins.

In many other ways, though, losing weight was akin to winning the lottery: after the initial euphoria, his expectations began to change. It no longer surprised him that people were willing, even eager, to speak to him at parties. In fact, there were times when he wished he could disappear into the corner again and pretend he were a couch or an oversized ottoman.

This was one of those nights.

He had arrived an hour early to help his mother supervise the hotel staff setting up the ballroom. They were expecting five hundred people, which was a testament to both the message of his charity— that no one should be without insurance—and the power and influence of his parents. His mother was ebullient, directing the waiters and making last-minute adjustments to the table settings. His father, to whom he hadn't spoken since their talk in the driveway the night before, was on his way back from the airport with a guest who, apparently, was too good for a taxi.

This event was, in many ways, the pinnacle of his mother's life. She had served on countless charity boards and helped with dozens of galas like this one but never for a foundation that had her own family name on it. He found her inspecting the bar, shimmering with joy and anticipation as she sampled the signature cocktail, something orange in color with vodka.

"Here," she said, holding a drink out to him. "Take the edge off. It's heaven."

Arlene wore a black evening gown with long, transparent chiffon sleeves, and a diamond necklace his father had given her for their twenty-fifth wedding anniversary. She looked as happy as he'd ever seen her.

"I'll pass," he said. He would need to keep a clear head. If they raised enough money tonight, he might be able to spend more of his time on clients instead of lunching with wealthy widows who kept their handbags in their laps while eating. "Let go of that," he always wanted to tell them. "People all over the world live on a small fraction of what you earn on your annuities alone. And they're just fine."

"I just went over the table placements," his mother said, taking another sip of the orange cocktail. "Oh, that's good . . . I hope you don't mind, but I've put Margaret and her husband with the Fosters. They're around the same age."

"Sure, fine." The Fosters were bores, but Fitz was in no mood to argue. His mother hadn't wanted him to invite Margaret and her husband at all, since their pockets were too shallow to pick, but he had pushed back. She needed a night out, one evening to dress up and forget about the past.

Fitz busied himself with final edits to his welcome speech as the ballroom began to fill with the elderly, who always arrived early. He looked across a sea of blue permanent waves and hunched backs. Then he noticed, standing out from them, a middle-aged woman alone near the kitchen door, her arms crossed. She wore a low-cut sequined silver gown, way too garish for the event. It was hard to tell from a distance, but she appeared to have a tattoo around her left upper arm. It couldn't be, but also had to be, Meredith. His stomach dropped.

When his father arrived, he would berate him for putting his mistress in the same room as his wife, but in the meantime, he had to get her out of there. He started toward Meredith when he saw Margaret come in through the ballroom's grand double doors.

She was swathed in a maroon, Grecian-style one-shoulder gown. Her hair was down and a bit disheveled. It looked as though she had driven to the gala with the windows open, but still, she was stunning. Her face was at once perfectly symmetrical but exceedingly complex. It seemed to have more planes and angles than the average face, which made people want to study it. Both women and men turned to look at her as she took a few hesitant steps toward the middle of the room. She appeared to be alone.

Margaret or Meredith. He had to decide which one needed his attention first. Before he could choose, his mother swept in and steered him by the elbow toward a corner filled with portly men sucking on cigars.

"Darling, these gentlemen have been asking for you," she said, before flitting away, her chiffon sleeves rippling.

It was five long minutes before Fitz could extricate himself from the cloud of cigar smoke. Back in the now-packed ballroom, he saw neither Margaret nor Meredith. He pushed his way through the conversation clusters slowly, his back patted along the way, until he was in the vicinity of the wide double-doored entry again where a tight crowd had gathered. Even with his height, he couldn't quite see whatever had commanded their attention.

Then his father came into view, his arm around a thin man in a sharp blue suit. Had no one told him this was black tie? He couldn't see the blue-suited-man's face, but the women in the crowd were smiling around fluttering fingers they had put up to their mouths. The man turned, and his profile was familiar. The nose was straight and elegant, Greek, but with a slight pinkness on the end like that of a possum. Then Fitz saw his full face, the ballroom lights bouncing off the bright white marquee of his smile.

It was Anders. *Fucking Anders.*

His mother was at his elbow again.

"We got him! You said you didn't know him, so I found someone who did. And he agreed to come for a very reasonable fee, happy to be back to visit his alma mater and all that."

Without changing his expression, Fitz felt the blood in his veins turn to lava and then to lead. His mother, who was beaming and receiving congratulations from everyone around her, had no idea that the peak of her social climbing had taken her onto a ledge about to break. Unknowingly she had brought a rapist into the same room as his victim. Unknowingly her husband's mistress was watching her from some unseen vantage point, no doubt assessing her smaller bust and the fussiness of the chiffon sleeves that covered up the loose skin around her elbows. And he, her only son, whose love she wanted most of all, stood there hating her for bringing this moment upon them.

Margaret. He had to get her out of there before she saw Anders.

He pushed his way back through the ballroom, searching for a glimpse of maroon. And there it was, the hem of her dress visible on one of the small second-floor balconies overlooking the ballroom. He rushed up the stairs to the balcony level as Margaret came into the hallway, her face distraught. He led her to an alcove near the bathrooms.

"I don't understand. Why is he here?"

"My mother. She didn't tell me."

Margaret contorted her arms to cover the bare shoulder that her dress revealed. She backed up against the wall as if she could disappear into it.

"I can't let him see me."

"We'll find some back way out. Where's Douglas?"

Margaret's mouth turned down in a way he had never seen before.

"Something came up. I only came by myself because I didn't want to disappoint you. And now—"

Fitz took a step back. He would ask his mother to stall for him and take Margaret home, but first he would ask Margaret for permission to confront the bastard. The room around him seemed to lose its solidity, molecules sliding away from each other.

"Let me talk to him, Margaret."

"Then he'll know I told you."

"He has to be stopped. Think of what he's done to your life. How many more people do you want him to hurt?"

"That's so unfair."

"Really, it's not. Think about it, Margaret."

"If you care about me at all, you won't do this."

Fitz jammed his hands in the pockets of his tuxedo pants.

"If I care about you? Margaret, I've been desperately in love with you since the first day I saw you, and I'm still in love with you. I want to do this *because* I love you. Because you can't carry this around anymore. You wanted to forget, but you haven't, and you won't. You have to face what happened, or you'll never get past it."

Darkness descended. Now that he had told Margaret what he thought she needed to hear, he was not relieved but terrified. Margaret looked at his wide-open chest, his exposed heart pumping maniacally, with shock.

"Oh," she said in a small voice. Fitz could see several emotions crossing her face—confusion, fear, panic—in roughly equal measure.

Then, pulling up her long skirt, she turned from him and ran, her spindly heels leaving deep imprints in the carpet.

On his way to find Margaret again, Fitz passed his father, who was bum-rushing an unhappy-looking Meredith toward the door, her silver-sequined, low-cut dress refracting the ballroom chandeliers in sharp little splinters of light. Evidently, she had come without his father knowing. His mother was standing with a small group talking to Anders, but Fitz could see that her eyes were trained like laser beams on Hamish. Soon, that mess would be out in the open, but he could not let his parents' drama derail his mission.

His new plan was to take Anders aside, claiming that he wanted to introduce him to a special donor. Then he would guide him to the lobby, where he would tell him his services were no longer needed. Out of respect for Margaret's wishes, he wouldn't say why. If he got up the gumption, he would land a punch on the marquee smile, hoping to loosen a tooth or two. But before he could reach Anders, Margaret appeared from the opposite direction, the maroon gown matching the color in her cheeks. She tapped Anders on the shoulder, and he turned with his movie star grin, ready to bestow it on whomever had been brave enough to approach him.

"And who do we have here?" he said. "Wait, I—"

Fitz's impulse was to get in between Anders and Margaret, but she had conjured a thunderstorm inside the ballroom. He could feel the air crackling with lightning, the anticipation of thunder. He stepped back, crushing the toes of a woman behind him.

"Remember me?" Margaret said. Her eyes had a stormy, yellowish light inside them, flashing a warning. "We dated once, just once, in college."

Anders's mouth turned up as if he were amused, but then fell. Confusion flashed across his face, then recognition. He looked around as if he might be rescued, which set the crowd murmuring.

"Of course, I remember. Hey, let's find someplace to talk," Anders said, smiling again, now acting the part of an old boyfriend who wanted to reconnect after all this time. He tried to put a hand on Margaret's arm, but she pulled it away.

"I'm fine where I am."

"Please," Anders said, his smile evaporating. "Don't."

"Don't what?" Margaret's voice shook, but her eyes were steady, locking Anders in place. "Don't tell everyone that you took me on a date—a first date—and drove me to a secluded spot in a city park where no one would see or hear? Don't say that you raped me?"

Anders began to look for an escape route, but the crowd had grown thicker and more agitated. Fitz could only see what was happening because he was taller than the people around him. This Margaret was not the Margaret he knew. This was some other Margaret who wasn't made of porcelain, or if she was, had decided to risk being shattered.

"Don't tell everyone that I found myself pregnant a few weeks later? You're a lucky man, you know that? I can't seem to carry a baby to term, which is the only reason I don't have your illegitimate child waiting for me at home right now."

Fitz felt his stomach drop and his knees go weak. Even he had never known how much she had suffered. Margaret's fists were clenched, her face tight, her eyes like the burning embers that started a forest fire after a lightning strike. Anders had gotten smaller in his effort to flee. He ducked down as cameras bulbs popped around him.

"Please, there are reporters here."

"I'm glad there are reporters here. They should know this. Your fellow actors should know this before they agree to work with you. I've been told you like them as young as possible."

Fitz stood in awe as Margaret beat Anders to a pulp without laying a hand on him.

"Not a word of this is true," Anders said, though he could not meet Margaret's eyes. The crowd surged toward him. Like the rodent he was, he found a small opening and darted into the lobby, then out the front doors of the hotel, before anyone could stop him.

When Fitz reached Margaret, she was shaking violently. He led her to one of the tables set for dinner and helped her into a chair.

"Let me get you some water," he said, and upon returning with it found Margaret holding a hand across her face as members of the local press tried to take her picture. He grabbed the closest camera and smashed it on the floor as the other photographers scattered.

"It's done," she said. "I'm done."

"I can't believe you did that. I'm so proud of you."

And he was proud, but he was also worried. In the same way that his confession of love had not freed him in the way he had hoped, all the condemnation she had feared was out there now, gathering in the dark. He had told her to be brave, but now that she had been, he was terrified of the consequences.

"I need to go home now."

She spoke in a monotone. The thunderstorm seemed to have used up all her energy. He wondered if she would ever get it back.

"Of course. I'll take you."

On the way out, they passed his mother drinking another of the orange cocktails. Her hair had gotten mussed, and she looked exhausted, as if it were the end of the night and not the beginning.

"It's all ruined," she said, looking around.

"I told you not to invite him, didn't I? But you had to do it your way."

He had a lot more to say, but he wanted to keep Margaret moving before she realized exactly what she had done. His mother touched his sleeve.

"What will happen?"

"It doesn't matter," he told her, gesturing to the ballroom, still recovering from Margaret's storm. The noise level had gone up as word of Margaret's confrontation with Anders spread. "None of this matters."

"Not this," she said. "I'm talking about my marriage."

"Oh."

His poor mother, always striving to manipulate every situation to her own advantage, could not make this one work in her favor.

"Did you know about this person?"

Fitz hesitated. He could pretend he didn't know what she was talking about, or he could tell her the truth. He wasn't sure which one was more cruel.

"I just found out."

His mother pulled herself up, straightening her delicate spine. She downed the rest of her drink, surprising Fitz with a fortitude he thought she saved for the misfortune of others.

"Well, she can have him. The house is mine."

—40—

Margaret

In the end, they did not believe her.

Fitz had offered to take Margaret to the police station on Sunday, the day after the gala, but she decided she should go alone, wearing clothes she would normally wear to the office, thinking that a skirt and jacket would make her more credible. In one windowless room after another, she sat with hands folded on her lap as police officers and prosecutors told her too much time had gone by. One by one, they shuffled papers and tugged on coffee-stained ties. There was no physical evidence or hospital record of a miscarriage, and when they contacted Anders, who had fled back to California, he flatly denied that Margaret had been unwilling. His story canceled out her story. Legally, the sum total was zero. It almost didn't matter since her accusations at the gala had made every tabloid in the country. Anders seemed to have gone into hiding, no doubt waiting for all the fuss to die down. Maybe it would, and maybe it wouldn't. She had no way to know.

When she was done at the police station, she walked back to get her car against a hot summer wind, her hair whipping around her face. Though it was a different season and a different place, the wind recalled the sadness of a Cape Cod weekend steeped in estrogen and Pinot Grigio and ripples of frigid water running over her bare feet after her third miscarriage. The loneliness of one heart beating instead of two. The disappointment, both hers and Douglas's, since her body had been the receptacle for both of their hopes and dreams.

Though it wasn't cold, the wind made her feel raw and exposed. As she passed a large Catholic church, a homeless man sitting on a small square of cardboard thrust a Styrofoam cup toward Margaret. Douglas often gave a dollar or some change, but she believed this only encouraged panhandlers and prevented them from getting the help they needed. Every year, she wrote a check to one of the local shelters to assuage any guilt, but this man stopped her with his eyes, the naked pleading in them. He was young. Maybe twenty.

"Anything you can give."

The cup was dirty and had fingernail marks on it, tiny crescents of desperation. In a dreamlike state, she reached into her purse and found a crumpled ten-dollar bill, tucking it inside the cup. The young man nodded his head. "Thank you, ma'am," he said. "God bless you."

As she neared the parking garage near the police station, she noticed that the sun was close to setting and it moved her almost to tears. Instead of finding her car, she kept walking, conscious of the sound of her heels echoing against the municipal buildings. The future stretched before her, shrouded in the falling light. The past was there, too, close on her heels, time pleated like a paper fan. Her father and mother walked behind her, occasionally reaching out to place a hand on one of her shoulders. She had never been convinced that life continued after death, despite her religious indoctrination, but her parents' presence told her that they had not disappeared into the nothingness from whence they came. They traveled the earth with her and always would. The children she lost with Douglas were there, too, a small girl skipping behind her, a tiny boy in a carriage. Their high, sweet voices could not be heard over the starlings that landed on tree branches over her head before taking off again en masse, their murmuration twisting across the sky.

She walked on, thinking now about her confrontation in the ballroom with a measure of awe and disbelief. It wasn't anger or bravery, she decided as she consumed the sidewalk in strides as long as she could take, but a question of control. After Fitz had said he wanted to fight for her, she wanted to fight for herself. Anders had robbed her of so much: her sense of safety, her willingness to give something of herself away without feeling she would lose it, her openness to love. In confronting him, she had reclaimed at least some of it. The secret was no longer pressing on her soul, and now that it was out in the open, she believed that other women would come forward in their own time. Even if they didn't, Anders would have to wonder how many women could or would bring charges against him for the rest of his life.

She thought about Douglas, too. When he had taken off on his recumbent bike on the night of the gala, she had chased him on a kid's bike purloined from Ollie and Tiffany's front yard, and there had been a moment, at the top of a very steep hill, where he had paused. She thought he was going to wait for her, to explain himself and patch things up, but he rode down the hill instead, never looking back, and she had decided not to follow. In that moment, she had realized how wrong she had been to marry him. She had chosen him because he was safe and pliable, the right kind of gauze for the wounds she was trying to conceal.

Douglas had contacted her the morning after her story became public, calling from Brooklyn, where he was staying with a friend.

"I wish you had told me," he had said on a phone line with the clarity of an old gramophone. She pictured him, for some reason, wearing suspenders and a fedora.

"I know that now. I should have."

"Why didn't you?"

"I don't know. I was worried you'd see me as damaged goods.

I wanted to put it behind me. I thought you'd blame me. All that. More. I don't know. It seems stupid now. Are you coming back?"

"I'm not."

"So, this is it?"

"Looks like it." Long pause. "We had a decent run, you know. It wasn't all bad."

That was the best assessment he could muster. She placed the phone gently on the receiver, knowing Douglas would wonder if she hung up or if they were disconnected, the anticlimactic end of a marriage. They could not and would not repair it, and that was for the best. He deserved someone who thought of him as above average.

She kept walking and found herself at the edge of Bushnell Park, where Douglas had proposed to her. Halfway through the park, her feet began to throb, so she sat on a bench with peeling green paint. As the sun began to dip below the city skyline, she shaded her eyes from the warm orange light with one hand. Physically, she felt fragile, as if she were elderly and not a young woman with most of her life ahead of her. Inside, though, she was renewed, relieved of the shame and guilt that had followed her since the night she had gone off with a boy she thought she loved.

Love was strange like that, both destructive and constructive. It possessed people and mangled their senses, but it could heal, too. As she sat on the bench, the wind subsiding now, it began to make sense: why she had always carried Fitz around with her, why she missed him so when they went too long without seeing each other, why she often thought about how he would react to something she had seen or done. Fitz, she now knew, had also given her the rosary beads, which had brought her back to her father, connected her to memories she had long since forgotten. Fitz was the part of her that was missing. He had loved her all along, even after she had married Douglas. He had tried to get her to do the right thing, but he had not forced her. He was an exceptionally patient man.

A soccer ball rolled toward her and, reflexively, she kicked it back to a group of kids playing nearby. Inside, her thoughts were coalescing around the idea that romantic love was not always of the *Thornbirds* variety. Love didn't have to be an inferno. It could also be an underground river, running strong and deep, rising into the light in unexpected places.

It struck her suddenly that she could not waste another moment, that life was apt to take radical turns, and that she could also decide to take one of these turns for herself. She took off her pumps and rose from the bench, flying in her stocking feet across the park back toward the parking garage. She ran across grass and tree roots and patches of dirt, her lungs aching, her purse banging against her side. She ran past the carousel and the playground and dodged trees and bicycles and trash cans. She ran with the kind of conviction that had eluded her since that terrible night in college. She was suddenly sure of something, and as she ran, the blue-black summer sky urged her on toward hope, and even with all its risks, toward love.

Acknowledgments

As always, my agent, Jess Regel, deserves a great deal of credit for how this book emerged into its present form. I appreciate her honesty when I went down various unproductive rabbit holes. Lord knows, Jess, this one took longer than it should have.

I'd also like to acknowledge editor Katherine Sharpe, who did an excellent job in guiding me toward a more cohesive vision for these characters, and copyeditor Jennifer Caven, who cleaned up the manuscript. Brooke Warner, publisher of She Writes Press, has a big job but still seems to find time for every author. She has changed the publishing world for the better.

In the course of this project, I lost my dear father, John Schoenberger. I saw him in the hospital a few days before he died, and one of his final questions to me was, "Sue, how's your book coming?" Then he listened patiently as I described all the steps before publication. He supported me every step of the way, and I miss him terribly.

My mother, Joyce, is still with us, cheering me on with a cadre of friends from Lacey Field, the small neighborhood where I grew up in New Windsor, New York. What a special place. You all have my undying gratitude for the way you look out for my mom and each other.

A few others deserve mention: Greg Dooman, from whom I stole the joke about Clydesdales; my sisters, Mary Ann and Nancy, and my brother, Johnny, who are the most supportive siblings anyone could have; my colleagues at Hartford Seminary, especially Tina Demo and M.T. Winter. They, along with my next-door neighbors, Bill and Michelle Souza, have listened to me fret about this book for years. You deserve some recognition for that alone.

About the Author

© Amy Mello Panucci

S usan Schoenberger is the award-winning author of *A Watershed Year* and *The Virtues of Oxygen*. With a linotype operator for a grandfather, she has ink in her blood. For many years, she worked as a journalist and copyeditor at newspapers including the *Hartford Courant* and the *Baltimore Sun*. She currently serves as director of communications at Hartford Seminary, a graduate school with a focus on interfaith dialogue. She lives in West Hartford, Connecticut, with her husband, Kevin. They have three grown children and a small dog named Leo.

SELECTED TITLES FROM SHE WRITES PRESS

She Writes Press is an independent publishing company founded to serve women writers everywhere. Visit us at www.shewritespress.com.

Again and Again by Ellen Bravo $16.95, 978-1-63152-939-9
When the man who raped her roommate in college becomes a Senate candidate, women's rights leader Deborah Borenstein must make a choice—one that could determine control of the Senate, the course of a friendship, and the fate of a marriage.

Shelter Us by Laura Diamond $16.95, 978-1-63152-970-2
Lawyer-turned-stay-at-home-mom Sarah Shaw is still struggling to find a steady happiness after the death of her infant daughter when she meets a young homeless mother and toddler she can't get out of her mind—and becomes determined to rescue them.

Profound and Perfect Things by Maribel Garcia $16.95, 978-1-63152-541-4
When Isa, a closeted lesbian with conservative Mexican parents, has a one-night stand that results in an unwanted pregnancy, her sister, Cristina adopts the baby—but twelve years later, Isa, who regrets giving up her child, threatens to spill the secret of her daughter's true parentage.

Center Ring by Nicole Waggoner $17.95, 978-1-63152-034-1
When a startling confession rattles a group of tightly knit women to its core, the friends are left analyzing their own roads not taken and the vastly different choices they've made in life and love.

The Trumpet Lesson by Dianne Romain $16.95, 978-1-63152-598-8
Fascinated by a young woman's performance of "The Lost Child" in Guanajuato's central plaza, painfully shy expat Callie Quinn asks the woman for a trumpet lesson—and ends up confronting her longing to know her own lost child, the biracial daughter she gave up for adoption more than thirty years ago.

As Long As It's Perfect by Lisa Tognola $16.95, 978-1-63152-624-4
What happens when you ignore the signs that you're living beyond your means? When married mother of three Janie Margolis's house lust gets the best of her, she is catapulted into a years-long quest for domicile perfection—one that nearly ruins her marriage.